Gestapo Lodge

Gestapo Lodge

Carlos Mundy

THAMES RIVER PRESS

Gestapo Lodge

THAMES RIVER PRESS
An imprint of Wimbledon Publishing Company Limited (WPC)
Another imprint of WPC is Anthem Press (www.anthempress.com)

First published in the United Kingdom in 2011 by

THAMES RIVER PRESS
75-76 Blackfriars Road
London SE1 8HA

www.thamesriverpress.com

© Carlos Mundy 2011

A CIP record for this book is available from the British Library.

ISBN 978-0-85728-387-0

To my father, Rodney Meynell Mundy, in loving memory.
To His Holiness the XIV Dalai Lama, my guiding light.
A S.A.R. El Conde de Barcelona, el gran patriota.

A S.M. El Rey Don Juan Carlos, el padre de la democracia.
To all the men and women who have sacrificed
their lives in the name of freedom.

Rodney Mundy in Madrid in 1941

ACKNOWLEDGEMENTS

Special gratitude to Phryne Alabaster Mundy for her recollection of those days and the part of her life she shared with our father; to Alicia Balenchana y Sandoval who was very helpful with her memories of Madrid during the Second World War; to my sister Charis for her editing work; and to my friends worldwide for their constant support and their empathy.

CONTENTS

Foreword   *xi*

1. Reflections   1
2. Carlos and I   2
3. Early Memories   13
4. The Côte d'Azur, July 1937 to October 1940   17
5. Shattered Dreams   27
6. A New Life   32
7. A Nest of Spies   41
8. Glittering Cairo   58
9. A Desert Liaison   74
10. Back in Spain   86
11. Going Home   105
12. A Short Visit to Paris and the End of the Second World War   113
13. The Nightmare Was Over   126
14. A Married Man   132
15. The Sixties   142
16. The Baron's Trial   150
17. An Irreparable Loss   158
18. Starting Again   164
19. Ghosts from the Past   174
20. Carlos and I   178

Epilogue   188

FOREWORD

When my father revealed to me in Costa Rica that he had been a member of MI6, I was fascinated. Since then and every time we saw each other, I urged him to write his story, to no avail.

However, after his sudden death I found to my surprise that he had been taking notes, and had even ventured to write certain passages of what was going to be his autobiography had he not died so unexpectedly. So, I was compelled, in tribute to his life, to take over and finish what he had started.

Borrowing from his autobiographical notes, writings and tales, and Phryne's recollections, I was able to picture a time past and construct the backbone of the story, but the material had too many gaps to be a biography; so, instead, I decided to write it as a novel. This allowed me the freedom to change the names of certain characters in order to protect the identity of their descendants, to fictionalise some of the different incidents, and to fill the gaps to the narrative's convenience.

As *Gestapo Lodge* is a work of fiction based on my father's life, I have made the creative choice of writing it as if the narrator were my father's consciousness remembering his life.

I hope you will enjoy the story as much as I enjoyed writing it. Some of the characters were main players in the history of the twentieth century. After all, they do say that those who forget their history are condemned to repeat it.

Carlos Mundy
Tangiers, July 2009

At the Naval Academy in Dartmouth 1936

1. REFLECTIONS

London, 27 October 1922, the place and date I was born… I do not have too many recollections of my childhood, nor of my life, but I will do my best to remember. Since I passed away, my memory has begun to blur and the line between fact and fiction seems to have slowly faded away.

Had I lived, I would be approaching my eighty-ninth birthday… I must confess I never looked forward to old age's tribulations and, with hindsight, I am glad it all happened as it did. I simply died in my sleep.

2. CARLOS AND I

My second son, Carlos, and I decided to go to Costa Rica for ten days before our holiday to Jamaica, where we were going to welcome the new year of 1992 with some family friends. We had not spent quality time together in quite a long time. My two other sons and two daughters had their own plans for Xmas.

We stayed for three days at the colonial Gran Hotel in San José, which proved to be an exhausting exercise with all the lavish entertainment in the beautiful homes of friends who had once lived in Spain, and the non-stop touring of the Central Valley. We visited the Poas volcano and were very impressed by the otherworldly setting. The sight of its sulphur pool surrounded by smoke and steam rising from fumaroles was such an awesome experience that a whole eternity will not erase it from my memory.

Nothing in our stay hinted that all the phantoms of my past were about to return. But return they did, and in the most unexpected way.

Carlos had arranged that we should go on 21 December to Puerto Viejo de Talamanca, a small village on the Caribbean Sea, only a few miles from the Panamanian border. Our friends in San José informed us that a devastating earthquake had hit the area a few months earlier and suggested we go to a resort on the Pacific Coast instead. But as Carlos had secured an article for a magazine about Puerto Viejo and its inhabitants, he insisted on sticking to our original plan, having made reservations to stay at the new Toucan Lodge; so, it was that on the morning of 21 December we set off in a rented four-wheel-drive vehicle for the Costa Rican Caribbean.

We took the Guapiles highway to Limón, which goes through Braulio Carrillo National Park. The scenery was one of rolling hillsides clothed with a thick emerald green mass of vegetation. Carlos was intent on stopping and walking the park's 700-metre Los Niños Trail, but I was adamant to reach our destination in daylight. Although I did not confess it at the time, I had done my bit of sightseeing, and I was looking forward to having a relaxing drink at the lodge.

We arrived at about three in the afternoon at the large tropical estate in which the Toucan Lodge stood, facing the beach. Our first sight of the lodge was of a wooden bungalow with a veranda, dining area, and reception lobby in the basement. Someone told us that the owner, a Costa Rican from San José called Martin Jiménez, had bought the land many years ago but had only recently developed it.

They were expecting us. A small well-built *tico*[1], in charge of the reception, welcomed us with a broad smile.

'Buenas tardes, señores. Did you have a nice trip? My name is José, and I am at your service,' he said, ringing a bell.

Billy came into the reception. He appeared so quickly that it seemed he had been standing behind the door, waiting for the bell to ring. He was a good-looking young houseboy, whom Carlos immediately speculated belonged to the Bribri Indian tribe. He showed us to our cabins and left, sporting a wide smile all the time. The bungalows were set amid lush vegetation, with toucans and parrots flying about the garden. Both my son and I were happy with the relaxed atmosphere and the beauty of the place, which were idyllic and enabled us to unwind from the trip. The lodge was quite charming and exuded good taste and refinement with a touch of understated luxury. Built of bamboo with a front porch, the cabins were simple but extremely cosy.

I was unpacking, merrily daydreaming of a pre-dinner whisky, when I heard a chilling scream—an expression of horror, such as I never thought I would hear again. I ran out of my room and saw Carlos running out of his, white-faced. 'What's wrong? Are you all right?'

'Yes, yes,' Carlos replied, still shaken. 'There's a large green-and-orange snake in my bathroom! It suddenly appeared behind me. I nearly got bitten.'

By then, José and a middle-aged Indian had joined us. We all went into Carlos's room, but there was no sign of the reptile anywhere.

'These snakes are quite poisonous but they seldom bite anybody—that is, unless they feel cornered,' said the Indian, looking into my eyes as if he

[1] How the Costa Ricans are known

were anticipating something I could not grasp, and showing no intention of hunting the snake down.

After José's friendly but long diatribe on the pros and cons of life in the woods, we decided Carlos would move into a new cabin and we would try to forget the incident.

Once we had settled in, we went off for a swim to refresh ourselves. We followed a narrow dirt track along the coast to Punta Uva because our friends had told it was the most beautiful beach in the area. It obviously had been a paradise, but the earthquake's devastation was evident. The floods that followed had washed thousands of tons of wood and debris down to the sea, which the tides had thrown back on to the beaches. In our eagerness to swim, we took a long dip in the warm clear waters while keeping an eye out for floating logs.

Back at the lodge, having showered and changed into loose clothes, we went to the bar, adjacent to the open-air dining room, to have a drink before dinner. I was struck with horror when I saw the man standing by the bar. He had a pair of Rottweilers by his side. He held his back tautly straight, had wavy blond hair, a sour expression, and was slowly sipping a beer as he watched the entrance. I looked straight into his icy blue eyes, and a chill went down my spine. The man, who was the owner of the Toucan Lodge, stood up to greet us. I hardly managed to force a smile.

He greeted us in a friendly manner. 'You must be los Señores Mundy. My name is Martin Jiménez. I am glad to have you here with us. José will shortly offer you welcome drinks.'

I do not think Carlos realised how stunned I was. Jiménez's face was disturbingly familiar, but I could not pinpoint where I had seen it before. That evening I was not very chatty and I could hardly eat my dinner. The sight of Martin Jiménez had deeply disturbed me.

I was unable to sleep that night. My restless mind travelled back and forth, rescuing from oblivion memories I had decided to forget long ago. Where did that face come from? I tossed restlessly in my bed, sweating with anxiety, unable to resolve the puzzle. My mind was like a wild horse, and no matter how much I tried, I was unable to tame it. At my age, I still remembered a face, but having met so many people during my life, I now had difficulty remembering the circumstances that surrounded each of them. I suppose, under normal circumstances, I would have not complained about this small handicap, but this was different. His face gnawed me, igniting all the fear I had bottled inside during the last decades.

Although there are few things I hate more than getting up early, I rose just after sunrise. Lying in bed had become a lethally dangerous exercise. I met Carlos for breakfast and we made plans for the day. It had rained all night and the morning was wet but it did not deter us from visiting one of the three Indian reservations in the Talamanca Mountains. The lands where these ancient people live are protected against commercial development in a variety of ways: all hunting is forbidden except the one practiced by the Indians for their survival, and access to the reservations requires special permits.

José suggested that we visit Mauricio Salazar. A Bribri Indian, Mauricio lived on a fourteen-hectare plot of jungle where he had built three charming thatched Indian-style bungalows. José had told Carlos that Mauricio had permits to visit the Kekodi reservation and could swiftly arrange permits for the other two. So I found myself following my son up a steep slippery path towards the Cabinas Chimuri, Mauricio's home.

When we arrived, I was completely out of breath. We were greeted by a charming German girl who we soon found out was Mauricio's girlfriend. She explained to us the difficulties involved in acquiring permits but insisted that it would be well worth it, as meeting the Indians would be an unforgettable experience and a walk through the rainforest would be thoroughly enjoyable. I had my doubts, as one is none too agile when approaching seventy, but Carlos was very excited. Nevertheless, we arranged that they would notify us at the lodge when the walk would take place. Mauricio, who was temporarily absent, would be our guide.

Once back in the car, I suggested to Carlos that we arrange a fishing expedition, as I had been told that there was good Atlantic tarpon in this region. So we went to see Willy Burton, a local fisherman and friend of José.

We followed the dirt track back along the coast, past Punta Uva, until we reached Manzanillo. Willy lived on a house on stilts that was on a riverbank close to the ocean at the end of the coastal track, along which you could walk to Panama. He was a small, stocky man in his early fifties who wore shorts and a pair of old Wellington boots, and revealed a tanned and hairy torso.

'*Buenos días,* I would like to go fishing one of these days. José says you can arrange it for me,' I said.

Willy had an amiable expression and a naughty twinkle in his eyes. He indicated that we follow him to a shack under which he kept a boat in need of a coat of paint. Pointing at it, he burst into hearty laughter.

'This is your vessel, *señor*, but the weather is not good now. The sea is rough because of the new moon. However, as soon as the weather changes, we will plunge into the sea. It'll be good for me to earn some dough!' He laughed again, probably at Carlos's expression of disbelief as he looked at the boat.

A striking old man, another Bribri Indian who was probably in his seventies, interrupted us. He was wearing only a pair of shorts and his long black hair fell over his shoulders. He introduced himself as Roberto, the shaman. While Willy and I discussed fishing, Carlos got into a lively conversation with our new acquaintance, and soon we received an invitation to visit him in the reservation. My son was thrilled and decided that his article would centre on him.

By the time we bade farewell, the weather had not improved; nevertheless, we went swimming to Punta Uva. My mind was set on persuading Carlos to go to the Pacific coast as soon as he had his article. It was too wet for my liking, but my desire to get away was more from uneasiness at the sight of Martin Jiménez than because of the weather.

Neither my children nor my wife knew anything of my past, as I had never wanted them to be involved. After 1977, I had decided to lay it to rest with great success.

I saw him again that evening. We were on our way to the car to go out for dinner when he stepped out of the lodge. This time he did not acknowledge us. He pretended he had not seen us, but I felt his piercing eyes set on me as we climbed into the car.

As we walked into a small restaurant lit with neon lights, Carlos blurted out, 'That man gives me the creeps!'

'I was just thinking the same thing,' I muttered.

God knows why we were in such an awful restaurant or why Carlos was asking for someone by the name of Johnny *El Guapo*[2]. We had a mediocre

---

[2] Good-looking Johnny

meal and later, as we were drinking tea, Carlos's friend walked in. He turned out to be a dealer in the sacred herbs of the Indians, which Carlos wanted to try. He explained it was part of his research. I did not think this to be a good idea, but I knew my son was headstrong and once he had decided to do something there was nothing I could say to make him change his mind.

While Carlos spoke to *El Guapo*, who, needless to say, was one of the ugliest people I had ever seen, I sat in silence feeling a bit dumb. Johnny had a generous smile, though, and did not seem to be a dangerous fellow. He was very dark skinned, and he explained his mother was a native and his father a Colombian. He suggested we drive him to a friend's house where he would collect some pot.

In spite of myself, I was quite amused by the adventure. The weed dealer had a great sense of humour, and before we knew it my son and I were enjoying his company and laughing our heads off as if we were high. We drove all the way up to a farm on a hill to find nobody was there.

On our way back to the restaurant to drop Johnny off, he abruptly ordered us to stop the car because he had spotted his friend, a Spaniard named Gerardo, who was delighted to hop into the car, take refuge from the heavy rain, and sell Carlos six dollars' worth of pot.

Back at the lodge, the sight of the two Rottweilers unsettled me again, and I had difficulty getting to sleep. I unsuccessfully tried to calm myself down through reason and logic. It was apparent from his features that Martin Jiménez was of German descent, but this did not necessarily make him a threat. Nothing appeased my fears, and my only comfort lay in the supposition that, due to the heavy rain, Carlos would soon want to leave to the Pacific.

Unfortunately, the morning greeted us with an imposing sun. Carlos came into my cabin urging me to get ready quickly, for he had planned a very tight schedule for the day. I was glad because he was going to get all the information he needed in just one day, but the sunshine destroyed all hope of him leaving of his own accord.

We drove to the path that led to Mauricio's small plot. This time he was in with his girlfriend. He had the permits with him, but he cautioned us that the trek would not be an easy one and that it would take a good two hours. Nonetheless, we set off on our way through the jungle. The flora and fauna continually called my son's attention, making our march painfully slow. After three long hours, we finally reached our destination.

The village was very small. The Bribri Indians lived as they had done for generations. Roberto gleefully greeted us the minute he saw us. As the wise man or witch doctor of the tribe, he possessed knowledge passed on orally from one ancestor to the next for many generations. He knew the spiritual and medicinal properties of every plant in the jungle.

Carlos was escorted around the small village while he took pictures and notes. When he was done, Roberto invited us into his hut, where we sat around a small fire.

'So you'd like to know what the gods have in store for you, would you?' he asked.

Carlos nodded with anticipation. The shaman took my son's hands and started chanting in a language unknown to us. Within minutes, he entered a self-induced trance, muttering words we did not understand. His voice changed, becoming coarse and loud. Mauricio looked worried but said nothing.

'What's he saying?' I whispered. Carlos also seemed to be in some sort of a trance, probably from the pot he had smoked earlier.

'Grave dangers loom over you… you must be careful…'

That was the last thing I wanted to hear. A hair-raising silence followed. Only the sounds of the jungle could be heard, mingled with the laughter of some children outside the hut.

I must have looked as worried as Mauricio when Roberto, opening his eyes, became himself again. He ordered a young girl, who was sitting quietly by the entrance to the hut, to bring a tray of fruits, which we shared in silence. After a while, Roberto gave Carlos and me an amulet each to ward off the bad spirits, saying that we were to wear them around our necks. We thanked Roberto and the most prominent members of the tribe for their kindness and left for Mauricio's home.

'What did he really mean, Mauricio?' I asked, rather concerned and upset at the shaman's economy of words.

'You should not worry too much. The doctor is an old man who speaks in metaphors. His medicine is only good for us Indians. We are quite superstitious,' Mauricio said, obviously hoping to calm me down.

'Well, we're OK now. Time is not linear. The dangers that loom over us must be the snake incident and, anyway, we have these now,' said Carlos, pointing at his colourful amulet gleefully.

I was dead worried, but I said nothing.

Before lunch, we went to the beach at Cahuita to swim and sunbathe. Only ten miles north of Puerto Viejo, and situated in the national park that bears its name, Cahuita is a charming village with a unique flavour. To the east of the village, a white sandy beach stretches for a mile and a half beside a gently curving bay. Although seriously affected by the earthquake, it still offered good swimming and plenty of shade. We spent a couple of hours dipping into the turquoise water, sharing family stories, and soon we forgot the morning's incident. Carlos had given me *The Spy Went Dancing* to read, the best-seller by Aline, Countess of Romanones. The American-born socialite had worked for the CIA in Madrid before marrying Luis Figueroa, Count of Romanones, and Carlos was a good friend of her son, Luis, Count of Quintanilla, and his charming wife, Inés.

What forces were suddenly at work and determined to make me remember my past? Was it what many New Age writers now call 'synchronicity'? The fact was, this book talked of a period of my life that I had not shared with anybody.

I had not known Aline in those days. According to her book, she arrived after I had already returned to England. What amazed me was that her job description was the same as mine had been. During the war years, she had met most of the same people that I had, and, later on in life, we had had friends in common and had moved in the same circles. I did meet her, though, in 1966 in Seville. I had seen her from behind. Jackie Kennedy, Fermín Bohorquez and Aline were riding on horseback in front of the Marquis of Atienza's carriage, in which my wife Pepita and I were riding. They were wearing the typical *traje corto,* or short jacket, with Cordobés hats. At the sound of the bells on the harness of our four *Cartujano* greys, they turned and smiled at us. Fermín, I knew well. He was a close friend of our host, the Marquis. The two ladies were surrounded by large crowds, as everybody wanted to get a close look at America's First Lady.

We met again that evening. After a memorable bullfight at the Maestranza, we were invited to the Palacio de Pilatos, home of the Duke of Medinaceli, head of one of the oldest and noblest families in Spain. Prince Rainier and Princess Grace of Monaco were also there. She was astoundingly beautiful.

I noticed that she and Jackie Kennedy did not seem to like each other as they sat either side of the duke. The truth is they did not even acknowledge each other's presence.

Having interviewed natives from the different Indian tribes, Carlos seemed quite happy with the material gathered for his article. He thought it convenient to write a travel piece on the area, so for the culinary section we decided to try the famous local dish, *rondon*[3], at Miss Edith's restaurant. Miss Edith was a large black mama who exuded so much charisma that she had no difficulty persuading us to return that evening for our Christmas Eve dinner, especially once she had made us taste her mouth-watering *Casado*[4], her deliciously coriander-flavoured *Ceviche*[5], and her renowned dessert, *Tres leches*, made with three different types of milk.

Back at the lodge, José informed us that a man, who had not left his name, had telephoned us from Spain and that he would call again at seven. Not a soul, with the exception of our friends in San José, knew of our whereabouts. The unexpected always creates a sense of unease, and this time was not to be the exception that proves the rule. However, I had not been trained to lose my cool and, seeing Carlos's worried face, I gaily said, 'Let's open a bottle of Dom Perignon. It's Christmas Eve!'

We sat at the veranda to sip the delicious, chilled champagne, which we had brought all the way from Europe together with a Christmas pudding from Fortnum & Mason's that José was keeping as a treasure for our Christmas lunch. I smiled at the thought of how we English love tradition. I had even bought the silver George V sixpence with me that, since my mother's days, had always gone into the family's pudding!

We had drunk half a bottle and were feeling relaxed and happy at being together when, at seven o'clock sharp, José answered the telephone and called my son. We both approached the phone, and Carlos picked up the receiver.

I asked impatiently, 'who is it? Who is it?' before he even had time to speak. Carlos did not reply. He became mute and motionless; listening to whatever the caller was telling him. After what to me seemed like a lifetime,

[3] Beef soup with potatoes, chayote, pumpkins and cauliflower
[4] Rice, black beans, beef, cabbage, avocado and plantain
[5] Chilled-marinated sea bass, shrimps and shellfish served with lemon, chopped onion and garlic

he thanked the man and hung up. He remained silent with a bewildered expression on his face. His lips quivered as if they wanted to form words but could not, and my heart sank, aching for my other children.

'For God's sake, Carlos, what is going on?' I asked angrily, shaking him from the shoulders, unable to face again the death of a loved one.

He looked at me in utter disbelief and burst out, 'Papa, we must pack and leave immediately! Something terrible is going to happen. Just pay the bill! I'll explain everything in the car.'

'What about your work?' I asked, irritated and not knowing what to make of the situation.

'Christ, go and pack! I'll explain later,' he ordered with urgency and contained desperation, hardly raising his voice.

At half past seven, having given José a flimsy excuse as to our sudden departure, we were on our way but without a destination. Carlos explained that the phone call was not from Spain and that the man had spoken in a whisper and tried to sound friendly although his voice was shrill and frightening. Apparently he was calling on behalf of someone who wanted to protect us. From what he was told, it seemed that Martin Jiménez was planning to have us busted for drugs, thus for our own good we were told to leave the lodge.

As it was dark and the roads were not safe, there was no way we could drive back to San José; so we decided to go to Cahuita, try to find accommodation there, and keep our dinner appointment at Miss Edith's.

We drove in silence. My worst fears were realised. Who *was* Martin Jiménez?

'It's probably just someone's idea of a bad joke. The hotel was probably overbooked and that freak thought it amusing to get rid of us like that.' Carlos broke the silence, hoping to release the tension.

'Damn!' I exclaimed. 'We forgot the Christmas pudding that we've dragged halfway round the bloody world!'

'But I did bring the other bottle of champagne!' grunted Carlos, laughing.

'Thank goodness for that. I definitely need a big drink as soon as we get there. Do you think this time they will let us finish the bottle without any upheaval?'

Finally, we reached Cabinas Atlánticas, a charming little lodge owned by a Canadian/Dutch couple. The family was already sitting down to dinner, so the husband, Louis, did not bother asking us to fill in the registration forms.

Just before nine o'clock we found ourselves sitting down comfortably at Miss Edith's and enjoying a delicious lobster cooked in coconut milk with spices, vegetables and rice, which we washed down with my favourite champagne.

Now that I felt more relaxed, I decided that I was ready to reveal the secrets of my past to my son.

3. EARLY MEMORIES

I do not remember the house we lived in near Barnstaple in Devonshire, but I do recall that my father rented Dunstrom Castle in Loch Awe (Scotland) for a short period. At the time, it seemed a terrifying dungeon; but in fact it may be quite a nice place now.

My father, Robert Charles Mundy, was fifty-two when I was born. In 1903 he had married a very wealthy lady by the name of Maud Andrew who, a year later, gave him a son called Basil. In 1920, by then a widower, he married my mother, Dorothy Sadler Phillips, the only child of a family that traced its lineage back to the Merovingian dynasty, or so they said.

Basil, though only sixteen, had inherited an immense fortune upon the death of his mother. But the minute he came of age and was able to dispose of his wealth, he dissipated it, leading a dissolute life, travelling extensively, spending millions on women and gambling until, having nothing left, he shot himself. The year was 1933. I was eleven at the time, and hardly knew him. A portrait of Basil at the age of five, painted by Joaquin Sorolla when he lived at my father's home in London, has always been in the family as a constant reminder of a life misspent.

When my mother married, her father decided that on his death the entire fortune would go to the Freemasons, though she would receive a generous lifetime allowance and the use of the Sadler Phillips' properties, but her children, if she had any, would not receive a penny. I suppose he was trying to protect me from myself, but I was not Basil.

My earliest memories are of my prep school, Elstree, in Hertfordshire, and of our house in Henley. The Old House at 2 New Street was a lovely Elizabethan corner-house painted white with black beams. It is still standing, and I hope it will do so for many more centuries.

Elstree was one of the best and most pompous preparatory schools in

England. In those days an old boy called Sanderson owned it, and later he passed it on to his son. At the slightest excuse they would have me, or anybody else they could lay their hands on, beaten across the backside a minimum of six lashes with a strong bamboo cane.

There was the usual collection of boarding school masters, one of whom was the history teacher, Mr Hardy, whom David Niven calls in his autobiography his 'most hated man'. Niven was at Elstree before me and I only met him some years later in Cannes.

Our home was a happy one, although my upbringing was more formal than strict. Dinner was always a formal occasion, even if we had no guests. The men would wear dinner jackets and my mother would appear in some stunningly beautiful evening gowns, most of which were made for her by Elsa Schiaparelli. Dot, my mother, was a born entertainer.

The Mundys descended from Normans who had accompanied William the Conqueror when he invaded England. Many members of our family have served the Crown. In 1522 my direct ancestor, John Mundy, was made Lord Mayor of London by Henry VIII and was later knighted for his services in 1529. We have given England high sheriffs, a governor of Jersey, an admiral of the fleet, an under secretary of state for war and many high-ranking officers in both the Army and the Navy. My family had been Lords of Markeaton in Derbyshire since 1516, and they had resided in the family home, Markeaton Hall, until 1929 when the sole female survivor of an elder branch without issue gave it to a certain Reverend Clark Maxwell who finally donated it to the Corporation in 1929. This upset my father terribly. Unfortunately, after the war, it was allowed to fall into total disrepair and was finally torn down in the sixties. Now, a park honours the family, but only the *orangerie* and the stables remain of its former grandness.

It was expected that I was to fulfil my duties to Crown and country in the Royal Navy when my turn came. My father was a major general who had been awarded many medals in the Boer War. A friend of King Alfonso XIII of Spain, he had also been awarded the very prestigious Cross of Isabel la Católica. Therefore, when I left Elstree at the age of thirteen, instead of going on to Eton, Harrow or Rugby, I was sent to the Royal Naval College at Dartmouth as a naval cadet to forge myself a career. The year was 1936.

Life at Dartmouth was quite exciting. The hard training included many sports. We had one of the best rugby teams that ever existed for boys our age, and we won plenty of games to boys one or two years older, which, at those ages, makes a huge, usually insurmountable, difference. Mark Sudden, one of the greatest Irish scrum halves ever, and a splendid person, coached us. I continued to be in close contact with my good friend Peter Learmond throughout the years. He was in the same three-quarter line as me when I played centre three-quarter, though I often played full back and occasionally forward. The war killed most of the others in the team.

I managed to avoid getting myself beaten at Dartmouth, but poor Peter was always punished for the most ridiculous things. The stupidest of all was for borrowing someone's tracksuit when his own was stolen. For this diabolical sin he was given twelve official cuts, as they were called, by a huge marine sergeant major in front of all cadets and officers. Holding a stick above our heads while trotting or jumping up and down for thirty minutes was a typical punishment for trivial offences. Naturally, I and everyone else were constantly punished in this way.

Whenever time and the officers permitted, we would go roller-skating on the lead roofs of part of the college. However, this led to long queues at the infirmary, as everybody ended up skinning the upper part of their thighs in falls.

Apart from the incessant parades, I remember having to dive every morning, even in winter, after wake-up call, through the dormitory pool of ice-cold water. The pool was only about three feet deep, so you had to stand in it and then dive through. Our superiors watched us with hawk eyes and made us repeat the exercise several times if we tried to con them. In the end, we would dive in just to save ourselves all the misery.

As it was a long way for my parents to come down from Frensham, Surrey, where we now lived, just to take me out for tea, they had the great idea, one July, of renting a small house on the other side of the River Dart, where we were taught sailing.

My mother had bought the house in Frensham when my parents left Henley. It had thirteen acres of gardens where she built a grass tennis court, which the weather hardly allowed us to use, and thirty-nine acres of fields that provided a little rough shooting: an odd rabbit, partridge or pheasant. There was a stream at the bottom of the property full of water rats and fish such as small roach. Nearby, mother built a cottage for our cook, a Gypsy called Bailey, whom we called Ma Bailey. She was the best cook we ever had.

The old house had a lovely entrance hall with a huge fireplace that in winter was always full of burning logs, and a large drawing room leading out on to a vast lawn bordered with flowerbeds. To the left of the drawing room was a good-sized oak-panelled dining room that led on to a smaller lawn with a large fishpond full of goldfish and a few Muscovy ducks. Opposite the dining room, at the bottom of the garden, was a large out house in which we built a music room that had excellent acoustics. It was my mother's sole domain where she centred her spirit playing her Blüthner grand piano. She had learnt to play in Dresden, becoming a virtuoso, and she had a beautiful mezzo-soprano voice, which her artistic friends had the privilege to enjoy on her frequent musical soirées.

In addition to Ma Bailey, who used one of the first Aga cookers with great success, we had a butler called Wilkin, five maids, and at least five gardeners. My father used to direct operations in the garden and worked on it a lot himself as, within his detached and pragmatic being, a sensitive and quite an expert gardener hided. He loved to get his hands dirtied in our exquisite orchard and to monitor the progress of the fruit trees growing against the walls of the vegetable garden closely. I myself had a penchant for gardening, having often mowed the lawns beside Ma Bailey's eldest son and tasted the unforgettable peaches we grew.

In July 1937 I had an accident that completely changed my lifestyle and, therefore, my future, when I fell off a small cliff at Mill Creek and badly injured the muscles and ligaments in my left arm and leg. As a result, I joined my parents for the summer holidays at their home in the south of France, very close to Monte Carlo. The doctors initially prescribed rest, followed by moderate exercise. I was treated by an Italian muscle and nerve specialist called Dr Lingueglia who recommended swimming for at least two to three hours a day in addition to rehabilitation exercises.

4. THE CÔTE D'AZUR, JULY 1937 TO OCTOBER 1940

Our summerhouse was set on lovely terraced land overlooking the bay of Cap Ferrat. My parents loved it, and we always extended our holidays as much as possible. It took me about a year to recover completely from the injury to my left arm and leg, which naturally prevented me from returning to Dartmouth. To tell the truth, I was not very sorry at being unable to continue with my naval training, as the South of France was much more entertaining!

A friend of the family, whom I called Uncle Jack and whose company my mother adored, joined us. It was not long before another friend, Princess Jane Magaloff, the widow of an impoverished Russian aristocrat, also became part of the family.

When my father passed away in his sleep, soon after our arrival in the south of France, he was only sixty-eight. My mother, not wanting to return to England, decided, as he had been so fond of the Côte d'Azur, to bury him in Nice and rent out the house in Surrey to Sir Anthony Eden, who at the time was Under Secretary of Foreign Affairs.

After a period of mourning, we continued with our lives.

I loved my new carefree life. I was nearly sixteen, handsome, spoke fluent French and Spanish, my beloved mother gave me an extremely generous allowance, and I felt like a man. That summer I had my first sexual experience, when a Hungarian countess who doubled me in age seduced me and taught me how to love a woman. Soon I discovered the secrets of seduction and apparently excelled at them.

The South of France was at the time a haven for the rich and famous; royalty mingled with American billionaires and impoverished Russian nobles. Everybody had a good time. I had many friends among the young scions of the Russian nobility, and we received many invitations, as we liked to party hard. Prince Basil Nakashidze, Prince Chervachedze, Prince Igor Trubetskoy and I were inseparable. We were known as the Four Musketeers! Being slightly older than I was, they taught me many tricks for living on the edge.

Many of these Russian families had lost everything during the Bolshevik Revolution and were now obliged to work in order to support themselves in exile. They worked as taxi drivers, porters at the top hotels, and waiters in the most fashionable restaurants, always displaying a great sense of humour. I found it highly amusing when former courtiers recognised them and addressed them by their formal titles; it always seemed to happen in the most awkward situations!

Igor Trubetskoy was in his late twenties, very handsome and utterly broke. He had quite a reputation with the women, and in the party circuit it was rumoured that he was very well endowed. One night, at a private party in a Russian restaurant, an eccentric gay American millionaire dared him to show it off and offered him a large sum of money if he did so. Igor got up swiftly from the table, went into the kitchen, and returned, a few minutes later, with his massive erection on a silver tray, surrounded by Beluga caviar. A perplexed silence took over the room as he nonchalantly went around the table asking us to help ourselves, which we did while trying to keep a straight face. I noticed some would rather help themselves to the hot-blooded sausage but my choice was clear: caviar for me, thank you.

At night, if no other plans came our way, we used to go to the Sporting Club in Monte Carlo and dance to the music of Lecuona and his Cuban Boys, undoubtedly the best Latino band that has ever existed. Afterwards, we would often go for a swim and then sleep on the beach until it was time for breakfast.

That summer was my initiation as a socialite. I mingled with people from a broad array of backgrounds, people who had different beliefs, passions, senses of humour and ways of looking at life. Soon I was to become a great adept at making small talk and reading between the lines.

On one occasion I went to dine at the palace in Monte Carlo with mother, Uncle Jack and Princess Jane. I think it was to celebrate some sort of anniversary of the Grimaldis and Prince Louis II was the host. I was introduced to Crown Prince Rainier who was just a year younger than I was.

On another occasion, at the Sporting Club, Igor introduced me to the Marquis of San Felice, who was Mussolini's consul in Monte Carlo. He was a man of refined features and of course a passionate fascist. He, in turn, introduced me to Baron Klaus von Jellenbach who, Basil Nakashidze explained, was one of the wealthiest men in Germany and an avid art collector. Little did I realise then that our paths would cross again.

"Rodney, would you like to spend the winter in France?" asked my mother unexpectedly while we were having breakfast on the veranda.

I was thrilled! "What a great idea. I feel so recovered that I can go skiing then." I said with enthusiasm.

"Its too soon for that," she said disapprovingly.

"Don't worry, I'll be fine and anyway it is still a few months away."

"Let the boy go darling. It will do him good," said Uncle Jack as he appeared with Princess Jane by his side having both just raised from bed.

" Oh Jack, you are going to spoil him. You are worst than Rodney," she said to Uncle Jack as he kissed her good morning on the cheeks and Jane winked at me in complicity.

My mother did spoil me in many ways but she was such a formidable role model that she knew that giving me such freedom would do me no harm. Uncle Jack was such a support to her and adored her. He took my father's place and though it was never talked about I knew that they were lovers. I was delighted to see her so happy. Delightful Jane was so very different from mother. She was outrageous, out spoken and terribly amusing with her husky un-refined accent in strike contrast to my mother's subdued although extravagant elegance, her discretion and her *savoir-faire*. This family set up raised quite a few eyebrows but mummy found it extremely amusing. I loved them dearly.

As soon as there was enough snow, I took off for Alp d'Huez, taking Igor as my guest. We stayed with friends of his, who owned a chalet, and we had a great time, enjoying the slopes as much as the party atmosphere.

One evening we met a stunning woman called Niloufer Mourad. She was the daughter of the Sultan of Turkey and had been married to the son of the Nizam of Hyderabad, who was one of the wealthiest men in the world but a notorious miser. She was in her early forties, and both Igor and I found her painfully attractive, especially as she kept us both at a distance. But we became very good friends and had a lot of fun together.

One day, to my surprise, she asked me to accompany her to Paris. How could I refuse such an enticing offer? Without a second thought, I left an unhappy Igor behind, and set off for the city of lights in the company of one of the most beautiful women in the world.

I was elated at being the chosen. My heart beat with anticipation, but my daydream soon ended when, the morning after our arrival, I discovered the reason for the trip. Niloufer showed me the most amazing emerald and diamond necklace. The deep green of the stones was the exact colour of her eyes. I presumed it had been a gift from the Nizam, who had owned a fabulous collection of gems, but I did not ask.

'Rodney, I need you to do me a favour. Take this to Van Cleef across the street and ask them to value it. It needs to be sold.'

I shall never forget the sales clerk's expression when he saw the necklace. It was so large and extravagant that his first impression was that it was a piece of costume jewellery.

We spent about ten days in Paris, which was the time it took the jeweller to arrange the money for the necklace. Princess Niloufer took me to her favourite restaurant, the Tour d'Argent, on the fifth *arrondisement,* which was owned by Claude Terrail. He would later become an important member of the resistance. I was surprised at his brother's not attempting to hide his pro-German sympathies. The Tour was nearly 350 years old and famous for its amazing duck dishes. Over the years, I became very close to Claude and dined in his restaurant with my three successive wives, though, naturally, at different periods of my life!

The winter passed peacefully and it was soon summer. Hitler's annexation of Austria and Czechoslovakia hardly seemed to affect us at all, as we lived in a bubble of champagne. In the Côte d'Azur it was business as usual, and I was ready for another crazy summer. As I had recovered completely from my injuries, I intended to get back into sports.

I played tennis every day with King Gustaf Adolf V of Sweden, who was a charming elderly gentleman. He lived close to us, perched like an eagle in the Château Eza, and was often a guest at my mother's soirées.

Apart from the swimming, which I continued to practise on a regular basis, I also did a lot of waterskiing and soon became one of the best water skiers on the coast. I taught many friends, including Lord Beaverbrook, who was not yet Lord B. I guess sports helped me survive through the summer's excesses.

In June, the most talked about news was that the Duke and Duchess of Windsor had taken an apartment at the Hotel de Cap d'Antibes while work was completed under the supervision of Elsie Mendl on the house they had bought, the twelve-acre Château de la Croé.

Mama's friends spent hours speculating as to what the house would be like, who would receive the duke and duchess, and how the British residents would react to their presence. The abdication crisis had been quite traumatic but it must be said in favour of the ex-king that, at the beginning of his exile, he behaved impeccably in order not to embarrass his brother, the new King George VI.

"I have been invited for dinner at Somerset Maugham's
The Duke and Duchess are the guests of honour." She announced excitedly while we were sitting for lunch.

"How wonderful!" exclaimed a beaming Jane. "What shall I wear, Dot?

" I am to go alone. I don't think Somerset approves of our little ménage-a-trois!" She said giggling.

" Anyway it will be a crushing bore but at least you will finally appease your curiosity," Uncle Jack said as he took his eyes from his paper.

" We will go out for dinner Jane and we will have a jolly good time." I said feeling sorry for Jane.

"I accept! With such a handsome young man I will be the envy of all the women." She replied trying to hide her disappointment

So, Uncle Jack drove her to Cap Ferrat at the arranged time. The next morning over breakfast she told us how uncomfortable she had felt when the duke insisted on presenting his wife as Her Royal Highness, despite the king not having authorised such royal treatment. My mother curtsied to relieve the charged atmosphere but felt ill at ease being so strict with protocol matters. She found the situation rather pathetic.

Our home was the venue of many garden parties, teas, and formal dinners. Among our regular guests were King Peter II of Yugoslavia and the Aga Khan III. The former I saw, many years later, a couple of times, in London where he lived at Claridge's after going into exile; and the latter, who had been president of the League of Nations, used to come with the beautiful Yvette

Blanche Labrousee, who had been crowned Miss France in 1930. In 1944, she married the Aga Khan, thus becoming the Begum of the Ishmaelites. King Zahir Shah of Afghanistan was also a regular that summer. Whenever he could escape from his responsibilities in Kabul, he enjoyed the South of France. History has been very unjust to him because he was an enlightened monarch who brought his backward country into the twentieth century. He should have never been deposed, as Afghanistan is still today suffering the terrible consequences. I was mesmerized by his conversation. In later years when he was in exile in Rome I was tempted to go and visit him and offer him my assistance but so many years had gone by that I finally never contacted him

Another fascinating person who was a regular visitor was Nicolae Titulescu. He used to sit with his charming family around our pool and hold court in French for the other Romanian guests that my mother always invited whenever he came. It amazed me how upper-class Romanians always spoke in French to each other, and I even wondered if they actually knew their own language. Titulescu was a statesman whose desire for peace, stability and good neighbourly relations was out of step with the rise of fascism throughout the continent. As Romania moved closer to Germany, Titulescu's close ties to France became a political liability and his king, Carol II, forced him to retire and leave Bucharest.

Titulescu wrote in my mother's scrapbook a phrase that has always marked me: 'To avoid war, one must not be afraid to wage it'. It was a pointed remark for those days. We had many political discussions and talked about the role of the League of Nations of which he had been president. He foresaw the disaster and devastation that was about to befall Europe.

By summer 1939 war was in the air, and people seemed very worried. Rumours abounded as to who had Nazi sympathies, and at my mother's parties the talk was of nothing else. I had discovered the good life and was determined to indulge in it for as long as my mother continued giving me the money or history allowed me to do so.

On 1 September 1939, German troops invaded Poland, whereupon Great Britain and France declared war on Germany. Our lives were soon to change dramatically. As we could still receive money from England and I was too young to go to war, we decided it was better to stay put and just wait the war out, as we sincerely believed it would be short.

Despite the overall atmosphere of gloom during the winter of '39/'40, we were all full of hope. We expected our troops to be victorious against the Germans but soon very anxious as we realised that we were no match for the well-trained and disciplined German war machine.

One day just before lunch mother stormed into the living room where I was having a sherry with Uncle Jack and Jane. She was clearly quite upset. "The Germans are advancing towards Paris and the Duke has sent Wallis to Biarritz and has abandoned his post."

"Calm down Dot, we wouldn't want them captured by the Germans!" Uncle Jack intervened trying to ease her distress.

"But he is liaison officer of the French and British armies! I've been told he has closed the house in Boulevard Suchet, and has followed that wretched woman to La Croé."

"They should have left long ago. What on earth are they still doing in France?" Uncle Jack interrupted her. "This is ludicrous! What if they were taken prisoners?

Jane and I agreed.

However, the Windsors seemed quite oblivious to this possibility. They finally came to their senses and left for Spain on 19 June, and we all felt relieved. At least they were in a neutral country and relatively safe until the king decided where they should go.

On 14 June 1940 Paris fell to the Germans, and a week later France was forced to sign the infamous armistice by which the country was divided: one half under the direct control of the Nazis and the other under Petain and his Vichy-based government. We soon heard rumours about what the new fascist government had in mind for citizens of unfriendly countries and for all socialists, communists, and people of political affiliations other than the far-right policies of the new regime. We were all to be rounded up and sent to prisoner of war camps in the centre of France until the end of the war. We soon lost all hope as now only Britain stood against Hitler.

After the Armistice our lives changed drastically and no one came to the house. So it was quite a surprise when one morning the servants announced the visit of Enrico Giglioli, whom we called Harry. He was the Italian Consul in Cannes and had been a regular at my mother's parties. He was in a cheerful mood and could not hide his delight at the prospect of a fascist Europe.

'Dot,' he said to my mother, 'you and your family are safe in the new order. I shall speak to the new authorities to make sure you are not disturbed so that you can live here until we win the war.'

She was quite fond of him because, like most aristocratic Italians, he had good manners and was a charmer, but she had always avoided discussing politics with him. Now she was prepared for a confrontation.

'Harry, your new order will not win this war. It is totally absurd. You have all gone crazy! I do not wish to be rude, but I must ask you to leave this house immediately and to never return, please, at least until we win the war. Sadly you are our enemy now.' The Italian Consul kissed my mother's hand and left without uttering another word.

The atmosphere was gloomy. Nobody could be trusted any more and we were very worried about our immediate future with neither money nor friends. General de Gaulle had formed a government in exile called 'France Libre', and resistance cells were soon created throughout France.

We never knew if it had anything to do with the incident with Enrico Giglioli or not, but a couple of days later the police came to the house and gave us fifteen minutes in which to pack and abandon our home. We were taken to the Hotel de la Barbacane, which was run by a friendly French family whom we assumed were pro-Vichy. We shared the hotel with SS officers. It was all rather awkward as I soon found out that the cook was the leader of the local *maquis* and held meetings in the cellar while we and the SS were upstairs! The Milice Française, which was the equivalent of the Gestapo, kept a close eye on us too. Danger loomed everywhere; the friendly cook told me people were disappearing after the militia had taken them in for questioning. We felt very uneasy when our passports were suddenly confiscated. Little did we know that things were about to get even worse!

Very early, one morning, the militia came to the hotel and dragged us out of our rooms. Mother became very agitated; she was furious. She was wearing her nightgown, and she considered it an unforgivable humiliation to be seen like that by all. She was a very dignified woman and loathed any form of bad manners. To her, this was the ultimate insult and she was outraged.

"How do you dare young man to treat a lady in such a manner?" The captain unperturbed by mother's ramblings muttered an order in German.

"Lets go back to our room, Jane," she ordered defiantly to a frightened trembling Jane. She then swiftly turned her back to the Captain and stormed back to the room.

The angry Captain followed and dragged her out violently by the arm. My mother was livid but maintained her dignity. But then the Captain did the most cowardly thing a man can do. He turned her around and slapped her across the face as he instructed his men something we did not comprehend. She fell to the floor. Neither Uncle Jack nor I could do anything as not only were we handcuffed but a menacing soldier also had a gun pointing at us. I had a feel of desperation. Princess Jane Magaloff leaped like a wild tiger towards the Captain and, had it not been for the rapid intervention of the *patron*, we would almost certainly have been shot on the spot. Uncle Jack and I with guns pointed towards us were unable to do anything

We were forced to dress immediately and pack our belongings. Then, we were taken in a lorry full of foreigners, guarded by five Gestapo officers and members of the SS, to an internment camp in Foix.

It was a very welcome surprise to come across my good friend Fred McEvoy on the journey.

Foix was a prisoner of war camp for foreigners that had many Spanish inmates, exiles from the Civil War and now undesirables under the Vichy regime. We were under the watchful eye of Petain's acolytes. We were their 'guests', as they were fond of calling us. We were fairly well treated, but there was not much to do and I became extremely restless at such inactivity. My mother, Uncle Jack, Princess Jane and I all shared a room with bunk beds and an outside toilet. Facilities were very Spartan in comparison with the luxuries to which we were accustomed, but at least we were all together and safe.

Fred and I were soon busily hatching all sorts of plans to escape from the camp. We held lengthy conversations outdoors, at which he confided he had plenty of money to bribe a guard. We spent some time figuring out which of them would be the ideal candidate, and we finally decided to approach a rather shy and friendly one called Jean-Marc, who seemed quite uncomfortable with his job. We could not have chosen better. Jean-Marc not only agreed to help us but also turned out to be a member of the resistance. He would not accept any money, only enough to arrange all the details of the escape and to pay the guide who would lead us through the Pyrenees into Spain.

'I can arrange for you to leave France for Spain through the mountains via Andorra. A friend of mine knows a Spanish guide who was a former captain in the Red Army. He received five death sentences and is the most wanted man in both France and Spain.' The next crossing was to be on my birthday, 27 October 1940, in just three days' time.

Our family farewell was a terribly sad affair. For the first time in my life, I was aware that I might never see my mother again and that my life was in dire danger.

"Please stay darling. You are so so young and your family needs you. Please!" She pleaded. "Its to dangerous."

"Mama, you will be fine here. Uncle Jack will make sure that you are safe but I have a duty. Please don't make it more difficult for me." She tried to convince me to stay, giving me all sorts of reasons why I should not leave, but there was nothing she could say that would make me change my mind.

Before sunrise, on the eve of my eighteenth birthday, Fred and I escaped from the camp with the help of Jean-Marc. My only belongings were a gold watch, a silver cigarette case that my father had given me, and an astrakhan fur coat. We walked through the countryside for a couple of hours and arrived at a marketplace where several members of the resistance met with us. It then took us two weeks to reach what we thought would be safety in Spain. The most wanted man was called Mario, and he went about his business while we followed him without a word. I told him that there was no need to murder us on the way, as upon arrival he would get the coat and watch as payment for his services. The other members of the expedition were a few Jewish families escaping from the Nuremberg Rules that deprived them of the most basic human rights.

The Pyrenees were heavily patrolled, and we were forced to travel at night in freezing temperatures and with hardly any food to put into our mouths. We hid for three days in Mario's home in the Principality of Andorra, which was neutral territory, before finally reaching the safety of Spain. The reason for this break was that I had started the trip wearing a pair of boots, and my feet became so sore that Mario decided I needed to nurse them and rest. I continued the rest of the march wearing some espadrilles.

5

5. SHATTERED DREAMS

Barcelona, November 1940

The party was divided up as soon as we entered Spain, illegally and without documents.

My good friend Fred McEvoy and I were taken to the home of the notary of Gosol where, out of sheer exhaustion, we slept for two days. Fred was an Australian who I had met when he had come second in a skiing marathon from Cannes to Monte Carlo that I had won. He was in his late twenties and was extremely popular with all the wealthy widows. He had explained to me how they were quite happy to pay him generous sums of money just to spend time with him. I could understand his success, for he was a very colourful character who looked like Errol Flynn and could charm the birds off the trees. He had plenty of money from his family; so he worked just for the fun of it. He had tried to convince me to join him in his lucrative profession, as he had more clients than he could cope with, but I had declined the offer, as not only money was not a worry in those days but mainly I had no shortage of women. We had not fully recovered when we went to meet the British Consul in Barcelona, Mr Scheuel.

The plan was for us to leave Barcelona harbour in a small fishing boat and be collected at sea by a British destroyer that would take us to the safety of Gibraltar. However, once on board, I realised something was terribly wrong. All of a sudden, the engine stopped, and the fishermen started making such a fuss that it attracted the curiosity of the police patrols, who approached and boarded us. It was discovered later that the British Consul worked for the Germans, selling those who escaped from France to Franco's police, who were working hand in hand with the Gestapo.

Fred and I had no papers; so I tried to bribe the person I thought was in charge of the operation. When the Civil Guard I had tried to bribe started yelling at me, we both understood we were in serious trouble. I signalled

Fred and we both jumped into the sea like lightning in the hope that we could swim ashore in the moonless night; but the sea was rough and cold.

I heard the crazed firing of guns. The guards were randomly shooting into the night, trusting that sooner rather than later they would hit the target. We were in serious trouble. The sea did not let me swim in a straight line nor did it let me advance much. I was frightened and knew that I had very little chance to get ashore alive. 'Me *rindo*, I surrender,' I started to yell.

Within seconds, the police patrol boat was upon me, blinding me with a strong spotlight as they dragged me on board. Fred was shivering in a corner.

We spent the night in a cell, accused of entering the country illegally, attempting to bribe an officer, attempting to resist arrest, and of being spies. A few days later, we found ourselves in Barcelona's notorious Modelo Prison with our heads shaved and sentenced without a trial to life imprisonment.

Our future was not in our hands; it depended on the outcome of the war, or so we thought at the time.

I was just eighteen. The idea of spending a lifetime in such a hellhole was more than I could bear. I missed my mother and wondered whether I would not have done better listening to her.

Our cell was filthy, smelly and lice-infested, with just a hole in the corner for a WC. There was not enough space for all of us to lie down at the same time, and we slept on the concrete floor without a mattress.

There were nine of us. One of our cellmates was a Frenchman called Jean-Pierre Melville, who later became a very famous film director. The others included a communist priest and some common criminals. I argued with the priest about theology as he tried unsuccessfully to convert me to Catholicism. Meal times were an exercise in active visualisation. We were given only a small piece of dry brown bread and a bowl of dirty water with a tiny morsel of half-rotten meat floating in it. Following the example of Jesus in the Canaan wedding, I tried to transmute, in my imagination of course and without success, the filthy soup into a succulent broth. But, and perhaps thanks to the priest who continuously prayed for us all, the guards were avid for a bit of extra money and bought us whatever we could afford. Fred and Jean-Pierre indulged in chocolates while I, not really knowing how long we would be there, bought an onion a day, which I ate like an apple, and I am certain that it kept me healthier than the others. Luckily, it was not hot. The cell was full of insect holes and, if it had been summer, we would have been eaten alive. We believed no one knew where we were, which only added to our desperation.

Once a week, a doctor in dirty white overalls would make his rounds. The guards would order us to pull our trousers down, and the doctor would inject us, using the same dirty needle, with some unknown substance. In spite of this, or because of it, we were continuously sick. The stench in the cell was unbearable. We were not allowed to wash, which made matters even worst. Fred, Jean-Pierre and I became close friends, and this camaraderie made our ordeal more bearable.

I spent hours recollecting the events that had landed me in that pigsty. Maybe Mama had been right, and I should have stayed with them in the camp. I missed her and the wonderful life I had once known as I cried myself to sleep.

The sameness of the long and aimless days in prison was broken one morning of late January. The guard handed our clothes back to us and informed us that we had a visitor. It was the British Consul in Cartagena, Mr. Leverkus, who was also temporarily in charge of the British Consulate in Barcelona. He explained to our delight that Mr. Scheuel had left his post in dishonor, having been involved in duplicitous activities and duly discharged. Mr. Leverkus had a strong German accent that caused us certain misgivings but, noticing our dismay, he quickly explained that although he had been the German Consul until Hitler's rise to power, he had been able to switch nationality due to his mother being English.

He was a very friendly fellow who could not offer us immediate relief; however, he promised that soon we would be transferred to the Naval Prison in Cartagena, which we would find much more bearable, and that he would speak to the British Ambassador in Madrid, and see what could be done to help us.

As promised, two weeks later we moved to our new abode. Cartagena was an important Spanish naval base and the prison was the responsibility of the Spanish Navy. Upon our arrival we were disinfected, washed, and given clean clothes.

Fred, Jean-Pierre and I were in high spirits; compared with the Modelo prison this was a five-star hotel. We were four to a cell, which had two bunk beds with sheets—an absolute luxury. We were allowed to exercise in the patio; the food tasted delicious; and we had access to cigars, cigarettes and other delicacies. Our wardens treated us with courtesy and we soon developed a friendly relationship. The three months spent in Barcelona were a nightmare l wanted to forget.

Our new cellmate was a Jew from Alsace called Fred Kempler. Nature had not endowed him with physical beauty, yet he had an enchanting smile and vibrant twinkling eyes. He was a very tough little fellow who, being no more than 5 ft 7 in tall, had become an SS officer, achieving an amazing and incredible feat for a Jew, especially as his features were distinctly Jewish. He had managed to get hold of a plan of the gun deployment along the Brittany coast and to escape via the same route that we had taken but, once he was in Spain, the police arrested him for not having any papers. He was tough, wiry and an expert in weapons, including knives.

Kempler had asked me to tell the British authorities he had some important information that he would give the British Ambassador if he secured his release, gave him British papers, and arranged for him to be taken to England. Therefore, the first day Mr. Leverkus came to see us, he arranged to meet Kempler, who would not tell anything he had not told me before. The Consul promised he would speak to the ambassador but explained there was not much they could do because he was a Frenchman.

Mr. Leverkus visited us quite regularly. He gave us fruit and sweets, and kept us up to date on how the war was going. He informed us that Winston Churchill, the British Prime Minister, had secured the friendship of US President Roosevelt, who was hesitant to enter the war but had ordered the American Secret Service to work in close collaboration with the British. Britain was under constant threat of a German invasion and London was being bombed on a regular basis. The situation was desperate, and I felt utterly frustrated, being locked up and unable to help.

Six months after our arrival, finally the good news arrived. The news we had been waiting so anxiously for. The British Embassy had secured Fred's and my release, and we would be leaving for Madrid the next day. Unfortunately, Fred Kempler and Jean-Pierre were to remain behind. I never saw Jean-Pierre again, although I did see most of his films.

The day before our departure, Mr Leverkus brought us some clean clothes for the trip. Fred and I travelled on a sleeper train from Cartagena to

Madrid. The civil guards, looking for communists, anarchists and all those without papers, constantly stopped the train and violently dragged them off it. Fortunately, we were carrying provisional passports; but, after our ordeal, the trip seemed endless, as we could not be sure we would make it to Madrid.

6. A NEW LIFE

As arranged, Captain Hillgarth, the Naval Attaché at the British Embassy, was at the station waiting for us. He was a tall, thin, handsome man with bushy eyebrows, a wide nose, and straight thin lips that made him look humourless. He was not the typical Englishman. Because of his dark looks, he could easily have been mistaken for a Spaniard. He was wearing an impeccably tailored suit that looked as if made to measure in Savile Row. With him was Alan Lubbock, the military attaché.

We were asked to say our farewells.

'Won't we be going to England together?' Fred asked, surprised.

'No. You will be driven to the airport now and Rodney will be taken to the embassy,' Lubbock replied.

'That probably means that they have good news for you, Rodney. News about your mother,' Fred said reassuringly. The farewells became quite emotional as we embraced. We had been through so much together.

After the war, Fred returned to the South of France where he resumed his life as a gigolo. We would meet again in the early fifties and sail on the Black Swan together. REMOVE THIS PARAGRAPH

Fred left with Alan Lubbock. An old polished Ford with diplomatic plates was waiting for Captain Hillgarth and a middle-aged Englishman with a northern accent drove us to the Hotel Nacional, opposite the station. 'All embassy drivers are English as we can't trust the Spaniards. They are all spies! By the way, I bought a suit for you. I hope it fits,' he said.

'Oh thanks. I don't have any clothes with me,' I said gratefully.

'You'll have to go shopping then. Madrid is now very conservative and jackets must be worn at all times. Please take a quick bath and change, as the ambassador is waiting for you.'

On the way to the embassy, I tried to engage the captain in conversation, but he hardly spoke. Alan Hillgarth seemed not to be very generous with his words or his smiles. The expression on his face barely changed. He spoke in a low-pitched voice and looked older than he was, as he admitted to being under forty. For some reason though there was something in him that I immediately liked.

My first impression of the city was most unfavourable. I had never seen anything like it. Madrid looked grim to say the least. The buildings were dilapidated and in need of paint. Most of the people I saw on the streets looked thin and tired and were shabbily dressed. The embassy was located on Calle Fernando el Santo, where I was to meet Samuel Hoare, the ambassador. As we turned the corner I saw the Union Jack and I somehow had a feeling of relief. The only reason for me to be taken to the embassy had to be to be given news on my mother. I was almost certain that I would soon be sent back to England to help in the war effort.

A pair of armed Guardia Civiles, in their green uniforms and wearing their bicorn shiny hats, stood guard. They looked so gaunt that they made me shiver. I would soon in spite of myself have to get used to seeing so many half famished people with terribly sad expressions on their faces on the streets of Madrid. Once inside the embassy I followed Captain Hillgarth to the ambassador's office. Samuel Hoare was sitting behind a large mahogany desk under a portrait of the king. He was a cultured, intelligent man who was a prominent member of the Conservative party. He had been Foreign Secretary and First Lord of the Admiralty with Baldwin and Chamberlain, and Churchill had only recently appointed him Ambassador to Madrid with the special mission to keep Spain out of the war. I later found out that his relationship with the prime minister was not as good as it seemed as apparently the ambassador was resentful at not having been appointed Viceroy of India.

As we entered the spacious room, he stood and shook my hand firmly as Alan introduced us. He smiled broadly. A small man, with thin white hair and expressive blue eyes, he was wearing a morning coat

The three of us sat comfortably in his study. I asked about my mother, but there were no news. My heart sank. A maidservant came in carrying a tray with tea. To my utter surprise the ambassador proceeded to explain the plans England had for me.

'You're a fine young man, and your family has served our country for generations. Now it is your turn,' he started saying.

'When do I return to the Navy, sir?' I asked, as I was eager to go back.

'We have other plans for you, Rodney. You are young, intelligent, speak good Spanish and have the right upbringing to infiltrate Spanish high society. I have heard that you have many social skills and we have decided that you are ideal for the job.'

'What job? What am I supposed to do?' I asked incredulously.

'Promote pro-British sentiments,' he said, adding after a fairly long pause, 'these are very dangerous times. We need you to stay in Madrid and obtain as much information as possible. It is vital for us to know who our friends and who our enemy's friends are. From time to time, we will feed you bits of information that you will nonchalantly reveal to certain people that we tell you. Now get a good rest and then go out and enjoy yourself. Madrid is a great city. I will give a dinner party in early October, at which you will meet the key people. At this time of year, all the wives and children of the most important families are in the north on holiday. They leave in July and return at the end of September. The husbands stay behind in Madrid with their *queridas*[1] and only join their families at weekends and for a few weeks in August.'

He laughed as he studied my face. 'So may I suggest that you get to know the city well and discover all it has to offer?

'Sir but I don't have any money?' I asked still shocked by what I was asked to do

'Captain Hillgarth will be your liaison officer, and he will give you money for your hotel bills and your expenses. You must inform him of everything you see and hear. Rodney, do not trust anybody. The Germans have spies everywhere.'

The Madrid heat was dry and unbearable, but it was so wonderful to be free that I did not complain.

The devastation of the city shocked me. During the Civil War it had been besieged for three years, and it had obviously paid a hefty price for being Spain's capital. The suffering that the people had endured was obvious everywhere. Women with patched and mended shawls, mostly dressed in black as a sign of having lost a loved one, and expressionless, beaten men roamed around the city. There were many skinny barefoot children dressed

---

[1.] Lovers

in rags begging in the streets or playing in the gutters. Most buildings were riddled with bullet holes if not destroyed, a reminder of the horrors of the conflict. Outside of the better areas, heaps of stones overgrown with weeds stood as mute witnesses to many fallen bombs. Public transport consisted of the underground, trams and some ancient taxis that, like the few private cars, ran on charcoal and weaved their way around mule-drawn carts and bicycles that criss-crossed the city, carrying all sorts of produce, while the nobility still moved around in their beautiful horse-drawn carriages.

Posters of Franco with the symbol of the Falange[2], the yokes and arrows, were plastered everywhere. Even the Nazi swastika flew beside the Spanish flag on a few buildings.

I soon discovered that, unlike in France or England, there was no middle class at all. The gap between classes was wide. The aristocracy was divided into two groups: the Grandees or Grandes de España, which included all dukes and a few other titles that had been granted this distinction by the different monarchs, and the rest of the nobility. The former ones had the privilege, under the fallen monarchy, of being members of the Council of Grandees, an advisory body to the Crown. They even could request an audience with the sovereign at any time, as they were considered cousins by the king. They also had the right to a diplomatic passport, which Franco duly supplied. This was because most of them had supported Franco during the Civil War against communism, but now some of them mocked him in private.

The summer passed very quickly. I visited the Prado Museum, which still had many empty spaces of the paintings that had been taken down during the war for safekeeping and had still not been re-hung. It was very quiet—hardly any visitors—and it had an abandoned feeling about it. I admired Goya's frescoes at San Antonio de la Florida. I also explored outside Madrid, and visited the impressive Escorial and the Segovia Aqueduct. But most of all I met with my liaison officer, as I had much to learn.

In one of my first meetings with Alan Hillgarth, who was wearing his naval uniform, he explained that Winston Churchill had recently reorganised the Secret Service and set up the Secret Intelligence Service better known as MI6. Alan's unofficial job in Madrid was to be in charge of MI6 and MI9

[2] The National Socialist Party that backed the Franco

operations in Spain. The latter consisted of rescuing refugees and prisoners of war and getting them to safety. Churchill had personally offered him the job and had called him to London.

"I met the Prime Minister for the first time in Mallorca were I had been appointed British Vice Consul in 1933." He told me during one of our meetings.

"So you passed the Civil War there?" I asked

"Difficult times those, young man. I suppose the bosses in London were happy with my work and I was offered the post here!"

One day at the end of September, after one of our meetings, I walked past the German school in Madrid and was shocked to see a large group of German youths, in Nazi uniforms, marching down the street and singing fascist songs. The next morning, when I went to see Hillgarth, Lubbock was there, and they put me in the loop by telling me that Franco had taken a pro-Axis non belligerence stance, which meant the Gestapo moved about freely and the German war vessels and submarines docked for supplies at Spanish ports along the country's western coast, Morocco and the Canary Islands. Landing strips had also been made available to German planes, and the Generalissimo helped Germany with strategic war materials, particularly the tungsten that was vital for armour-piercing shells and armour plating. He also permitted the installation of German observation posts, radar installations, and radio interception stations. The reason for this was that Franco had received a lot of support from Hitler and Mussolini during the Civil War and he felt indebted to them; that was why he had sent a unit of over 18,000 soldiers, known as the Blue Division, to fight alongside the Germans in Russia.

'This neutrality is just a joke. Imagine, every week the Gestapo gives the Ministry of the Interior a list of undesirables,' Alan Lubbock exclaimed. 'You can just imagine what happens to them!

'The Prime Minister was very worried when Franco met Hitler in Hendaye last October. The possibility that he would finally be persuaded to join the war had never been closer. However, he has yet not made up his mind. Franco is a very shrewd man and knows rebuilding Spain has to be his main priority. The country is in no position to start a new war. We know that the conditions he demanded for his participation were too much for Hitler to accept, at least for the moment. But things can change if he feels that the Germans have the upper hand in the war, so you can imagine how worrying the whole situation is. Of course it does not help our cause that the newspapers and the radio are widely pro-German.'

I had never reflected on the political situation of the moment; I was, after all, quite young. What I had been told and asked to do made quite an impact on me. This was in fact my first real responsibility. One has to be inside an intrigue before one can appreciate the thrill of it.

Historians now speculate whether Franco was well aware that his conditions would be unacceptable or whether he was just being greedy. However, the possibility of Spain's joining the war on the German side had been very real during the first part of the conflict and, consequently, Madrid and Lisbon, being neutral, had become operation centres for the intelligence services of the main players. It had been Churchill's idea to set up a network of civilian spies without the knowledge of the Spanish authorities.

Alan Hillgarth brought me up to speed on the schemers and plotters in Madrid, explaining in detail, while showing me photographs of the various people. There had even been a plan the Germans had hatched to kidnap the Duke and Duchess of Windsor. I was stunned by what I learnt.

The former king and his American wife had arrived in Spain on 25 July 1940 in their Buick, followed by an immense amount of luggage. On their arrival, Samuel Hoare informed them that Churchill wished them to return immediately to England.

"Madrid is full of German agents. The German Embassy is the largest in the world and the ambassador, Baron von Stohrer, and his wife not only were guests at the houses of the most prominent Spanish families, but also have direct access to General Franco and his wife, Doña Carmen. They wielding unparalleled influence, while our Ambassador is rarely invited to the Pardo Palace, the centre of power. They also work in close collaboration with Ramón Serrano Suñer, Spain's Minister of Foreign Affairs and who is Franco's brother in law"

"That must be most frustrating for the Ambassador." I interjected.

"Well he knew that Madrid could prove too much of a temptation for the Duke and Duchess, who could easily fall prey to all the flattery and adulation. During their stay they had been received everywhere as if he were still king, and the duchess was treated like his queen, even by some of the remaining members of the former Spanish royal family, such as the Infante D. Alfonso de Orleans. Miguel Primo de Rivera, Marquis of Estella and son of the founder of the Falange and Doña Sol, sister of the Duke of Alba visited at their hotel suite and, it was rumoured, gave them the fascist salute! A very real danger existed of them being lured into the arms of the Germans with the promise of being restored to the throne. After all, the duke's admiration for Hitler was no secret, nor was the duchess's hatred of Britain."

While Captain Hillgarth was telling me all this, I realised how extremely concerned he was. He was barely able to conceal his indignation but, being a true Englishman, he managed to control his feelings. I was struck by what a highly disciplined man he was; a trait he had undoubtedly learnt in the Royal Navy. I did not interrupt him

'During their nine days in Madrid and under the close scrutiny of the ambassador,' he went on explaining, 'they visited the city, went to a bullfight, were invited to a flamenco evening by the Count and Countess of Herentals, and were wined and dined by the most prominent fascists. our efforts to persuade them to return to England did not bear any fruit. Alas, the duke demanded to know exactly what post he would be appointed to and was adamant that the duchess be addressed officially as Her Royal Highness!'

'I would have thought that being a duchess, for an absolute nobody like her, would have been sufficient honour,' I could not help myself repeating what I had heard my mama say so many times.

'In hindsight, however,' he continued saying, undisturbed by my inappropriate comment, 'I now believe that His Majesty should have been more generous in this affair. It would have been in our interest to grant her the damned title she so covets, and thus to have lured them both to return home. It would certainly have saved everybody a lot of aggravation. I think that both queens have much influence on the king and they did not want the duchess anywhere near him. They wished at all costs to prevent the duke's presence from overshadowing that of His Majesty, but in my opinion the medicine has been worse than the disease.'

'So what happened?' I asked impatiently.

'They were finally persuaded to leave Madrid and in early July they moved to Estoril where they stayed at a villa owned by Ricardo Espiritu Santo, one of the wealthiest men in Portugal and a close friend of Sir Walford Selby, our ambassador there, who had arranged it all. It was in Estoril that the duke received the news from England that they were welcome to return but there would be no royal treatment for the duchess. The decision was final. The Prime Minister, fed up with the duke, sent to Portugal a common friend, Sir Walter Mouckton, to offer him the Governorship of the Bahamas and to inform him that British Intelligence had uncovered signs of a Nazi plot to kidnap them and hold them hostage.' He stopped, took a deep breath and continued, saying, 'the duke apparently shrugged the news off lightly.' I was beginning to realise that they found themselves between a rock and a hard place: on one hand, we were pressuring them to take the post in the Bahamas as soon as possible; and on the other, the Germans and their friends were sending envoys to persuade them to return to Spain.'

'This is incredible!' I said

'We found out later that the German Foreign Minister, von Ribbentrop, had outlined a plan in a telegram to Baron von Stohrer. The plan was to have the Count and Countess of Herentals and other Spanish friends of the duke to invite them for a fortnight's visit to Spain so as not to raise their or the British authorities' suspicions. Once in Spain, they were to be persuaded to remain there, even if it meant that the Spanish authorities had to arrest them. Under German influence, the duke would be made to see that the Germans wanted peace and that it was the Prime Minister who stood in the way. The Germans wanted to force peace on us at whatever cost and were prepared to offer the duke the throne, allowing him to make the duchess his queen.'

I was flabbergasted. I sat in silence and looked at Alan in disbelief.

'The duke would have found this plan very appealing; but it is still unknown whether he himself had any part in it. It was no secret how attractive a return to Spain seemed to him, nor that he loathed the idea of being sent to a remote outpost of the Empire such as the Bahamas. Baron Oswald von Hoyningen-Huene, the German Ambassador in Lisbon, was a regular at the dinner parties they gave in the Espiritu Santo villa.'

I could not believe what I was being told. The fact that the former king could bring himself to allow to sit at his table the ambassador of a country with which his own country was at war, struck me as incomprehensible. My mother's attitude towards Harry Giglioli came to my mind. She had put her patriotism before our personal welfare, which was impeccable behaviour.

'Fortunately for us, the duke had left both their passports at the embassy in order to obtain return visas for Spain and France, and Sir Walford Selby had not returned them. It was at this point that von Ribbentrop, aware of the impasse, arranged for senior agent Walter Schellenberg to go to Lisbon and organise a secret operation to kidnap them and take them to Spain. He was working directly under Himmler's orders.'

'But how could they carry out such a plan?' I asked in bewilderment.

'Portuguese friends within the aristocracy were to invite them to a shooting expedition at a mountain estate close to Spain. The border police had been bribed to look the other way while the duke and duchess entered Spain. They were to be escorted to Madrid under Spanish military protection as guests of the Spanish government. The Germans were to keep their intervention secret and have the couple under surveillance. Fortunately, the whole plot collapsed when, after much hesitation, the duke finally accepted the post in the Bahamas. Frantic last-minute efforts were made and the Spanish interior minister, Serrano Suñer, sent the Marquis of Estella to try to persuade them to change their minds on the very eve of their departure for Nassau. They were told that our government planned to have them murdered. Obviously, he was unable to show them any proof, as it was a complete fabrication by German intelligence.

To our relief, in the end, they set sail for their new post, though, unbelievably, keeping von Ribbentrop under the mistaken impression that they were still open to other possibilities. You can imagine, Rodney, how uneasy we have all been with this entire affair and I am sure by now you realise how valuable all the information you will gather will be for us.'

I had to admit that I fully shared the Naval Attaché's indignation, as the whole incident had put Britain's war effort in jeopardy. How could the Duke of Windsor possibly consider that Hitler could reinstate him on the British throne with Queen Wallis at his side? I wondered whether he had gone mad.

7. A NEST OF SPIES

The dinner at the embassy went very well and the ambassador and his wife, Lady Maud, a large plain but charming woman, introduced me to all their Spanish friends. I have learnt to love Madrid and felt quite at ease amid the very polite *madrileños*. The autumn temperature was very pleasant, and the intense blue of Madrid's clear and crisp sky bewitched me then as much as it does today.

That October I was very busy accepting invitations to different parties, where my host generally introduced me to the whole family, knowing within weeks all of Madrid. I went to partridge shoots in the countryside, which were quite an elaborate affair. Nonetheless, rural life in Spain was very primitive. Most *fincas*[1] had no electricity or heating, and barely any plumbing. To make matters worse, the roads leading to them were quite dreadful. The landscape of the countryside was empty, broken by a few peasants riding their donkeys. They all looked rather famished and sad. I have never been a good shot, but I went through the motions and got on splendidly well with my hosts.

On most evenings I would start the night with a drink at the bar of the Palace Hotel, where Hungarian pianist Jorge Jalpen played. He was a highly accomplished musician who excelled at the classics. I soon got used to dining at eleven, which I found extremely civilised. Afterwards, I would go with my new friends to Villa Rosa, the fashionable nightclub, where one could also have dinner.

I took eagerly to my new job, and was soon in full waltz with Madrid society. I think the combination of my age and my cosmopolitan education opened all doors. I befriended not only with people my age but also their parents, who loved to talk and gossip with a foreigner.

[1] Country estates

The first thing I learnt was to be very discreet. The Gestapo had many informers among Spanish civilians, so I limited myself to listening, observing and making small talk. I got used to being watched and followed, so I had to be extremely cautious.

The chic thing to do in the afternoons was to go for tea to a tearoom named Embassy, situated on the very central Paseo de la Castellana and owned by a delightful Irish lady called Margaret Taylor.

MI9 had the task of rescuing prisoners of war and helping Jews and gentiles escape from the Nazis, Spain being a natural evasion route. I soon learnt that Embassy had become the most active escapee rescue centre in Spain. Although the Spanish government accepted their entrance, their evacuation to Portugal and Gibraltar had to be clandestine as the Gestapo was well informed of most activities, and the rescue of Jews through Spain would have not been accepted. It was an amazing feat and a paradox that such a frivolous place was the centre for such humanitarian activities.

The mixture of Embassy's clients was incredible. Mingling with the old-time aristocracy were many Germans from the embassy at 5 Paseo de la Castellana, the English crowd with their Spanish friends, and die-hard *falangistas*[2].

Prince Max von Hohenlohe was always passing messages to us, in an effort to persuade the ambassador to push for peace, which he naturally refused to do. I once bumped into an Italian princess, accompanied by none other than Countess Ciano, daughter of the Duce. This explosive cocktail of people explains the highly charged atmosphere of Embassy that was in those days quite a remarkable place. Margaret Taylor was the sole captain of the ship.

I remember one afternoon having tea with friends among who was Pepe Ruiz-Gimenez, whom we called Opus Night, and his brother Joaquín, known as Opus Day, and who went on to become Spanish Ambassador to the Vatican during the fifties. They were both highly intelligent members of Opus Dei, a Catholic sect that is still very influential in Spain today. Sitting at a large table opposite us was Alan Lubbock, with Michael and Elisabeth Creswell, the Babington-Smiths, David Thompson and a Spanish couple whom I had met at a dinner party at the British Embassy. I was aware they

---

[2] Members of the National Socialist Party

were discussing the best ways to save the many Jews and other refugees who had reached Spain without any papers. The presence of the most prominent members of society sipping tea and nibbling on cucumber sandwiches was an excellent cover for the clandestine activities that went on there.

I was not involved in any way with MI9 but knew of their work. Michael Creswell was the head of the organisation in Spain and he did a splendid job. To aid him in his difficult task, Creswell recruited a number of Spanish civilians with conservative views. Leftists were out of the question because the Spanish police had them all under constant surveillance.

Every week I reported to Captain Hillgarth, of whom I was becoming quite fond. We casually discussed many subjects. He told me about his life, starting from Osborne Naval College, which he had entered at the tender age of eight, passing through the Riff Rebellion in North Africa in which he had fought in the twenties, to his time as a gold prospector in Bolivia and his success as an adventure novelist. He gave me some of his novels to read which I thoroughly enjoyed, especially *The War Maker*, which was set in Spanish Morocco and which he autographed for me. It is one of the treasures of my library. Alan was a highly accomplished man who treated people in such a way that it made them feel completely at ease. His sense of humour was very British, dry and ironic and I liked it as it made me feel at home; at times I was unsure whether he was joking or deadly serious.

Our meetings were often interrupted by calls from the Prime Minister and soon I became aware that Alan was receiving direct instructions from Downing Street. He found the information I passed on to him very useful, or so he said.

As the ambassador had foreseen, no one considered me a threat. I was able to move easily in all circles and also befriend many German sympathisers who were all charming to me.

I was enjoying myself very much and lived well on the generous allowance the embassy gave me. One thing that fascinated me about Madrid society was how they loved mingling with the Gypsies, whom they invited to their homes to dance, sing and party. The Gypsy matador, Gitanillo de Triana, whom I went to see at the Ventas bull ring during the San Isidro festivities, though illiterate, had knowledge of life equivalent to that of any philosopher. I sometimes went with him, Lola Flores, Manolo Caracol and Imperio Argentina, who had an overwhelming personality, to the flamenco *tablaos*[3] that only Gypsies and artists frequented. I was learning a lot about Spanish culture and as the days passed I appreciated it more and more. I was fascinated!

Chicote was a bar on the Gran Vía where men went to meet the most beautiful women in the city. In the basement, the owner, Pedro Chicote, had a drink museum full of unique bottles from all over the world. He also ran a black market operation. In those days, penicillin was in great demand and very difficult to obtain, so those families that could afford it bought it there at exorbitant prices; payment in works of art and jewels was accepted. I have to say, I found this situation quite unacceptable, but it must be understood that Spain had just emerged from a terrible war that had left the country devastated and in ruins.

One evening in Chicote, Dionisio Sanchez, who worked for MI6, introduced me to one of the most sophisticated and elegant women I have ever met. Her name was Felisin. She was in her mid-twenties and a Balenciaga model. She looked irresistible in her Balenciaga dress, which emphasised her delicate long neck. That same evening I went to her apartment and we spent an unforgettable night together. The attraction was mutual, and we continued our rendezvous on a regular basis until I left Madrid.

She never charged me a peseta, and I treated her like a lady and a close friend, taking her out to dinner, showering her with presents, and dancing with her at Villa Rosa. She was a mine of information, as she had a wide variety of clients. Captain Hillgarth was delighted with the information that I got from her.

Until I had arrived in Spain I was not really familiar with its recent history. I had heard my mother say that it had been terribly sad when the king had gone into exile as he was such a charming gentleman but we never discussed the reasons. So once in Madrid I was giving a crash course on the events of the years that had led to the bloody Civil War that cost Spain over a million lives.

The Civil War had wrecked Spain, the infrastructure being ruined during the conflict with the result that there were two Madrids: one was the dramatic Madrid of the majority of the population who could hardly make ends meet; the Madrid of people who went hungry, suffered the bitter

[3] ???

winter cold and had no access to medicines or education; people who were victims of the bad harvests and the scarce food rations; a city where packs of wild dogs attacked the starving population at night in the dark alleys—a real nightmare not much better than the terrible war that they had recently endured. In contrast there was the Madrid of the privileged few to whom I had been accepted with open arms and who bought everything in the black market and enjoyed life as best they could oblivious to what was happening around them.

The regime was also divided in two camps. On one side stood the fascists of the *Falange* party, the only legalised political party, who were besotted with Hitler and Mussolini, wanted to turn Spain into a National Socialist state and who were trying with all their might to win the struggle for the Generalissimo's ear and persuade him to enter the war on the Axis side. On the other side stood the monarchist, traditional conservatives who had supported Franco during the war but admired Britain and its class structure and were waiting eagerly for the return of King Alfonso XIII. They despised the fascists, whom they found vulgar and common, although most of them where not too keen on democracy. They were adamant that Spain should stay neutral, and worried that entering the war would consolidate the *Falange's* power and would prevent the king from returning from exile.

Spanish society was now rigidly ultra-conservative and governed by strict Catholic principles. There was little room for reconciliation as Franco cleaned the country of all he considered undesirables. The strict Catholic principles meant that for a young man of my age the only way to satisfy a strong sex drive was to be fortunate enough to know someone like Felisin or one of her friends. My friends' daughters or sisters were completely out of bounds, although I must admit I flirted very innocently with some of them! It was governed by a double moral standard. Prostitution was illegal, but certain women were protected by men in high places and were able to carry on their business undisturbed. As these men gave them money and financed their homes, they felt they had the right to have sex with them whenever they had the urge. In this way, beautiful women from poor families became the lovers of prominent men in society. As their lovers, they were taken out to places where the men would never take their wives, and they led comfortable lives. Most of the wives were aware of this arrangement, but ignored it as just an accepted fact of life in Madrid's high society.

One day, I was having lunch with Pepe and Joaquín Ruiz-Gimenez at Edelweiss, a German restaurant on Calle Jovellanos, which has not changed in the slightest since those days. It was the favourite restaurant of the German residents and their friends, as the food was genuine German staple. It was and still is excellent: herrings, sauerkraut and many other delicacies.

As we lunched, a tall, well-dressed man approached our table, and I was finally introduced to the Count of Herentals. The Ruiz-Gimenez brothers later explained that the family had come from Spanish Flanders originally, with the first count receiving his title from Phillip II. The current count owned a beautiful palace in Madrid and a country estate in Toledo, where he and the countess entertained lavishly. They had two sons similar to me in age.

'My wife and I are giving a small dinner in honour of Baron Klaus von Jellenbach, who is a good friend and our guest for a few days. I would be delighted if you could come,' he said.

My friends, having a prior engagement, declined the invitation, but I accepted readily. I was certain it would be a very interesting evening and I was not to be disappointed.

The home of the Count and Countess of Herentals was a small palace on the Paseo de la Castellana. A fairly large park with ancient trees surrounded it. Unfortunately, so many of those palaces have since been destroyed to make way for large, characterless modern buildings.

I was invited to many Madrid homes and I have to say that most of the times I found the interior decoration quite dreary; I have always disliked heavy Castilian furniture, and I was not accustomed to be surrounded by so many religious paintings and artefacts. As winter was approaching, they were inevitably cold and damp, as coal was heavily rationed. Thus, I was not prepared for the exquisite taste of this home or for their display of luxury. Magnificent paintings and tapestries hung from the walls, while Bohemian chandeliers full of candles gave the house a sedate atmosphere from another era. Jorge Jalpen provided the entertainment. He played pieces by Mozart, Wagner and other German composers exquisitely on a grand piano.

The countess was petite but had a strong personality not overshadowed by that of her husband. She wore an exquisite evening dress and a stunning diamond necklace with matching bracelet that glittered in the candlelight. Her vibrant eyes were almond-shaped and their colour complemented her beautiful olive complexion. She was a charming host who promptly introduced me to the other guests.

'Rodney, let me introduce you to our guest of honour, Baron Klaus von Jellenbach, who owns a magnificent collection of paintings, probably one of the best in the world'

'You exaggerate, my dear,' he said as we shook hands.

'We were introduced once before, in Monte Carlo, by the Marquis of San Felice,' I said.

The baron seemed to remember me.

At that moment, Jose Luis de Arrese, a top *Falange* leader arrived. The conversations just about ceased as a big the other guests made a big fuss about him. In an amazing twist of fate, I would marry his niece in 1955. I knew from Alan Hillgarth that he was a very influential man in the regime, and a few years later, he became the housing minister.

I had been served a Scotch when a very attractive woman approached me from across the room. She must have been in her early thirties. Her fabulous red hair fell loose over her shoulders. She was wearing a sleeveless black gown with a fine gold and diamond choker, which had a diamond brooch in the shape of a swastika. Her pale skin, covered in freckles, and her delicate feminine appearance belied the strength of her character, as I was soon to discover. She had a broad smile lacking in warmth. I felt that she seemed very much in control.

'My name is Gisela von Krieger, Rodney,' she said, introducing herself in perfect English with a heavy German accent.

'Have we met before?' I asked politely.

'I saw you in the South of France, but we have never been formally introduced, although we do have some friends in common.'

'And who are they, may I ask?

'Harry Giglioli and the Marquis of San Felice.'

'They are friends no more. Both are my enemies now, and so are you,' I said provocatively.

She laughed seductively and took a sip of champagne.

'I have always found you very attractive. In addition, you are quite daring for someone your age. Do you like older women?'

'I like all types of women, even those who are the enemy! But what is such a beautiful lady as you doing in Madrid?'

'I am a spy,' she said jokingly. 'Ah, I see that you don't believe me?' she asked teasingly. I found her easy sense of humour very sexy, and she knew it as she continued to play with me. She was in control.

'I am in fact an art consultant and a close friend of Klaus. I am staying at the home of the German Ambassador and shall be in Madrid for a few weeks. You must meet them—they are a very nice enemy couple.'

Gisela introduced me to Baron and Baroness von Stohrer who, I knew from the reports at the embassy, were very close to the centre of power in Madrid. I had seen them having lunch at Edelweiss and Horcher, the luxury German restaurant on *Calle Alfonso XII*, but we had not been previously introduced. They were a formidable fascist couple, always trying to recruit people to embrace Nazi ideals. They hosted lunches and dinners to which most of the ministers and their wives were invited, and they lunched with Mrs. Franco at the *Palacio del Pardo* on a regular basis, no doubt to ensure that she used her powerful influence over her husband in the right direction. They had been very active in the Windsor plot revealed to me earlier by Alan Hillgarth.

We exchanged some pleasantries and then Gisela took me by the arm and led me to a corner where we chatted happily until a rather unpleasant-looking man in an SS captain's uniform interrupted us.

'This is Captain Hans Vogel,' Gisela said, frowning.

The captain kissed her hand. 'What a lovely surprise, Gisela. What brings you here?' he said, raising his eyebrows.

'Hans, can't you see we are having a conversation? And you know very well what I am doing here, so if you don't mind…'

There was certainly some sort of tension between them. Captain Vogel moved on without uttering another word, and Gisela muttered something in German to herself that was obviously not pleasant.

My situation suddenly dawned on me. I was only going on nineteen, and yet there I was in a foreign country, working for my government, and surrounded by extremely charming people, most of whom were, almost certainly, extremely dangerous. I thought about my mother, Uncle Jack and Princess Magaloff. I wondered if they were still alive and I felt a pang of loneliness.

'Rodney, what is bothering you?' Gisela asked with a kind of alluring sweetness in her voice. At that moment, the count approached and whisked her away to introduce her to some of the other guests. We were about twenty people in all and I knew several of them. I could see that most were Nazi sympathisers and that they felt very much at ease because they knew each other well.

I was sitting alone, observing everything, when the countess came up and introduced me to a distinguished Hungarian of medium height. He was about forty and had a broad smile.

'This is my dear friend, Laszlo Szekeres. He is a magnificent painter. You must come to the opening of his exhibition next week.'

'I will be delighted to do so,' I replied.

Laszlo was a refined man who wore an impeccably tailored suit. *Definitely a gentleman*, I thought.

'Savile Row?' I asked.

'No. Cutuli. He is a local tailor. He has nothing to envy in Savile Row though. I'll take you to meet him, if you want.'

'I'd be delighted.'

We had a drink together and soon discovered we felt a great affinity for each other. We had a friend in common, Prince George Govecki, a journalist whose *nom de plume* was Armand Arronsart and who was a great grandson of the poet Mickiewicz. We had both stayed at his estate near Vilno in Poland[4].

'It's a small world,' he said.

'Who is that very tall man with such a stern expression?' I asked intrigued by the presence of the unfriendly looking bloke who I had yet not been introduced to.

'Oh, he is Hans Thomsen, the head of the Nazi party in Spain. Not someone you would like to meet. A nasty fellow!'

'And tell me,' I asked in a matter-of-fact tone, 'what do you know about the baron?'

'Well, Rodney, it is an old title, and his family was quite prominent under the late Kaiser. He is very influential now and very wealthy. Over the last few years he has managed to acquire an outstanding art collection: Braque, Picasso, Kandinsky, Manet, Ingres, Corot, Courbet, Léger, Tintoretto, El Greco, Degas, Monet, Renoir. You name them and he has them.'

[4] Now in Lithuania

'How come?' I asked.

'He is a close friend of Göering and they both share an insatiable appetite for art. Most of his best paintings were apparently given to him for safekeeping by Jewish acquaintances, first in Germany and later in Poland and France, and he has shared them with his master, who permits and encourages the spoil as long as he gets first choice. That clown in Berlin admires his patriotism!' he added sarcastically.

'So he has no intention of giving the paintings back to their owners once the war is over?'

'My dear chap, you are so naïve. Those poor Jews are all probably dead by now!'

Over dinner, Baron Stohrer tried to convince us that Britain would soon lose the war and that it would be in our best interest to seek peace with Germany. He went on and on about Hitler's plans for Europe and even tried to persuade me that we English were blind for not seeing the greatness of his master plan. I kept my eyes and ears wide open while I made polite conversation.

As I was taking my coffee in the smoking room, Gisela von Krieger joined me again.

'Are you enjoying yourself?'

'I am, very much so.'

'Well, Rodney. The best is still to come.'

That night she took me to the von Stohrer's residence. I knew I was entering a snake pit but could not refuse the invitation, and the challenge excited me in more ways than one.

Her body was that of a goddess, with small and firm breasts. Every single inch of her entire lustful body was covered in freckles. Her big green eyes were full of desire for my body that she grabbed with hunger, tearing off my clothes and kissing me passionately. There was no feeling between us, only unrestricted carnal desire.

'I want to tie you up and blindfold you,' she said suddenly but firmly. I shuddered with excitement, probably because I was walking on thin ice. She took a silk scarf out of a drawer and I dutifully let her cover my eyes. Then, with another scarf, she tied my wrists in front of my body. I felt her nails softly scratch my chest all the way down to my navel. She kissed me and I kissed her back. Her tongue was caressing my gums. She then kissed my ears and blew the air of passion into them. It felt so, so good! She got herself behind me and started licking with her warm tongue the back of my neck all the way down my spine. I gasped with pleasure when I felt her tongue on my hole. Then, she turned me around forcefully and took me in her mouth. I was so hard with excitement that I was on the verge of crossing the gates of bliss.

'You like it, Rodney, don't you?' she whispered in my ear.

'Yes, I do very much,' I said with a gasp. I was about to come and she must have felt it too because she let go of my hard member. She pushed me on the bed violently and then she mounted me. She rode me like an Amazon and after a period of ecstasy, we simultaneously reached the point of no return.

I have to admit it was a night I would never forget.

It was now December 1941, and up to now, the news from the front had not been very encouraging, as the Germans appeared to be unstoppable. After the Japanese attack on Pearl Harbor, the skeptic Americans finally joined the war on the side of the Allies and we all became more optimistic. Nazi propaganda was everywhere and the Spanish press did very little to report British successes.

That December was bitterly cold and it snowed on and off continuously. The power cuts occurred regularly. I went to the cinema on several occasions with the intent of watching the No-do, the government news broadcast. The scenes of bombed London devastated me. According to the broadcaster, it was only a matter of time before Britain lost the war. The fascist propaganda was incredible: a bishop blessing the opening of a factory in Bilbao; a battalion of *Falange* Youth wearing their uniforms parading in front of a beaming Caudillo and his wife; the ever present dictator and a delighted Doña Carmen entering the Cathedral in Burgos under a canopy followed by bishops and cardinals for a Te Deum. Spain had been saved form the claws of communism and Franco was the father of the nation, its saviour!

Hitler had scrapped the plan to invade Britain after realising the huge cost involved. Even so, the Luftwaffe had bombed and destroyed many British cities between September and November, yet had not succeeded in breaking our fighting spirit. Much to Germany's surprise, and despite our isolation and painful exposure to the Luftwaffe, we did not surrender.

My life continued much the same. I still had no news from my mother, but I tried to convince myself that no news was good news. Therefore, I went on with my routine: golf most mornings in *Puerta de Hierro*, which is still a very sophisticated sports club just outside Madrid; then lunch at L'Hardy, Botín or some other fashionable restaurant, followed by a siesta in the early afternoon. Most days, I would go to Embassy for tea, to the Palace Hotel for a few drinks and then, after dinner, to the favourite nightspots. Chipen, on *Calle Peligros*, was a noisy restaurant very much in fashion where I ate on a regular basis. Once a week I would meet Alan Hillgarth at his office. He had become something of a father figure to me.

I became good friends with Laszlo Szekeres and naturally attended his exhibition, which was a huge success. He was a good horseman, and I accompanied him to the Alberto Aguilera stables, where he rented a horse. He introduced me to Beltran Osorio, Marquis of Cuellar, the son and heir to the Duke of Alburquerque, who was an excellent rider and later became world famous at the turf. The Alburquerques lived on an enormous estate in Algete, outside Madrid. They were a lovely family and very anglophile. Inés, the duchess, reminded me very much of my mother.

I also met Cayetana Fitz James Stuart, the Duchess of Montoro, heir to the Duke of Berwick and Alba, who was also a very keen rider. I had the pleasure to be invited to their home for tea and contemplate their exquisite art collection. Cayetana, upon her father's death, would become the most titled woman in the world.

Most of these people dreamed nostalgically of the restoration of the monarchy. King Alfonso XIII had died in February in a hotel in Rome, and his son, Don Juan, was now their rightful king.

Laszlo and I went out together on many nights, and sometimes we would take Felisin and her friends to dine at Horcher, one of the capital's most sophisticated restaurants. People would whisper as we walked in. Some of the men felt obviously most uneasy with our presence, but Felisin was so graceful and elegant that there was never an awkward moment when we introduced her to the wives of men she knew very intimately. Both Laszlo and I thought it was all extremely amusing. We enjoyed the provocation and got away with it. Laszlo was very generous and in his company the champagne, a rare and expensive item in those austere days, flowed freely.

I could not stop feeling somewhat guilty though. Each time I moved around the city, I was reminded of the reality of the situation. The signs of poverty and misery were everywhere. The shop windows were half empty, beggars huddled together trying to keep warm in doorways and I was heart broken each time I saw the barefoot, wild-faced children with their bloated stomachs. And the awful reality was that Madrid was half-starved; the fascist economic policies of self-sufficiency and the chaotic and very corrupt distribution system did not make matters any easier for the needy. However, the small elite to which I was fully integrated went about as if all this had nothing to do with them.

One Monday morning, I received a call from Alan Hillgarth and he invited me for lunch at the Ritz Hotel.

'I will pick you up at two-thirty at your hotel,' he said. It was the first time we were meeting outside of the embassy.

At the agreed time, a large black Packard stopped at the entrance of the Hotel *Nacional*. In the car with the Naval Attaché was Alan Lubbock. Located at the *Plaza de la Lealtad* opposite the Palace Hotel where I used to go regularly, the imposing hotel was a favourite haunt with the Germans and Italians.

The dining room was elegant with many fascist officers in uniform accompanied by a few well-dressed women. Alan was wearing his too and with all his medals.

'A little provocation is good!' he said, lowering his voice to a whisper as we were shown to our table by the maître d'.

Sitting at a table close to ours I recognized Hans Thomsen sitting with a well-dressed woman whom I assumed was his wife.

'Is he as dangerous as he looks?' I asked

'More!' Both Alans exclaimed unanimously

'But why does the German Nationalist Party have a leader in Madrid?'

'Thomsen has to make sure that the German community hear is totally loyal to the party. Himmler signed a pact with the Spanish government in 1938 by which any German suspect of not being loyal to the Third Reich could be arrested and deported to Germany without trial. Needless to say that after the Civil war all German residents here at least pretend to be loyal members of the party or else!' Alan Hillgarth clarified.

'Rodney, as you can see we are outnumbered here. There are also very few Spanish. The ambassador likes that we come here every now and then. He will be joining us in a moment with Lady Maud. Before they arrive Alan has some news for you.'

'Yes, Rodney,' said Alan, 'I have just returned with *Lalo* Martinez-Alonso from the camp in Miranda del Ebro. The situation is really quite serious there. There are more than 3,000 prisoners, yet the facilities are for only 500.'

'This is a camp for prisoners of war with no papers,' Hillgarth clarified, 'and we with the Americans are in charge of the general well-being of the prisoners. We try to have them released and then we help them leave the country as fast as possible.'

'Who is this "Lalo"?' I enquired.

'He's a Spanish doctor and a close friend. He is very active in MI9 and is doing a great job helping us get people out of the country. I'm sure you'll meet him soon.'

'What does this have to do with my work?' I asked.

'Rodney, you will be glad to know we have finally, after so many negotiations, secured the release of your friend Alfred Kempler. He is quite ill though and will have to stay at Dr Martinez-Alonso's home until he's well enough to travel,' Alan said sternly. He suddenly coughed to signal the arrival of the ambassador and his wife.

That December, while the Americans were mobilising for war, Alan Lubbock came by my hotel on the 23rd. I would finally be seeing Fred and I was so excited.

'It would be nice if we could meet for tea today. Let's say at seven at Embassy.'

At the agreed time, I arrived at 12 Paseo de la Castellana. Alan was sitting with the lovely Margaret Taylor. I joined them at the table.

'He can't wait to see you, Rodney,' she said softly. 'Right now he's upstairs, as he will be spending a couple of days with me. It is probably better if you join me for dinner tomorrow. It's Christmas Eve after all—I am Irish, you are British and on your own. Our friendship will not be cause for suspicion.'

The following morning I went to buy some presents for Margaret and her young daughter, Consuelo, and naturally for good old Fred, whom I considered a hero.

It was my first Christmas in Madrid. There were not many lights in the streets, with the exception of a few lighted shops. Spain was slowly rising from its ashes and the official attitude was one of complete austerity. It was very quiet in the streets and it was raining solidly. A pair of Guardia Civiles huddled under their green capes. I had arranged a taxi to pick me up at the hotel. On the way, we passed a gasogene stuck in the middle of the street and a desperate, soaked man trying to start the engine. I felt sorry for him.

At about eight, I arrived at Margaret's house. The moment he saw me, Fred threw his arms around me and we hugged while he cried like a child.

'Fred! It is so good to see you. Finally, you are on your way to freedom,' I said, happily.

'Let's all sit down and have a glass of port to celebrate this most auspicious reunion,' said Margaret, who had been watching us with a broad smile.

We followed her into the sitting room. The house, decorated in a very English style, was elegant yet subdued, with no concessions to extravagance. There were several floral motifs and it felt cosy and homely. Consuelo, Margaret's lovely little girl, came to wish us good night before her nanny whisked her off to bed.

Dinner was an extremely pleasant affair. There was a warm sense of family and the traditional English food was delicious. Fred recounted how he had been released from Cartagena and taken to Miranda del Ebro where he had fallen ill with TB which was rampant in Spain. Apparently, Michael Creswell had stumbled on him lying in the hospital during one of his routine visits to the camp. The British immediately took hold of the excellent opportunity and had him released to them on medical grounds. Fortunately, the Gestapo never discovered who he was and what information he possessed.

'I'll be quite glad to leave this country. I haven't been treated too well,' he said as he forced a smile. 'Miranda del Ebro was a nightmare! The fact that we did not know when we were going to be deported or shot did not make things any easier. I lived in a constant state of fear. However, after dinner I am leaving at last, Rodney.'

'Well, my friend, you'll soon be a free man.'

'The Spanish press is manipulating public opinion by saying we are Freemasons and responsible for the Civil War. They now blame us for Spain's economic problems and use the same rhetoric against us as the Nazis do. I have been told that all the ministries have been ordered to comply with Gestapo policies. It is absurd! The government is using the same anti-Jewish rhetoric as in the time of Queen Isabella, the Catholic!'

'This madness will soon be over, now that the Americans are joining in the war,' I said hesitantly, trying to boost his morale.

Fred went on, as if he needed to get things off his chest. 'The Spanish Ministry of Foreign Affairs has even made it a crime to sell to European Jews passage on Spanish vessels leaving from Portugal. They want us all dead. Wiped out!' he added bitterly.

'A bright future lies ahead of you,' said Margaret reassuringly.

She served a delicious Christmas pudding with homemade brandy butter, and to our delight, Fred drew the lucky sixpence. This was a good omen indeed.

At exactly midnight, a car with diplomatic plates pulled up in front of Margaret's home. The rain had shortly ceased. Making sure there was nobody on the streets, and with most caution, we bundled Fred into the car. Then I heard Margaret whispering, 'God bless you!' We both knew he would still face many dangers before arriving at the border, as the Civil Guard had many roadblocks.

Despite the bitterly cold night, and as the skies were now clear, I walked back to my hotel thinking about Margaret and the group of Spaniards who were helping so altruistically in rescue operations that were saving thousands of lives. These were true anonymous heroes.

The following day I had an unexpected call from Alan asking me to go to the embassy. I was in for a surprise. I took a bath, dressed, and soon afterwards was in his office.

'Do we have any problems?' I asked with concern, as soon as I entered the room. Captain Hillgarth was sitting behind his desk and stood up to greet me. King George stared at me from the portrait behind him.

'Merry Christmas, Rodney!'

'Do you have any news about my mother?' I asked hopefully. They had obviously not summoned me just to wish me a merry Christmas.

'No, I'm afraid I don't. I called you because we have a delicate mission for you. We are delighted with your work and—'

'What mission?' I interrupted with eagerness.

'You are to return to London immediately and then you will be flown to Cairo.'

'Egypt?' I grunted.

Alan said nothing but offered me a John Player's, the cigarettes that I smoked ever after until I quit when I was reaching forty. I accepted it and he took one too. We both took a deep puff and a cloud of smoke filled the room.

'Your mission is to befriend a young Spaniard who we believe is working for the Germans. His name is Francisco de Beaumont. Sir Miles Lampson, the ambassador in Cairo, will brief you as soon as you arrive there. The war in the desert is not going well for us. Rommel, whom we call the Desert Fox, is a very able commander with great tactical awareness and a natural flair for mobile warfare. We cannot afford to lose the Suez Canal to the enemy and we must do our utmost to stop any intelligence information from reaching him.'

'Why is he called the Desert Fox?'

'Because he is as cunning as a fox and he constantly improvises and uses any trick to outsmart us and he is successful on many occasions,' Alan replied, wearily.

8. GLITTERING CAIRO

I left Madrid on Boxing Day without having a chance to say goodbye to anybody. I was mainly concerned for Felisin, who I was certain would be terribly worried. It was agreed that the ambassador would make excuses for my sudden disappearance.

Four days after arriving in London, I took the Imperial Airways flight to Cairo where an embassy car was waiting for me. A young Foreign Office chap was there to collect me at the airport. His name was James but I do not recall his surname. He was in his mid-twenties, pleasant looking and rather pompous.

Everything seemed fascinating; the colours, the sounds and smells were as if from another world. We drove through the bazaar area where the men were wearing *djellabas*[1] and I could hear them speaking in Arabic, a language that was completely foreign to me at the time. The streets were full of camels and donkeys used for transport.

'This area is called the Mouski,' James said, breaking the silence. 'This is where the ancient mosques are.'

'It's amazingly interesting! I must come and visit,' I said.

'I wouldn't recommend that. We are not particularly popular with the Egyptians.'

'How is that?' I asked with genuine curiosity.

'The wogs[2] think the Germans will liberate them from British oppression.'

I did not like his tone of disrespect, which I soon discovered was quite generalised among the Brits and based on an obvious superiority complex and a misconceptiom. I let him know my opinion that to be respected one had to respect.

---

[1] Long, loosely fitted, hooded outer robes with full sleeves

[2] The term stood for 'Working on Government Service' but it was used in a derogatory way to mean 'Wily Oriental Gentlemen'

The scenery soon changed dramatically. The donkeys and camels gave way to Rolls-Royces and Bentleys, and the streets took on the appearance of a sophisticated city like Paris. The men were elegantly dressed in linen suits and I saw many chic women in front of Circurel and Le Salon Vert, which according to James were the top department stores. We passed through Suleiman Pasha Square, which he said was the city's glamorous commercial centre. Here everybody was speaking French and appeared quite oblivious to what was going on at the front.

'There are some really fancy brothels near the hotel. We can have a night out if you feel up to it,' James said, smiling.

The car stopped at the entrance to the Shepherd Hotel, which faced the Ezbekkiah Gardens, Cairo's Tuilleries. James escorted me to reception and then, before leaving me to go up to my room, showed me around what would be my new home for an unknown period. The Karnak Ballroom and the Moorish Hall were quite outstanding.

'Maybe we can have a drink together at the Long Bar this evening, unless Sir Miles has other plans for you,' James suggested cheerfully. 'I shall wait here for you while you freshen up, and then we shall go to the embassy as soon as you are ready.'

Sir Miles Lampson was much taller than I was. At around six-foot five, he was a towering figure with a majestic bearing. He rose from his chair to greet me in his office while saying, 'Well, well, who do we have here? Alan and Samuel Hoare have highly recommended you, young man. They seem to believe you are perfect for this mission, are you not? '

'What would you have me do, sir?'

'You are about the same age as the boy.'

'The boy? What boy? You mean Francisco de Beaumont?' I asked confused.

'No, no, no. Farouk, the bloody king.'

Why did he have to follow the same pattern of disrespect for the Egyptians, for their king? I asked myself, feeling quite annoyed.

'Captain Hillgarth told me that His Majesty is very much loved by his people,' I said, trying tactfully to show him how I felt.

'He is! Very much loved by ignorant people who consider the Germans are their saviours. Bloody idiots!' I could feel that the ambassador was irritated, but his arrogance made me feel uncomfortable. 'The German propaganda machine has led them to believe that Hitler was a Muslim born in Egypt. Fools! They do not realise that if the Germans take Egypt, the first thing they will do is depose their beloved king and replace him on the throne with his fascist uncle.' He paused and then asked as an afterthought, 'did you know, Rodney, that they call Hitler, "Mohammed Haider"? We think your new *friend* Francisco de Beaumont may have a lot to do with all this rubbish propaganda. We also believe he could be passing very sensitive information to Rommel. We suspect he must be a German agent.'

'But if you are so certain, why don't you bag him?'

Sir Miles took a few seconds to reply. 'We are not certain. We need proof, dear chap, and that is where you come in. It is not easy. To start with Francisco de Beaumont is close to the king. He is also under the protection of some of our friends.'

'What do you mean, Sir Miles.'

'Some of the emerging Arab sheikhs, whom he has befriended, protect him. He currently lives in Dubai but is constantly on the move between Cairo, Teheran and Baghdad. In Baghdad he is now close to Prince Abdal-allah, the Regent who is our ally. It is all rather complicated as you can see but we believe his scheming could be undermining our war efforts. It's difficult to know what his up to. He is even a good friend of the Duke of Aosta, who as you might know is the Italian Viceroy of Ethiopia. Nice decent chap, the duke! Pity he's on the wrong side.'

'I'd like to hear more about de Beaumont, Sir,' I said.

'Here, read these papers. But to put you in the picture, he is twenty-five. His family descends from François du Beaumont, who arrived in Madrid in the cortege with King Joseph I, Napoleon's brother. This charming and debonair character married into the Spanish aristocracy and stayed on after the French were driven out of Spain. Francisco's father died shortly after he was born, and his young mother then married a German count and went to live in Berlin with her new husband thus our man is fluent in German, French, English, and Spanish, of course. He is a charmer and moves like a fish in a pond in the upper circles of society. He is the darling of the Egyptian aristocracy. He is known to have no scruples and can be very dangerous. So your job is to get us proof of his activities.'

'So what's the plan of action?' I asked eagerly.

'Your mission is to befriend him. Your cover is that of a young and ambitious war correspondent. You must make him believe that he can get some interesting information out of you while in fact, hopefully, it will be the other way round. We need to know what he is up to before we decide what to do with him. It should not be a difficult job for you, young man. He is now in town, so you must meet him. Enjoy the city's decadent nightlife. If you are as good as Alan says, you will have no problem succeeding in this mission.'

'And how will I do that?

'I am expecting a lovely lady very shortly,' he continued. 'Her name is Irene Guile. She is from Alexandria and comes from a very prominent Venetian Jewish trading family. The king is infatuated with her beauty and sophistication. As she is as worried about the Germans as we are, she is aiding us in ensuring the king does not lean towards the Axis. She is highly popular and will find a way of introducing you to our man.'

A knock on the door interrupted our conversation, and James walked in, accompanied by a stunning woman. Just one look into her eyes, and I could understand how she had won the king's heart. She was not only beautiful, but had that kind of allure that makes some women extremely special. She offered me her hand, and I kissed it.

'So this is the charming Rodney, Sir Miles?' she asked the ambassador.

'Yes, my dear, and now we depend on you to introduce him into the right circles, if you know what I mean.'

She smiled at me.

'Tomorrow I shall send my car to pick you up at the hotel at eight. We will be going to a very special soirée at Princess Shivekiar's palace. You will never forget this New Year's Eve party.'

Princess Shivekiar's palace stood just a few blocks from the Shepherd Hotel. The wealthy princess had been married to her impoverished and loathed cousin, Fuad, before he ascended the throne. King Farouk was very fond of his stepmother, as she gave for him the wildest parties, put women in his path, and encouraged him to gamble. Apparently, it was the princess's way of wreaking revenge on the Fuad dynasty. She had the reputation of being rather Machiavellian, and many people questioned the king's good judgement when he had restored her to full palace rights.

I was ill-prepared for the dream-like setting that awaited me at the palace. It felt like if I had stepped into the *One Thousand and One Nights* tales. The palace glittered in the night with myriads of lights. There were coloured tents placed around the park where the party took place. An army of exotically dressed servants served gallons of pink champagne of an exquisite vintage while three different and magnificent orchestras played the latest tunes. Irene had not yet arrived, so I wandered around the party and noticed that some very sophisticated and good-looking women were eyeing me. Being the new boy in town had its advantages after all. I felt good in my white dinner jacket. The party seemed an exercise in glamorous excess, the like of which I had never seen before.

Suddenly the music came to a halt, the chit-chat ceased and the band struck up the Egyptian national anthem. The king had arrived with the ravishing Irene Guile by his side. Many of the guests stood on their chairs to get a better look at the couple, whom they watched in admiration. Irene looked like a queen. She was wearing a long, ivory-coloured robe embroidered in geometric patterns. The amazing dress could very well have been a creation of Elsa Schiaparelli, my mother's favourite couturier.

'They are lovely, aren't they?' I turned and found myself looking at an attractive and elegant woman who was behind me. She smiled flirtatiously. 'My name is Helen Mosseri. I am a friend of Irene's and she has asked me to look out for you. You must be Rodney.' She had an intense gaze and exuded charm. She was rather tantalising. I kissed her hand.

'You speak remarkably good English, though I detect a slight Greek accent,' I replied.

'Yes, I am Greek. My family are the Polymires. Mosseri is the name of my late husband.'

'Oh, I am so sorry. May I be bold and say that you are a beautiful widow though!'

'Yes you may, and I may say you are a handsome young man! You will be very successful in Cairo if you stay with us long enough. Come. Let me introduce you to His Majesty.' We walked over towards the king and Irene. They both looked at us. Irene's smile was beautiful.

'Your Majesty,' she said, 'May I introduce you to Rodney Mundy, a very likeable Englishman?' The king seemed to be in an excellent mood. He smiled broadly and we shook hands while I lowered my head out of respect. All eyes were now on me.

'You could not have a better introduction card than Irene and Helen,' the king said cheerfully, putting his arm around me with such unexpected familiarity that I felt rather awkward. Irene winked at me, while Helen kissed her on the cheeks. The king and I walked forward in this way, and I could feel the gaze upon us. No doubt everybody was wondering who I was. The king suddenly burped. It took me by surprise. I was aghast, not knowing how to react. He laughed. The two beautiful ladies giggled with embarrassment. I later found out that he used to do this on purpose to annoy people. It was some sort of a test. King Farouk was about my age. He was handsome and possessed a worldly charm and as king he felt he could get away with these small pranks.

'Some Englishmen don't please me too much. Your ambassador, for instance, particularly irritates me,' he said suddenly becoming serious.

'I am sorry to hear that, Your Majesty,' I replied, not knowing very well how to react.

'Helen, darling, why don't you introduce Rodney to some of our friends?' Irene asked, in an effort to change the subject swiftly.

I took my leave of the king and strolled around the party arm in arm with Helen, who introduced me to the crème de la crème of Egyptian society. First, she introduced me to our host, Princess Shivekiar, a small and frail old woman of remarkable character who undoubtedly was a plotter and a schemer. One only had to observe her as she talked to her guests. I also met her son, Prince Wahid—whom Helen said was allegedly having an affair with Queen Farida, the king's wife—Victor Smaika, the famous playboy and friend of Barbara Hutton, and some of the most prominent Jews such as the Lambrossis, Victor Harari, the Cattawis and Baron George de Menasce. Finally, I was introduced to my prey, Francisco de Beaumont.

We hit it off immediately. He was well bred, articulate, highly sophisticated and cheerful, so I did not have to make an effort to like him. I knew that I had to be cautious because he was, after all, supposed to be not only very shrewd but the enemy too. Helen, obviously well informed by Irene, left us together to dine on the magnificent selection of French, Italian and Russian dishes served in the different tents. We spoke in Spanish, which pleased him, and he asked me a lot about Madrid, where he had not been since his childhood. As planned I told him that I was a war correspondent, and from him I learnt that he was a pearl dealer who spent quite a lot of time in Dubai where he was a close friend of the ruling sheikh.

'You must come and stay with me. Dubai is a very interesting place.' I agreed to go when and if my work allowed me to do so, knowing all too well that it would not happen.

'Would you like a cigarette?' I asked, searching in the inside pocket of my dinner jacket.

'What have you lost?' he asked, seeing that I could not find what I was looking for.

'I've misplaced my silver cigarette case. I am certain I put in my pocket. It would be quite upsetting as it was a present from my father!' I replied as I frowned, startled. He started to laugh and could not stop. 'You have just been a victim of the king's long hand.'

'You must be joking!' I said in astonishment as I frowned again.

'The king thinks it's a very funny joke! He is very good at it. They say he received lessons from a master thief he had pardoned from the Turah prison.'

'You are teasing me,' I said in disbelief.

'No. It is absolutely true, Rodney.'

Years later, in 1954, in a twist of fate, I bought back the cigarette case at an auction at Sotheby's. The army had organised it after the king was overthrown, with articles from his personal collection.

Just before the midnight chimes we refilled our glasses with champagne to toast the New Year, while an extravaganza of fireworks lit up the Cairo night. The contrast between Cairo and Madrid could not have been greater.

On January 1st, I decided to explore Cairo and get my bearings. James took me to play golf at the Gezira Sporting Club. There he introduced me to Jacqueline Lampson, Sir Miles's charming young wife. She was the daughter of Sir Aldo Castellani, doctor to the Italian troops, which was no doubt very difficult for Sir Miles to digest. I was disappointed to discover that both native Egyptians and the Turkish aristocracy were excluded from the club. This attitude of superiority would surely prove to be a formula for disaster in the future for us. I believed that winning people's hearts had to be a much better policy. I had heard my father complain at home on many occasions about this attitude. The things he used to say about the treatment of the Indian princes were the same as the shameful behaviour that I was now witnessing first hand in Egypt. Like him, I could not come to terms with this bigotry towards natives and even toward members of ancient aristocratic families whose only crime, as far as I could see, was that they were not white.

That evening, I invited James over for dinner at the hotel, and afterwards he took me gambling at the Royal Automobile Club. It was surprisingly unstuffy and rather fun, and was allegedly the king's favourite gambling den. After I had lost at the roulette, James decided to take me to visit the red light district, which was known as the Fish Market. It was the seediest place I had ever seen. Heavily made-up young girls catered for the many Commonwealth and British soldiers stationed in the city. We witnessed several brawls between drunken soldiers and locals. Violence here was the order of the day, and the murder of both whores and soldiers was not uncommon. James, considering these brothels beneath our station, decided to spare me the unpleasantness of visiting any of them. Instead, we toured the fancier ones that were popular with the officers and were run by European madams with *filles de joies* from many different nations. Cairo was undoubtedly a city of pleasure and very unlike Madrid. In spite of the many temptations, I indulged in no sex that night, but a few too many drinks.

I slept well and woke up late. After a hearty English breakfast, I visited Ismail Pasha Square near the banks of the Nile and then went to the Egyptian Museum, where I was awestruck by the treasures of the ancient Egyptian rulers. I also visited the Cathedral of All Saints, not far from the Kasr-El-Nil Barracks, home of the British Army, before wandering through the Garden City where the embassies and residences of the rich were located.

I could see that modern and ancient Cairo did not mingle, which, I soon discovered, was a sore point with the man on the street, who resented the British troops' overbearing presence and obscene disregard for the king. Although a neutral country, Egypt felt like part of the British Empire. No wonder the locals believed their admired king was the only person who could liberate them from us. I realised for the first time that our old imperialistic attitude was definitely hurting our cause.

Venturing bravely into the Khan el-Khalilli bazaar, I bought a cotton *djellaba* and, putting it on, I amused the locals, which only goes to show that making a small effort of integration helps people accept you. I did not feel threatened at all at any time. Quite the contrary—I managed to speak to some of the locals who, although friendly towards me, were quite blunt about their feelings, they got the message across to me as best they could that we were no better than imperialist pigs—an animal not much liked by the followers of Mahoma. What could be expected from people that came from a land where pigs are lawful food?

Later in the afternoon I ventured to the historical Cairo: the Al Azhar and Sultan Hassan Mosques, the Ben Ezra Synagogue, the Coptic churches and the medieval gates of Bab Zuwayla. Time passed in a flash and, as night fell, I heard the wailing of the muezzin over the city when I decided to take a taxi back to the Shepherd. I created quite a commotion when I entered wearing my *djellaba*.

The following day I could not resist visiting the Cairo of antiquity: the Pyramids and the Sphinx, a dream for any traveller, which left me utterly in awe. I could not help asking myself, how could such an ancient civilisation have built such architectural marvels?

That evening, on 3 January at the appointed time, Francisco met me at the Long Bar for a drink. His insolent indifference struck me though he was in a cheerful mood and most friendly towards me. After a couple of whiskies he took me to dinner at the Auberge des Pyramides, which was one of the most popular nightclubs with Cairo's *jeunesse dorée* and well known for its excellent food. While we were waiting for our meal, sipping cold Chablis, the orchestra played 'I Get a Kick Out of You'.

'The king is here,' said Francisco, suddenly.

Everyone stood up as King Farouk was escorted to his table, accompanied by a once-again ravishing Irene and a large entourage of friends that included the lovely Helen Mosseri. He was really a king taken out of a picture book: handsome, charming, wealthy and with a practical good sense of humour.

After dinner, a waiter asked us to accompany him to the king's table. The group was in a jolly mood. Farouk sipped orangeade while the rest of us drank champagne. We talked about cars, his passion. He seemed rather immature for his age and I could see he was quite desperate to fit in and be part of the gang. He was smoking a huge cigar, much to Irene's irritation, and he laughed as he shot bread pellets at anyone who seemed too pompous for his liking. I must admit there were many of them around us! I found the whole thing quite hilarious, as the king cracked endless jokes and puns at everyone's expense, including his own. I noticed that he was very fond of Francisco, with whom he confided several times during the evening.

'I am leaving for Aswan tomorrow,' the king said. 'You should come, Francisco, and bring Rodney with you. We will be there for a few weeks.'

'Unfortunately, I cannot go, Your Majesty, as I must return to Dubai in a few days. But, Rodney, you should go,' Francisco said, turning to me.

'There is nothing I'd enjoy more, but I have just arrived and my bosses in London would not be too happy...' I said to the king, apologetically. The truth is that I could not think of anything better to do, as Helen would certainly be there as well. 'I will accept Your Majesty's invitation at any other time with pleasure,' I said.

'What a pity! We shall be going now.' Farouk got up, and soon after he had left with his group, we left the club too. However, for Francisco and me the night was only just beginning.

The Opera Casino owned by Madam Badia was located in Giza. Francisco said it was Cairo's popular headquarters for the *beau monde*.

Everyone acknowledged him as we entered, and we were escorted to one of the best tables close to the stage where a lovely belly dancer in high heels performed her sensual art. She moved her pelvis rhythmically as she looked at the crowded floor of the club flirtatiously. I feasted my eyes on her magnificent body, and her sensual movements turned me on. Her movements were those of a classical ballerina with a mixture of Latin American rhythms, which made her dancing very original. Francisco touched my elbow and laughed.

'She is lovely. Her name is Samia Gamal. But wait until you see Tahiya Carioca!'

Tahiya came on next, and Francisco was right. She was even more alluring. She swirled around the stage raising her thin arms and covering her eyes with her perfectly manicured hands at brief intriguing moments. She was the sexiest of creatures. She smiled invitingly as she shook her breasts, jerked her hips, and rolled her belly in an indescribable way that had all the men in the audience thinking of only one thing: possessing her. Waves of excitement rippled through my body as I fantasised about making love to her. She danced until she seemed close to ecstasy. The crowd cheered her on as the music reached its climax and she kept thrusting her pelvis in a perfect rhythm and then, suddenly, the stage lights went out. The roar of applause was deafening.

'Enjoying yourself?' asked Francisco with a grin. 'I can see you need a woman tonight. I'm going to take you to meet a friend of mine who will take care of your needs.'

The gaiety of the Cairo night was terrific and quite unbelievable when you stopped to think that a savage war was taking place. Only the uniforms at the clubs indicated that a conflict of some sort might be taking place somewhere far away.

Much as I tried to engage Francisco in a discussion on current events, he always managed to lead the conversation to more mundane matters. He came across as anything but a spy, but I had been forewarned that he was a master of deceit, so I kept my guard up. In Cairo as in Madrid everyone was suspicious of everyone else.

When we entered the Kit Kat, one of the king's favourite nightclubs, Francisco was welcomed again as a favoured patron, and again we were escorted to one of the best tables. He ordered a bottle of champagne. The cabaret venue was quite a place and like the city itself, it was full of intrigue as at night most people in Cairo sought relief in revelry. The showgirls were performing anti-Nazi vaudeville skits, which were very popular although offensive to many, as most Egyptians considered the Germans their liberators from British shackles.

'This place is full of spies!' Francisco said after our second glass of champagne. 'Even those Hungarian showgirls are spies.' I jumped at the opportunity that the conversation offered.

'Who do they work for?' I asked.

'For the Germans, of course,' he said cheerfully. 'And those women sitting over there are the Endozzi sisters, who work at the Italian Embassy.'

'Are they spies too?' I asked, in disbelief at my new friend's sudden revelations.

'They work the Italian population in Cairo and Alexandria and inform their government about who are pro-Axis and who are not.' I smiled inwardly at the similarity between their work and mine. I felt that Francisco was probably expecting me to lower my guard and tell him something that could be useful to him, but as he seemed relaxed and chatty I tried to get some more information from him.

'Tell me, why do the Egyptians call Hitler, "Mohammed Haider"? I find it quite extraordinary.'

'It's a German master plan! Somehow they have managed to make them believe that he has Muslim origins.'

The arrival of a remarkably voluptuous and sexy young woman interrupted our conversation. I estimated her to be in her late twenties. Of medium height, she had long, thick black hair that fell loosely over her shoulders.

'Rodney, please meet my good friend Naima. She is one of the most famous exponent of the *danse de ventre* in the country,' Francisco said, as he pulled a chair over and invited her to sit down. Pouring her a glass of champagne, he whispered in my ear, 'She'll be yours tonight.' She was certainly very attractive and immediately showed signs of having a strong personality. Without really acknowledging me, she addressed Francisco with a touch of sarcasm. 'What a pity your friend is British, as he is rather good-looking.' She then put her hand on my knee and moved it slowly upwards.

'So what is a young man like you doing without a uniform?' she asked me.

'I am a journalist.'

'Well, tell your readers that we want our country back. If you promise to do so, I will make you a very happy man.' She teased me as her hand continued upwards until it nearly reached my crotch. By now, I was extremely excited and had an erection. She had her hand on me and she smiled at my uneasiness.

'Not bad at all. You are a big boy.'

I blushed, but tried to regain my composure.

'We live in dangerous times and, like it or not, the survival of Egypt goes hand in hand with the defeat of the Germans,' I said with conviction. Francisco, who had been surreptitiously watching me and paying attention to every one of my words, laughed, aware of my difficulties.

'Naima has a lovely *dahabiya* on the Nile. We should go and have a nightcap at her place.' I agreed, and the two of us followed him out of the nightclub. While we were waiting for his driver, a tall, handsome, blond bloke appeared, accompanied by none other than Gisela von Krieger.

After our night together, Gisela had lost interest in me and we met at only a few social functions. I presume she collected men like trophies much as many men of my generation collected women, but each time I saw her I could not help becoming sexually aroused.

'Why, darling, how lovely to see you!' she cried, kissing Francisco on both cheeks and feigning surprise.

'Let me introduce you to my friends, Gisela von Krieger and Paul Roberts. Gisela works for an important art collector, and Paul... well, he's an American and is enjoying this great city.' Naima kissed Paul, so I gathered they knew each other quite well.

'What a happy coincidence, Gisela,' I said, as I kissed her hand.

'What brings you to Cairo?'

'So you two know each other?' Francisco interjected.

'Yes, Francisco, Rodney and I know each other from Madrid.'

Something about the casualness of the encounter made me believe it was not by chance but rather some sort of set-up. I gathered the friendship between Gisela and Francisco meant they both were working on the same side but I could not place Paul Roberts. Was he just a victim squeezed for any useful information he might have had?

'We'd better move on. Why don't you join us for a drink on Naima's houseboat?' Francisco suggested.

'What a good idea. Ideal!' Paul exclaimed. 'Close to home. I am her neighbour,' he added.

Naima's *dahabiya* was moored by the bank of the Nile: a papyrus-lined oasis. Creeping hyacinth and guava trees, virtually blocked out Cairo's crowds and noise. I could not believe I was looking at the longest river that flowed into the Mediterranean. The sky was studded with stars and it was all quite romantic. I was already a bit tipsy, but was still sober enough to know that I was in dangerous if charming company.

Naima led us over the gangplank, across the deck, and down the stairs to her cosy private world.

'Make yourselves comfortable,' she said, disappearing behind a curtain. 'Francisco, be a darling and fetch some champagne from the fridge. You know where the glasses are.'

The room was luxurious and exuded oriental charm. Persian carpets with exquisite patterns covered the floor. We took our shoes off and sat down on large cushions. The champagne cork flew up and hit the chandelier. I was feeling rather randy and felt a bit disappointed that there were five of us in the room.

She came back into the room wearing a satin nightgown that revealed the shape of her small nipples. She sat down next to me and without a word kissed me on the lips. I helped her out of her gown, quite oblivious of the others, as I sucked her brown nipples, making her groan with pleasure.

Then, out of the corner of my eye, I saw Paul and Francisco. They were naked, kissing, and playing with each other. I had never seen another man erect, not even in my boarding school days, and the disturbing sight made me feel rather uncomfortable. Gisela approached them and, falling on her knees, she caressed both their members touching them with her lips and tongue.

I was aghast. Naima tried to recapture my attention but I felt uptight. I downed my champagne in one gulp and poured myself another glass, which I also drank, hoping to overcome my prejudices. I was in unfamiliar territory.

'Relax, Rodney, relax,' Naima said before kissing me again. Her skin was soft all over. She had shaved off all her pubic hair. She excited me and I was not prepared to let her go. She undressed me. I was feeling dizzy and my head started spinning. I was losing my mind. Where was I? I tried to struggle but was unable to do so. I could hear voices but I could not command my body. I felt that I had entered a dark tunnel with no light at the end. I could sense that Gisela was over me now. Both she and Naima were kissing each other and then kissing me, their hands all over my body. I finally had to surrender, as I had no strength or willpower left. I managed to open my eyes, regaining briefly my bearings, and glimpsed Francisco and Paul going through my clothes, still naked and erect.

'Nothing!' I heard them say and then I drowned in the sea of forbidden pleasure.

The sunlight coming through the hatch hit my face. I had a terrible headache and could hardly move. My clothes lay in a pile beside me on the floor. A naked man's body also lay close to me. He was sleeping. I could feel his breath close to my face. There did not seem to be anybody else in the room. I could hear a low rumble of voices in the distance. The Nile was alive.

Memories of the night before poured in. I felt my head was about to explode. I saw images of the king, Irene, Helen. I could hear the music and saw the sensual dancing. Then there were the faces of Francisco, Gisela, Naima and Paul, and I heard their laughter. I felt I had to get out. What had I done?

They must have drugged me, I thought, as I tried to justify my irresponsible behaviour.

I started to dress hurriedly. There was no sign of the others. I looked behind the curtain and saw Naima fast asleep on her bed. Gisela and Francisco had already gone. In utmost silence I tiptoed around the room and searched the pockets of the jacket and trousers that lay in a pile on the floor and that obviously belonged to Paul. I found only a note written in German. It looked like a list. Who was Paul, I wondered? I had to get back to the hotel and speak to Sir Miles. I walked towards the exit and, just as I was about to leave, I heard Paul's voice.

'Don't move. Where do you think you are going?'

I turned around and saw that he was pointing a gun at me.

Something in his attitude revealed that I had it all very wrong. 'Who are you? Why are you searching my clothes?'

'Take it easy. I am a friend! Our countries are fighting on the same side.' I tried to remain calm. I was rather confused and I could not think clearly. My words seemed not to change his attitude. I tried to hide the list but he already knew I had it.

'You sneaky bastard! So Gisela was right. You do work for British intelligence.'

'Paul, you are an American! You are one of us,' I exclaimed again.

He laughed. 'You are quite wrong, dear chap. It is unfortunate that you know too much for your own good, Rodney. Place that note back where you found it.' I did as I was told, moving very cautiously. It seemed to me that behind the superficial calmness he was rather upset.

'What a pity! We could have had a good time. But I can't let you leave now.'

'What do you mean?' I was trying to figure out what was going on. My head throbbed. I hoped Naima would wake up but she probably had drunk too much and was oblivious as to what was going on.

'Come on Paul, put the gun down. Don't joke with me.' I tried to remain calm but I heard the click of the gun.

'Don't move or I'll shoot!' he hissed. Was he about to shoot or was he going to keep me there until Francisco returned and they figured out how to get rid of me? Their cover had been blown and they could surely not let me go. I could not take the chance so I decided to take a gamble.

'You bloody pervert! That's what you are. What did you do to me last night?' I shouted. Driven by the force of my fear, I leapt towards him. The sheer surprise and the impact of my body against his made him fall backwards.

'Nothing!' he screamed as he hit the floor. I heard gunshots. Warm blood poured over my stomach. I saw Naima's stunned face out of the corner of my eye... and then I had no doubt that I was dying as I entered a tunnel of total darkness.

9. A DESERT LIAISON

I woke up in a spacious room tastefully decorated with antiques. I admired the portrait of an attractive woman that was hanging on one of the walls. I was clueless as to my whereabouts. I felt a sudden pain in my stomach and noticed a stain of dry blood on the bandage.

'That is my mother.' The voice sounded familiar. I turned and saw Francisco standing in the doorway, smiling.

I was very confused. 'Where am I?'

'Don't worry, Rodney. You're safe.' He walked over to the bed and sat down, placing his hand gently on the sheet covering my knee.

'What are you doing? Don't touch me! Where am I?' My uneasiness betrayed me.

'You are lucky to be alive. You suffered an accident.'

'An accident?' I asked in bewilderment, 'I don't remember…'

'You really don't remember?

'But what happened?'

'You were shot and I saved your life.'

'Why did you do that?'

'Well, let's just say that I like you. Don't you remember what happened the other night? It was quite a party…'

Images suddenly started pouring in but I was very confused. 'You are just a bunch of decadent perverts!' I blurted out angrily.

'Well, you too seemed to enjoy yourself if my memory doesn't fail me… orgies are as old as mankind!' Francisco's cynicism upset me.

'You drugged me!' I retorted angrily, realising what had happened.

'That's beside the point.'

'Where are we?' I asked impatiently again.

'We are at my home in Dubai and it's January 1942. You did, after all, accept my invitation. You have been out for a few days!' He grinned. I was under his thumb and he knew it. He was in total control and obviously enjoying himself.

I fell silent while I recollected my thoughts. Madrid, Cairo. So many things had happened since I had crossed the Pyrenees. I wondered if my mother was still alive. I hated the war and all it had done to my lovely life.

'Does anybody know where I am or what happened to me?' I asked, trying to seem more relaxed, though I was certain my face reflected my strained worry.

'No, Rodney. You are a missing person. They have probably stopped looking for you, thinking you are dead by now. Many people disappear in Cairo's Fish Market; it can be a dangerous city. Now, you and I need to chat. Tell me what you were doing in Cairo. I know you are not a journalist. You see, Gisela and I are close friends.'

So he knew. Gisela obviously did.

'You are right. I am not a professional journalist but, as the British Ambassador in Madrid is a family friend, he found this job for me. Madrid was too dull and I wanted to leave. Given the situation in Europe, Samuel Hoare, who is like a second father to me, decided that Cairo was a good place for me to go to. Journalism was only the excuse.' I tried to sound as convincing as possible, hoping he would believe me.

'Don't give me that crap! I know what you are! Nevertheless, now that you are here I do not give a damn. You are no threat to us and you cannot harm our interests. Don't look so bloody worried, you are safe with me.' Francisco stood up and came closer. He put his hand on my head and passed his long fingers softly through my hair.

'You are very attractive, Rodney, and when you recover you owe me one.' He lowered himself, kissed me on the cheek and left.

I knew I had to escape. However, I felt weak, was in enemy hands, and in a foreign country where I did not know a soul. I remembered Sir Miles at the embassy in Cairo had mentioned that Francisco lived in Dubai. I had asked a few questions about the country; so I knew at least that, together with its larger neighbours, this tiny sheikhdom had become vital to our government due to its strategic importance on the route between East and West. Since the mid-nineteenth century when they had signed a treaty with us, these states had been known as the Trucial Sheikhdoms, and we had agreed to protect their coasts from any aggression by sea and to help them fight any attack by land. In exchange for our protection, their rulers had agreed not to dispose of any territory, except to us, nor to enter into any relationship with other countries without London's consent. In other words, they were satellite friendly states; so I only needed to get out of the house and reach the political agent or the British Army barracks. But how could I achieve this, being wounded, in pain, and virtually a prisoner? I was sure Francisco would return to get his dues sooner rather than later.

Just as I was thinking on ways to escape, a young Bedouin girl, not older than fifteen, entered the room with a tray. She had amazing dark eyes accentuated with kohl[1] and wore her silver jewellery with pride. When I saw the food, I realised how hungry and how weak I was. I managed to sit up in bed, and the girl observed me as I feasted on lentils with chard and lemon, broiled lamb, *tabbouleh*[2], pitta bread and a plate of dates.

'Do you speak English?' I asked her.

'A little,' she replied to my surprise.

'I need your help. Do you understand?'

'Yes,' she said

'Bring me some women's clothes, please. Will you help me get out of the house?'

'Very dangerous. Dangerous!'

'Please!' I pleaded. She was my only ticket to freedom, my only chance. She took the empty tray and left the room. I felt gloomy, as I doubted she would help me.

Thoughts of Francisco turning me into some sort of sex slave crossed my mind. As I was already officially dead, I had no chance of anyone coming to my rescue. He could easily rid himself of me whenever he pleased, and in my current state, I was not much of a match.

I did not have any more visitors until that evening an elderly, overweight woman brought me my dinner, cleaned my wound, and changed my bandages. The palms of her hands were stained in intricate designs. She did not speak a word of English and was not particularly friendly. I was terribly disappointed. By now, I had given up any hope of the Bedouin girl

---

[1] Natural black eyeliner used by Arab men and women

[2] A refreshing parsley salad with lemon juice

ever returning to help me. I started thinking of England, my childhood, and eventually I fell asleep.

Someone shook me and I woke up. By the light of the flickering candle, I was able to recognise her. It was the Bedouin girl. She put her fingers to my lips and helped me put on a dark dress. She then placed a *burka* over my head so that it covered my face. As I stood up, I realised how weak I was. I could barely keep upright; the wound was still tender and it hurt. Taking my hand, she led me in nearly total darkness along a corridor and then down some stairs. The house did not seem very large, as it was not long before I could smell the scent of flowers in an interior courtyard. When we reached the main door, a man was waiting for us, and the girl turned back and left.

Walking was agony for me, and the man had to support me by the arm as we progressed silently. We walked through narrow alleys, past houses built close together. The night temperature was very pleasant. A north wind blew freely, and the generous light of the full moon made it easier to move. We walked through a maze of streets until it seemed we were on the outskirts of town. Finally, we reached a large tent shared by both men and beasts. From what I could gather, it was made of animal skin and hair. Inside, a group of men sat around a fire, together with a few camels.

'*Salaam alaikoum*,' said the man as we entered.

'*Salaam*,' they responded in unison.

I was pushed into a corner of the stable, where he forced me to sit down. After a few words in Arabic, a man who seemed to be in charge gave my guide some coins, and he left. I thought it was odd, but at last I was safe and on my way to freedom. I assumed they would hand me over to the British as soon as the city awoke. I felt tired, but happy to have survived the ordeal.

The men spoke among themselves, laughing as they sipped their tea, but I could not understand what they said. Through the window of my *burka* I could see they were all young, sturdy, and heavily armed with weapons I had never seen before: double-edged blades with hilts of horn inlaid in what seemed to be silver[1] and axes with steel heads[4]. They looked quite lethal. They were six in all, had thick black beards, and wore traditional dress[5].

[3] Khanjars

[4] Yirz

[5] Kandura

I only had to glance through my *burka* to see that the chief had a sinister appearance. He stood up and walked towards me. He lifted his white *kandura*, revealing that he was wearing nothing underneath. He laughed and said something to the other men that sounded obscene. He had a big stomach and a nasty looking erection. His eyes were full of lust. Something was very wrong. Two of the other men walked towards me and dragged me to my feet. I was shaking. They started tearing my *burka* off. I was in grave danger and utterly terrified. They were obviously expecting me to be a woman. I had been sold to a bunch of dangerous ruffians. This time I would not be able to escape.

The two men pulled my *burka* off while their leader stroked his penis in anticipation. When he saw my unshaven face, he jerked back as if struck by lightning and shouted to the others. I could not understand what he had said but he was livid. I could see the horror and disappointment on his face at having been so deceived. He grabbed a shovel and hit me hard across my chest. I fell to the ground. The other men started cursing and kicking me all over. I felt my wound open and blood gushing out once again.

I opened my eyes, and the first thing I saw was the smiling face of a middle-aged nurse. I was not sure where I was, if I had I fallen into enemy hands or if I was in friendly surroundings; but at least I was alive and had survived the ordeal.

'Welcome back. What is your name? Do you speak English?' she asked softly.

'Thank God! You are English! My name is Rodney Mundy,' I blurted out with relief. 'Where am I?'

'You are at the British Garrison Hospital in Dubai,' she said kindly. 'What happened to you, Rodney? You were very lucky that our boys found you in time. You were haemorrhaging very badly.'

She must have seen how worried I was because she took my hand in hers. She seemed a compassionate woman and it felt good to let her take care of me. I tried to assemble my thoughts but could not.

'I need to talk to someone, someone in charge... an officer... perhaps, I should call Madrid... the embassy. They have to be informed immediately.' I rumbled incoherently as I tried to remove the drip from my arm.

'That is enough, Rodney. Relax, be a good boy,' the nurse ordered, while injecting me with a tranquilliser. When you get better, I will get someone from the political agency to come and see you.'

Several days had passed, although I was not certain as to how many, when I received a visit from an officer by the name of Smith. I was already feeling stronger thanks to Mary's care and the frequent visits from the doctor. I had received three gun wounds in the stomach, not one as I had previously believed, but, miraculously, the bullets had not touched any of my vital organs.

I told Smith my story, leaving out some of the more sordid details that I preferred not to remember.

'I say, dear chap, that's quite a story. I shall inform Cairo immediately, and the political resident. As soon as the doctor says that you are well enough to leave hospital, I will come and pick you up,' he said cheerfully.

'What news do you have from Cairo, Major Smith?' I sighed.

The major thought for a while before answering. 'Nothing very encouraging! The pro-German student demonstrations seem to be at fever pitch. The Egyptian Prime Minister resigned, and Sir Miles, wanting to make sure that his successor was our choice and not King Farouk's, was behind the coup. We surrounded the Abdine Palace with our troops and forced the king to accept a pro-British Prime Minister, which I am told has left the Egyptian Army in a highly volatile state with many officers apparently wishing to avenge their national honour. These are very difficult times for us, dear chap!'

I could well understand the frustration of the Egyptians but, with the Germans on our doorstep, the decisions that Sir Miles had to take must have been very difficult indeed.

'Major, what are you going to do about Francisco de Beaumont?'

'I shall of course inform Cairo of your findings, but I am afraid that even if he is a German spy, as you seem to think, there is not much we can do about it over here. He is well liked by the Sheikh, and he is one of the most important pearl merchants in town.'

I wanted Francisco locked up, and the major's rather patronising tone angered me. I felt very impatient and frustrated. I was wondering if my loathing was personal but I blurted out anyway. 'It is not a question of what I think, Major Smith. He is a German spy for God's sake and he is very dangerous! You must do something.'

A week later, Smith drove me from the hospital to the home of a British gold trader who had a thriving business in Dubai, thanks to the Sheik abolishing all import and export tariffs.

Alistair Sinclair came from a prominent Scottish family. He was an unmarried adventurer who claimed to descend from the Merovingians, which sort of made us family. His house was in the Shindaha area on the Western Bank, a narrow strip of land that separated the sea from the creek and was the town's smallest area but its main residential district. The living quarters consisted of three wind towers laid around a courtyard with the doors, the lattice screens and the balustrades made of teak.

Alistair and I liked each other from the start. His eyes were brimful of alert intelligence. We spent many an evening talking about the good old days over a few whiskies, amid the flickering light of candles as in those days they did not have electricity.

I soon found out that not only we were neighbours of the ruler, Sheikh Saeed bin Maktoum, but also that the Scotsman was a close friend of his, often consulted for advice on a variety of subjects.

Because we British considered the Trucial States as having merely strategic importance for the route to India, we were not involved in their internal affairs, as we were in Egypt. Dubai was just a port of call for the our ships on their way to India, and during the war we increased our presence there and installed defence measures, fearing the Germans might go after the oil in Persia and Iraq.

Although a small old-world town, Dubai certainly had a cosmopolitan atmosphere and an air of tolerance. Unlike Cairo, it was not sophisticated, but it was quite fascinating, with a large Indian population that mingled not only with us British but also with the Persians, Baluchis, and Arabs from different parts of the Middle East. The centre of town was Deira, where the *souk* comprised over 350 stalls. The area was a maze of narrow covered passageways, where it was very easy to get lost. Many of the artisans had no shops but simply worked on a vacant piece of ground as close as possible to their clients.

Donkeys and camels provided the main transportation on land, and crossing the creek involved an arduous journey around its end or a ride on a small wooden boat. The town was dominated by the old fort, the watch towers and the *barajils*, or wind towers—the most distinctive architectural element of the houses, designed to deflect the wind downwards to cool the rooms below.

Alistair had instructed one of his trusted servants to take me all around town. The muezzins wailed all over the city several times a day calling the pious to prayer. One Friday we went to the Grand Mosque. It was certainly a very impressive and elegant building, with its minarets and fifty-two domes. As I looked towards Mecca and did as all the worshippers, I felt a sense of belonging that thrilled me. This alien culture fascinated me, and I was very impressed by the Arab women, their elegance, and flamboyance, which they carried off with great modesty.

On 21 February, while Alistair and I were having breakfast, the servant announced the visit of Major Smith. He seemed in high spirits and did not allow anything, not even a cup of tea, to delay him from delivering his message.

'I have good news for you, dear chap. In four days' time, you will fly back to London from Sharjah and will then proceed back to Madrid. I'm told they are eagerly awaiting your return there.'

'And what are you going to do about Beaumont?' I enquired again when Alistair had left the room.

'Still waiting for orders from Cairo, I'm afraid. Don't worry, we will eventually take care of him.' That Francisco was still at large angered me.

Once the major had left, Alistair, the adventurer, gave me a wonderful surprise. 'Tomorrow,' he said, 'I have been invited by His Highness to hunt houbara[6] with falcons. His young sons, Sheikhs Rashid and Khalifa, will be there and I think you will enjoy meeting them.'

'I'd love to go,' I said excitedly, 'and before I leave I would very much like to go out one night on a pearl-fishing expedition. Can you arrange that?'

'I most certainly can.'

Sheikh Saeed's hunting camp was on the outskirts of town. Alistair introduced me to him and to his two sons. They both seemed focused and intelligent and I found Rashid to be a visionary. His dream of what Dubai could become overcame all timidity and broke all limits.

The Sheikh was an uncomplicated man and one could easily see that he relished the simple pleasures of life, his favourite pastime being falconry.

---

[6] A large bird of the Bustard family

Soon after our arrival Francisco de Beaumont appeared. The Sheikh and his family greeted him warmly, and this only confirmed that they enjoyed a close friendship. The minute he saw me, he walked straight towards us.

'Good morning, Alistair! I see you are taking good care of my friend Rodney.' He was full of scorn, no doubt annoyed at me having outsmarted him and upset his plans. His eyes flicked. 'Rodney, I would like to have a word with you in private,' he said to me in Spanish.

Sensing the tension, Alistair discreetly moved on to speak to some of his other friends.

'Why did you leave like a thief in the middle of the night? I told you, you were safe with me.' He suddenly sounded quite desperate. 'Rodney, I love you! Can't you understand that?'

This confession was definitely not on the agenda and it left me speechless for a moment. 'No, I can't,' I said coldly. I was aghast. 'You must be out of your bloody mind! I am not a queer. And even if I were, do you think I would be interested in you? You are my bloody enemy!'

He grabbed me by the arm rather violently. 'Please, Rodney, please!' pleading desperately.

'Leave me alone, you are sick!' I pushed him off, calling the attention of several guests who looked at us with curiosity.

Realising that we were being watched, Francisco regained his composure immediately and, whispering in my ear a threat: 'Watch out! You will pay for this! Even if it takes me a whole lifetime, one day you'll regret it!' Then he turned around and just walked away.

'What was all that about?' asked Alistair as he approached me.

'You'd rather not know,' I said.

The hunt was about to start. The guests had all finally arrived, and the splendid Arab horses, from the ruling family's stables, were ready for us to mount. I was not much of a rider but I did my best and concentrated on not falling off my horse, which helped me put the incident with Francisco at the back of my mind. There was something in his eyes when he threatened me that made me believe revenge would be the main motor of his life, but somehow I felt pity for him.

'Falconry is a very noble art. The falconer is seen as a figure of authority, and as he controls his falcon so does he control his territory,' Alistair explained from atop his beautiful grey stallion.

We all placed ourselves around Sheikh Saeed as the hunt was about to commence. The chief falconer, who was responsible for the bird's daily training, handed the Sheikh his bird. The falcon had on its head, covering its eyes, an *al burgu*, a hood of decorated leather, which the Sheikh removed slowly.

'Yalla!' he shouted. In a split second, the falcon flapped its great wings with regal grace and launched itself powerfully into the sky. We all looked up as an exciting chase took place among the birds. The Sheikh broke into a gallop and we all followed while he tore across the desert, watching his falcon hunt the *houbara*, which on several occasions managed to escape by a hair's breadth. The chase continued until the prey, no doubt exhausted, began to slow down, at which moment the falcon swooped down and pulled it to the ground. The Sheikh's presence on the spot within seconds of the falcon's pouncing on the *houbara* ensured that the animal would be killed according to Islamic custom.

'That was amazing!' I said to Alistair, as we tried to recover our breath after galloping several miles.

'It teaches endurance, skill and patience. All of which are the virtues that make a good ruler.'

'And is he?' I enquired with genuine curiosity.

'Exceptional, I would say. And his son Sheikh Rashid has all the potential to be one too.'

'I have to say I was quite impressed by the brief conversation I had with him when we arrived. Thanks for bringing me, Alistair. The sight of the falcon soaring upward from the Sheikh's hand was breathtaking, and I shall always treasure the memory of such an unforgettable experience.'

'It's my pleasure, dear friend. Wait until you taste the delicious meat of the *houbara* that will be served when the hunt is over. I am glad that you have had the opportunity to experience the inborn Eastern sense of sacredness in the relationship between host and guest.'

Pearls were the region's main export and many of the merchants had made veritable fortunes with them. They were considered the Sheikhdom's aristocracy and most were from the Ban Yas tribe to which the Al Maktoums belonged. Although the main pearl-fishing season lasted only from May to September, some boats went out to sea all year round, and it was on one of these that Alistair had arranged for me to sail. Francisco de Beaumont was one of the few Europeans to have his own fleet of boats and, like the other merchants he provided the capital and the equipment in return for a majority share of the profit obtained from the sale of the pearls. For centuries, the best pearls had come from these seas, but now there were genuine worries that the much cheaper cultivated pearls from Japan would affect the market very negatively and, naturally, the ongoing war did nothing to help business.

In spite of this, the crew on the boat that I sailed on were extremely cheerful and friendly although, as they spoke no English, we could barely understand each other. We set sail early in the morning, but not before having a large breakfast, as no food or drink would be consumed until sunset.

Until we were well clear from the harbour, heavy oars, each manned by two oarsmen, propelled the boat, and they invited me to be one of them. The crew looked healthy, strong, and showed unusually fine muscles, overall. They sang the pearl-fishers' song as we rowed.

The divers wore pegs or clips on their nostrils, and had protective leather sheathes on their fingers and big toes to enable them to separate the shells from the rocks. Each one of them descended on a rope with a heavy stone attached to the end and, when they reached the bottom, I helped the men on board haul up the ropes. All the divers had a string bag slung around their necks, which they would fill with shells. The bags were attached to ropes held by the men on board, the pullers. When the divers were ready, they pulled on the ropes to signal us to draw them up. The men went underwater for well over a minute per dive. This procedure was repeated throughout the day, with the divers going down quite deep more than thirty times, having in between descents very short rests. After each dive, the shells were heaped on deck.

At sunset when the day's work was over, we opened the shells under the vigilant eye of the captain, putting the pearls away in his sea chest and throwing the shells back into the sea. Alistair later explained that the divers believed that oysters fed on empty shells and that drops of rain caught by the oysters were turned at night into pearls.

After a long day's work, we ate the meal of rice, dates and fish that was consumed with such hunger that it seemed we had not eaten in months. The men thought I was rather strange when they saw me eating the oysters I had reserved for my meal but, using body language, I managed to persuade them to try some and, to my surprise, they seemed to find them as delicious as I did. What a pity I did not have a lemon or some chilled white wine with me!

As night fell, we returned with the high tide. The sound of the sailors chanting and the splash of the oars carried across the still water to town. The sky was full of stars such as can only be seen in the desert. It had been a wonderful experience, in which the men made me feel welcome. It probably was the first time a white man had joined them on a fishing expedition.

10. BACK IN SPAIN

It was already spring. Alan collected me at the airport and dropped me at my hotel. He was happy to see me and could not wait to hear all the details of my ordeal. Unfortunately, he had no news from my mother. I promised I would visit him in his office the next afternoon. The first thing I did when I found myself alone in my room was to call Felisin, who was so happy to know I was well and eager to see me. I was in need of an embrace, of feeling the closeness of a woman. She had been very worried by my sudden departure and not even Alan's reassurances had calmed her down; so she was delighted to hear my voice.

'How about having lunch tomorrow?' I said. 'Where would you like to go? It's Thursday, so how about L'Hardy?'

On Thursdays, this very well known restaurant that still exists served their famous *cocido madrileño*, a delicious stew of chickpeas, chicken, ham, leeks, carrots and cabbage. The meal has its own rules: first, you have the soup with vermicelli, then the vegetables and chickpeas, and finally the meat. The dining room was always noisy and full of familiar faces.

I picked Felisin up at two-thirty sharp. It was a lovely sunny day, though still fresh. She had sounded very eager to tell me something that seemed to be bothering her. I had never seen her during the daytime, and although there is a saying that at night all the cats seem grey, she did not disappoint me. She was wearing a burgundy two-piece suit and a mink collar. Around her long, gracious neck, she wore a delicate string of pearls. Her hair was up in a bun, under an elegant little hat, and she wore just the right amount of make-up. She had so much allure that she would have made an excellent wife for a member of the nobility had it not been for her profession and her coming from the wrong background, which in Spain, in those days, was an unforgivable sin. Felisin never ceased to surprise me with her elegant manners and candid charm, and had she ever visited the South of France or Paris, she would have conquered the highest levels of society.

I kissed her hand and, as we walked to the restaurant as I told her briefly about my trip to Cairo, so that she would not have the need to pose me any questions.

'Rodney, I know you are not a student, and that you are up to something, but I'd prefer not to know about it. A woman like me needs her sixth sense in order to survive; besides, a young man would not be here during the war. You know I am very fond of you. You are the first man who has ever made me feel that I am worth more. You have always treated me so well and with such respect—'

'You are better than a duchess to me, my dear,' I interrupted, taking her delicate porcelain hand and raising it to my lips.

'I need to tell you something, but I don't know if I should. I have not been able to sleep since I heard about it and I don't know what I should do.'

'You know you can trust me. Are you pregnant, my dear?' I asked, prepared to take the responsibility of fatherhood even if the child was not mine.

'No. It is not that. Don't worry.' She took my hand and smiled reassuringly.

'It is something terrible that could start the civil war again. There's a plot to murder Franco and to restore the monarchy,' she whispered in my ear. I knew her well to know how frightened she was.

'What? Who told you this?' I asked in bewilderment.

'I can reveal the sin to you but not the sinner. You should know that. But what should I do, darling?' I held her hand reassuringly. She was shaking.

' Don't utter a word to anyone at all. Promise! Tell me everything you know and the forget it. Its for your own safety. Please! I implored.

'They know about the plot,' she said mysteriously.

'Who knows, Felisin?'

'The Falangistas.'

'And what are they going to do?'

'I don't know but I am sure it will be something with terrible consequences.'

After lunch, much to my regret I had to walk Felisin home and take a taxi to the embassy. Sex had to wait, as Alan was expecting me. Speculation is definitely the enemy of peace of mind. I could not believe that only a day after my arrival I was already embroiled in another dangerous plot.

'Rodney, take a seat and make yourself comfortable. I can't wait to hear everything.'

'Alan, I'm afraid Cairo will have to wait. I have just been informed of some extraordinary news. Felisin has heard from one of her well-placed clients in the government that they've uncovered a plot to murder Franco and restore the monarchy,' I said excitedly.

Captain Hillgarth did not respond. His jaw dropped. From the fearless man that I was used to seeing I saw a very worried one. He was in some kind of a dilemma. I felt a lot of tension in the room. He lit a John Player's and offered me one. He took a deep puff then, clearing his throat, he finally spoke.

'Listen, Rodney. Your work in Madrid and Cairo has been excellent, the information you bring us is very useful, and I have precise instructions from the ambassador not to involve you in any risky operations. He wants to protect you because of your age but this is getting more and more dangerous. However, under the present circumstances, it is probably better if I explain to you the situation. You are a man now and I will take full responsibility of what I am about to say.'

I listened attentively and in silence.

'In April last year we devised a plan to persuade the more moderate members of the army to support the restoration of the monarchy, if and when the timing was right. A few months earlier, Himmler had visited Madrid and held top-level meetings with Serrano Suñer and Franco, so we got to work. You may be aware that thanks to the influence of generals like Aranda, Beigbeder, Kindelan, Varela, Ponte and Solchaga we have succeeded in getting General Valentín Galarza, a royalist who is totally opposed to Nazism, as Minister of the Interior.'

'How did you arrange that?' I interrupted.

'That's what we are here for! To prevent, at all costs, Spain entering the war.'

'And the plan?' I enquired with genuine interest.

'The plan was momentarily shelved, but since the Americans entered the war, Berlin has renewed its pressure on Franco to join the Axis. Therefore, we have started working again.'

'How did you manage to be so persuasive?' I interrupted.

'We had a very large amount of money at our disposal for this project and, though they are mostly good patriots, none of these generals are insensitive to money. These are difficult times for everyone. We are paying any voices in the government that can argue for Spain staying out of the war. So now, with the collaboration of the CIA, the operation is once again in full swing. Part of the army is prepared to rise up if, and only if, we feel that Franco plans to join the war. The plan is for the British Navy to invade the Canary Islands and establish a free Spanish government headed by the Don Juan as king, with Pedro Sainz Rodriguez as prime minister. I might add that we feel this could occur at any moment. Have you heard what Franco said yesterday to his troops in Seville? He promised the Germans a million men to defend Berlin whenever they were needed! The prospect of Hitler and the Caudillo in eternal friendship is quite appalling, as you might well imagine.'

'This is a very big fish indeed!'

'Too big and too dangerous! Do not breathe a word about this to anybody. We must warn the Americans that it is probable that Franco knows about the operation. We must do nothing else at least for the time being. I feel sorry for Don Juan, as he will be bitterly disappointed!'

That night I felt very restless. I had too many things on my mind. I had still no news from Foix so I was dead worried about mother, Uncle Jack and Princess Jane. I could not believe that by now the embassy could not at least confirm that they were still there; so I started fearing the worst and feeling somewhat angry with Alan and the lot. I needed a stiff drink so I went to Pasapoga, a glittering nightclub where married men took their lovers. I was sitting at the bar with Laszlo, when we saw Gisela walk in, accompanied by Hans Vogel in uniform, the SS Captain she had led me to believe she despised and Hans Thomsen and his wife. He was wearing a swastika armband on his dinner jacket. What was she doing back in Madrid, I wondered. Did she have anything to do with what was going on? She saw us and walked straight towards us.

'Hello, Rodney. What a small world! You seem to be everywhere. You know Captain Vogel and these are my friends Hans and Lizzie Thomsen.' She said charmingly.

Both Laslo and I greeted the Thomsen as politely as we could and then I said coldly to Gisela, 'And so do you.' The memories of Naima's houseboat all too fresh.

'You look ravishing, my dear! Travelling suits you,' I said sarcastically.

'And so do you, darling! I have heard you had just vanished from Cairo. I am glad you have not left us altogether... at least yet,' she mused in her usual provocative manner.

'Well, you should know my dear!' I could not hide my irritation.

'Of course, we do seem to move in the same circles.' She winked as she passed her finger over her juicy red lips. She was wearing a long red velvet dress open on one side. Her shoulders were bare and the diamond swastika brooch was pinned strategically on her bosom. She had remarkably long legs and once again I felt a tinge of excitement in spite of myself.

'So what brings you to Madrid this time?' I asked.

'Well, you know—art. Art makes me travel extensively. I am now looking at some Spanish paintings that Marshal Goering is interested in buying.' She seemed genuinely surprised to see me, but nothing in her voice or demeanour denoted that she held Paul's views about my activities. I wondered how Francisco had explained our sudden disappearance.

'Tata!' she said, turning around with a brisk, sexy thrust of her hip, letting her long leg out, in full as the maitre d accompanied them to their table.

Laszlo looked worried but remained silent for a while, before muttering, 'I don't like this.'

'What don't you like, my friend?' I asked.

I was becoming quite good at getting people to confide in me. I felt that we all needed to talk. Unable to trust anybody, we tended to keep our fears, worries, and most intimate thoughts to ourselves.

'Rodney, I know I can trust you. Listen to me carefully and please don't repeat it. I am an undercover agent and I work for the CIA. There are just a handful of us here in Madrid,' he said with an exquisite candour. His confession took me completely by surprise, and he must have seen my look of bewilderment. I said nothing.

'You need to know that Gisela is a very dangerous woman.' He went on, 'She is Himmler's right hand and her presence here in Madrid indicates that something is about to happen. Did you know that Vogel is the head of the SS in Spain? Those two used to be lovers. And then Thomsen. They are up to something.'

'Gisela told me she hated the chap,' I replied nonchalantly, before I added by way of an afterthought, 'I wasn't aware of any of that, but, Laszlo, why do you tell me these things?'

'Rodney, you know why. We fight on the same side.'

Could I trust Laszlo, I wondered? I felt certain I could, but one could not be too careful. I was not about to reveal my activities to him even though he seemed to know. I felt he had been unnecessarily careless in speaking to me so openly although, I suppose, it is only human nature to want to share your worries with others.

'You see, Rodney, I'm in charge of preparing a coup against Franco and setting up a democratic government that will support the Allies.'

I could not believe my ears! My friend Laszlo was the man in charge of the entire operation! We remained there for hours, while he filled me in on all the details of what was known as Operation Relator, parts of which I already knew.

Laszlo's revelations had come as a huge surprise. As far as I was concerned, if anyone in Madrid was not a spy, it was he, which only goes to show how difficult our work was and how good he was at it. I never told the embassy that I knew who the CIA agent was, as I felt it would not help matters but would probably only make Laszlo more vulnerable. He was a friend who in a moment of weakness had felt the need to talk, and I left it at that.

The following morning I felt I needed to think things over quietly so I decided to take a stroll in the Retiro Park, the meeting place for the respectable women in Madrid. Because of the good weather, many nannies were pushing prams carrying the newborn babies of the elite. Quite a few pretty-looking younger women with their mothers giggled and whispered as I passed. I smiled at them and they blushed.

I wanted to investigate further. I felt an enormous curiosity as to how the events would develop and I knew I would be leaving soon. I decided that the first thing I was going to do was to go to Felisin's house. I felt a strong sexual desire as I thought of her. After some glorious lovemaking, I told her I was really a journalist in search of a good story and she appeared to believe me. She promised to let me know if she heard anything that could help me write my story.

My intention was to spend the next few days visiting the places that the Germans most frequented. I arranged to have lunch at Edelweiss opposite the Zarzuela theatre, and in order to allay any suspicions I invited Gonzaga and Pelayo, sons of the Count of Herentals. By now, I knew that the count was Himmler's man in Madrid, so I thought this quite a clever move on my part.

The Herentals boys were very handsome and extremely refined and well educated. They had their father's large blue eyes, but whereas his were despotic, theirs were full of warmth. One lad was my age and the other was twenty-one. They spoke fluent German, French and English, which was very rare in Spain in those days. They were both unwillingly studying university careers imposed on them by their autocratic father, whom they disliked intensely, while living under the constant protection of their mother. In the count's presence, they were not allowed to express their inner feelings and they lived in constant fear of his rages and tantrums. I felt quite sorry for them. We had in common a love of women and sports, and I really enjoyed their company. Initially, we avoided discussing politics, but as we grew to know each other better, they began to confide in me. They hated the Germans, maybe as an act of rebellion against their father; so every now and then they would give me very important information. The Herentals palace was the centre of German espionage in Madrid.

On that day, Edelweiss was unusually busy and there were a surprising number of men in German uniforms.

'So what have you been up to?' I asked, as we enjoyed our first glass of Riesling.

'You tell us. We've been told you're having an affair with Felisin.'

Gonzaga, the eldest, was the more outspoken of the two, while Pelayo was the artist and a trifle shy. I had seen some of the paintings he did without his father's knowledge, and could see he had great talent. To boost his morale I had bought two of them, which are still in my possession. For the Count of Herentals all artists were *maricones*[1], which traumatised poor Pelayo. The two brothers were very close and felt quite at ease in my company, as they felt they could be themselves and I encouraged them to be so.

'You Spanish like your gossip!' I said, laughing. 'She's a friend,' I added nonchalantly.

'But are you having sex with her?' Gonzaga asked excitedly.

---

[1] Queers

'I won't lie to you. The answer is yes, and she's quite amazing.' The conversation went off in that direction for a while, and they talked about their sexual fantasies as we had a good laugh together.

'It's very odd to see so many Germans in uniform, don't you think?' I asked.

'You're right,' said Pelayo.

'Do you want to know something, Rodney?' asked Gonzaga.

'I'd be delighted.'

'I'll tell you a secret if you promise to introduce Pelayo and me to Felisin. We want to have sex with her.'

'Together?' I asked, feigning surprise, and we all laughed at the thought.

'OK. You have a deal. It better be good, though, Gonzaga',

'Yesterday, my father had a meeting with Gisela von Krieger and Captain Vogel. The German Ambassador, Hans Thomsen and some officers also came to the house.'

'Did I ever tell you that I had sex with her, too?' I interrupted him with the intention of getting them to relax even more and lower their guard, and thus tell me everything they knew. During the next ten minutes I told them all about my sexual experience with Gisela in Madrid, which had them both mesmerised.

'Sorry, Gonzaga. Go on,' I said after I finished narrating my sexual encounter.

'I overheard everything they discussed yesterday, and you are in for a shock, my friend.' The waiter who brought the main course interrupted him. We waited, sipping the wine, and then he blurted out, 'the Germans are plotting to kill Franco!' I tried to conceal my surprise at what he was saying.

Gonzaga was of course unable to tell me the details of the plot, but it appeared that Hitler had lost his patience with Franco and wanted him to commit himself firmly once and for all to what I later learnt was called Operation Felix, under which the German army would march from France through Spain, conquer Gibraltar and advance on North Africa.

I took the story straight to Alan, and it was news to him too.

'I'm afraid you know too much for your own good, Rodney.'

'But, Alan, don't you think it's a paradox that both we and our enemies want to get rid of Franco?'

'Well, our objectives are very different. It only shows us how Franco is a very skilful political tactician who is balancing the factions that make up the regime and at the same time has angered both sides! I can only presume that the Nazis are fed up with the dithering and want to have him replaced by someone like General Muñoz Grandes who would go along with their plans. If they do so, it would put our own plans in jeopardy.'

'What plans?' I asked with interest.

'The plan to land Allied troops in North Africa.'

I sat there and listened while he told me of plans that would change the course of history, and I felt immensely proud to be helping the cause of justice and freedom.

'We, on the other hand, want to restore the monarchy, which is after all the traditional form of government in this country. We really don't want to back a fascist dictator. With Prince Juan as king, we would invite the political parties to return to Spain and hold democratic elections.'

'They are definitely very different objectives, and it amazes me that they both involve Franco being eliminated. Do you think he has any inkling about this plot?' I enquired.

'I've no idea, son, but if the Falangistas know what Felisin has told you, what is certain is that everybody must be very busy right now. Franco still believes in an Axis victory. I will inform the prime minister and the CIA immediately. Rodney, it would probably be advisable to consider sending you back to England as soon as it is feasibly possible. I think your staying here would make you very vulnerable. Your cover has now been blown so I will talk to the ambassador about it. In the meantime, as always, be very careful and keep your eyes wide open.'

Everywhere I went I could feel tension in the air, and I do not know if it was my imagination running away with me or whether it was genuine. The atmosphere was gloomy. Every morning when I woke up I expected to hear the news of a coup against the dictator. I just hoped it would be our coup. However, the days passed and nothing happened.

I had heard nothing further about my departure and had not asked. Captains Lubbock and Hillgarth were both very busy those days. I tried to keep a low profile and make myself as useful as I could while continuing with my regular routine.

One evening I invited Felisin to the Teatro Real for a production of

Puccini's *Madame Butterfly*. She had never been there and was terribly excited at the prospect. I knew her presence would again raise more than one eyebrow but that amused me very much and anyway I did have strong feelings for her. Before the performance, everybody stood up as the orchestra played the national anthem and most of the audience raised their arms in the fascist salute. Felisin looked stunning. She had such a sense of style and was so elegant that she made most women in the audience look plain. The evening was a success and ended with a splendid night of lovemaking.

About two weeks later, I met Laszlo for tea at Embassy. I could see immediately that he was in a state of shock when he walked in.

'They've k-killed him,' he stammered.

'Whom are you talking about?'

'I've just had a very brief encounter with my contact in the Spanish army on the Puente de Segovia. He was my go-between with General Aranda. We barely exchanged a glance when I passed him an envelope. I had started walking towards the Plaza de Oriente when I heard a scream and saw him fall from the bridge. I am sure they must know who I am, now. I'll be next!' I could see fear in my friend's eyes.

'Calm down, Laszlo. Did you see anybody push him?'

'No.'

'He could have jumped. If he knew they were on to him, jumping might have been a better option than being interrogated by Franco's police. This is war and we are all in danger,' I said. 'Let's not panic. Go to your embassy, inform them, and then go home. I will see you soon.' I made an effort to reassure him but it did not help. I realised that what I was saying was utter nonsense.

Easter came and the city went completely dead. Franco's ultra-conservative government went into mourning for the suffering and death of Christ and all flags flew at half-mast. Absolutely everything closed, even the restaurants and cafes. The radio stations played martial music. I had never seen anything like it in my life.

During Holy Week, the most important churches in the city paraded their statues of Christ and the Virgin, which competed with each other in extravagance and luxury. Their velvet and silk robes, embroidered in gold and silver, were encrusted with precious stones. The statues, carried through the city on heavy floats, were supported on the shoulders of about twenty men. Each float was covered with hundreds of lit candles. The processions moved slowly to the sound of a slow regular drumbeat. Behind the statues, men paraded orderly, wearing purple robes with hoods that resembled those of the Ku Klux Klan and carrying long tapers. Every now and then the floats would stop for the bearers to rest, and someone selected for the occasion would sing a beautiful *saeta* in honour of Christ or the Virgin Mary. When the song was over, the bearers would lift the float again and carry on, watched by thousands of awed *madrileños*. The women traditionally wore black, with their hair caught up in *peinetas*[2] and *mantilla*[3]. The theatrical religious devotion of the masses was very moving, even to an agnostic like me.

On the evening of Glory Saturday, the cinemas and theatres opened with a new show, and the city came back to life, as Spain prepared to celebrate Christ's resurrection.

During the Easter holidays, I did not see Laszlo but I knew he had gone to Seville to enjoy their famous Holy Week.

On Easter Monday, which was no longer a holiday, I was summoned to the British Embassy for a meeting with the ambassador, whom I had hardly seen since my arrival, with the exception of a few brief encounters.

It was a warm spring day and as I had some time, I decided to walk part of the way before taking a taxi. Round the corner from the hotel, a family dressed in rags was hunting in the rubbish bins for scraps of food. A pair of Guardia Civiles approached them and, using force, made them leave. It was heartbreaking but that is how post-war Madrid was. The bureaucracy was completely corrupt and rations did not get to the people who needed them more: so many disturbing contrasts between the privileged few and the rest.

When I arrived, he was waiting in his large study with Alan Hillgarth. They both rose from their chairs to greet me.

'Well, Rodney,' he said without a preamble, 'I've been following your progress and I'm very proud of you. Captain Hillgarth has told me that you have surpassed our highest expectations. Your reports and the information you have gathered over the past few months have been very useful and have

---

[2] High combs
[3] Lace hand-made headscarves

saved many lives. However, you could be in danger if you stay in Madrid any longer. It has been decided that the time has come for you to leave Spain. We would like you to consider joining the firm as soon as you return to England. If you agree, you will be sent to Fort Monckton to receive proper training, and by January you can start active service in London.'

'I would like to stay here a bit longer, sir. I know everybody now and I think I can still be very useful.'

Samuel Hoare looked at Alan Hillgarth and smiled. 'I'm afraid that is completely out of the question. The embassy is under a lot of pressure. We have pro-Nazi protestors outside on a daily basis now, and six of our men have been murdered in the last month alone. Only yesterday, a large group of Falange youths voiced their anti-British sentiment in front of the embassy. 'Gibraltar Español!' they screamed. It was rather nerve-racking and the Civiles just stood and watched. I am afraid that I cannot allow it. You must go.'

I was disappointed but I understood that not only for my own good I had to leave.

'I will gladly join MI6 and serve my country then, sir. When am I to leave?'

'Soon. Alan will let you know.'

I went straight to see Felisin. I had become so used to her lovemaking, and missed her caresses and the warmth of her body. Each time we were in each other's arms, she surprised me with something new and taught me many of her most intimate secrets. It is to Felisin that all credit is due for my success with women later on in my life.

'Felisin, I will be leaving Madrid very soon. My work here is over,' I said, as we lay naked in bed.

'Have you finished writing your articles?' she asked.

'Yes. I am returning to England. I also want to find out where my mother is. I hope she's still alive.'

I kissed her. She was a delightful creature. Her cosy little flat, not far from the Barrio de las Letras, was home in Madrid. She had her head on my shoulder and I stroked her hair. I told her about my life in the South of France, how I had escaped through the mountains and ended up in a Spanish jail. She laughed and kissed me tenderly.

'Let's celebrate life! Let's drink a toast to our paths having crossed!'

She got out of bed. The satin sheets fell to the floor. Her body would have delighted Leonardo. She knew I was watching her, and she swayed her hips in a way she knew made me crazy. She returned with a chilled bottle of champagne and two glasses.

'What a luxury, my love!'

'You won't believe who gave me this, Rodney,' she said, handing me the bottle to uncork. 'Last night at Chicote I met this German officer called Hans Vogel. Do you know him?'

I filled the glasses and we toasted and drank. 'He's a very dangerous man,' I replied after the toast.

'He invited me to spend some time with him, and suggested we go to his flat. He gave me a lot of money upfront; so I was expecting something kinky. You know what strange sexual tastes these Germans have. Anyway, I went along… after all, that's my job.'

'Did he hurt you?'

'No, Rodney. To my surprise he wasn't interested in having sex with me at all.'

'So what was he after?'

'Information! He gave me 20,000 pesetas and has offered me 100,000 if I got him what he is after.'

'And what is that. Do you have it?'

'No I don't, but I will certainly do my best to get it for him.'

'What does he want to know?' I insisted.

Felisin hesitated for a moment and then turned serious. 'You remember the story I told you about a plot to kill Franco and reinstate the king?'

'Yes, I do. It was obviously just a rumour.'

'No it wasn't. Vogel told me the plan was aborted because Franco had found out about it. Right now someone has a huge amount of money that was supposed to be used to finance the plot, and the Germans are after it.'

God, she knew too much for her own good. I wondered how I could protect her. I needed to warn her, but how?

'Felisin, promise me that even if you find something out you won't say a word to Vogel, or anyone else for that matter,' I said gravely.

'Why? That money would change my life. It would allow me to stop working! To leave the country.'

'You know that I do care for you, and believe me that money would be your ticket to the grave. Promise me. Please promise me that you will forget it completely,' I pleaded.

'OK, beautiful. I promise!' She kissed me and turned over me. Her sensual body covered mine. I embraced her and this time we made love hurriedly but with a passion that I had never felt before. Then after a sublime orgasm, I rushed out of her apartment. My head was spinning as I contemplated my choices. I would definitely have to see Laszlo immediately and, naturally, inform the embassy. Once the Germans knew he had the money, he would be dead, and they were bound to know eventually. I now had no doubt that his contact had been murdered by the Gestapo or by Franco's secret police. It seemed it had probably been a Gestapo job, in which case Laszlo's life was certainly at risk. It all now began to make sense to me. I had just managed to listen on the BBC radio station that the Nazi offensive in Russia was not going well and was an enormous drain on the resources of the Third Reich. The Falange's newspaper *Arriba* of course reported the opposite, as was to be expected. The Spanish National Socialist Party still hoped for a German victory and a fascist Europe.

I figured that such a vast sum of money would enable the Germans to carry out their plans in Spain, including murdering Franco and replacing him with Muñoz-Grandes or Serrano-Suñer and the Falange would certainly go along with the plan. The situation was extremely critical.

As soon as I arrived at my hotel I called the embassy, but was told that Captain Hillgarth would not be in until the next day. I urged the secretary to let him know as soon as possible that I called. There was no way I could reach him other than through the embassy and time was of vital importance; accordingly, I decided to go to Laszlo's apartment to tell him everything I knew. I had not seen him since our night out at Pasapoga and I assumed he had returned from Seville by now. I hoped he had.

I took a taxi to Calle Garcia de Paredes where he lived in a modernist building from the turn of the century. Many bourgeois families lived in buildings of that type.

As I walked in, the *portera*[4] was mopping the marble floors. 'Buenas tardes, Señor.'

'Buenas tardes, Remedios. Is Señor Szekeres in?'

---

[4] Caretaker

'Yes, Señor Mundy. He has three visitors: a very tall man, much taller than you, an officer and a very elegant lady. She has lovely red hair!'

I had not time for the usual small talk and gossip. My heart was pounding as I took the elevator up to the fifth floor. I hoped I had not arrived too late. As the lift rose, I heard a door slam and people running hurriedly down the stairs. I could not see who they were through the lift's stained glass windows; nevertheless, I had no doubt as to the identity of the visitors.

When I got out off the lift, I saw that Laszlo's door had been forced open. I walked into his apartment, calling out to him.

The flat had been ransacked. Things lay broken and scattered all over the floor. The sofas in the living room and the mattress in the bedroom had been cut open, allowing the feathers to take over the rooms. They had been very thorough in their search. Laszlo's favourite armchair was covered in bloodstains and a piece of rope on the floor indicated that he had been tied up and probably tortured. Had they found what they had come for? If the Gestapo were now in possession of the money, the German coup to replace Franco would be carried out very soon.

'Laszlo! Laszlo! Where are you?' I called out.

I tried to remain calm but I was shaking. It was one thing to pass on information to my superiors, but quite another to be in the midst of what probably was the murder of my friend.

The sliding doors leading on to the balcony were wide open, and the curtains billowed in the spring breeze. I went onto the balcony and looked down. There it was, my friend's body lying on the pavement in a pool of blood, surrounded by passers-by and the police. I realised I was in serious trouble and, not knowing what to do, I walked back into the living room where I saw something glittering on the floor. It was Gisela von Krieger's diamond swastika. I picked it up and hid it in my underwear, thinking it would be safe if I were searched.

Within minutes, the police stormed into the apartment, followed by a hysterical Remedios.

'Poor Señor Szekeres! I know you did not kill him, Señor Mundy. You were his friend. It must have been those German visitors who ran out of the building, overturning my bucket on to the floor I have just cleaned.'

'Be quiet, Señora,' the police captain snapped at the caretaker. 'Go and wait downstairs. We will need you to answer a few questions.'

When Remedios left, still blabbering on, the captain switched his attention to me and had me searched.

'Your papers,' he demanded in a firm voice.

I was in trouble. To be caught without papers in Spain meant immediate arrest and questioning, and I had left my passport at the hotel when I had rushed out.

'I am a British citizen. I am staying at the Hotel Nacional, and my papers are in my room. I am a personal friend of the British Ambassador and I would appreciate it if you get in touch with the embassy,' I said firmly, hoping they would not automatically arrest me.

'Señor, you are under arrest on suspicion of the murder of Señor Szekeres.'

I was handcuffed and rough-handled out of the apartment by two sturdy police officers in their grey uniforms with a menacing expression.

'But you heard what Señora Remedios said,' I interjected sharply. 'When I arrived, I heard people running down the stairs. She will confirm what I say,' I protested.

'You can explain everything to the *comisario*.'

I was taken to the cells in the basement of the Interior Ministry in the Puerta del Sol—the same place where the communists had their torture chambers after they had taken over the republic.

As I feared, I spent over a week in solitary confinement in the eerie basement of the police headquarters. The police did not allow me to call the British Embassy and the thought that the Germans might have got the money and succeed in the coup while I was wasting away, was agony. Though I was not tortured, listening to the screams coming from other cells made me feel very uneasy as to what was in store for me.

The *comisario* was a very unpleasant man with an inclination for cruelty. Though rather frail, he wielded great power in his little kingdom. He sported a neatly trimmed narrow moustache and wore an old brown suit, which showed signs of having been mended several times by a submissive wife. He struck me as being someone who had a price; however, after my experience in Barcelona, I dared not bribe him in case I only made matters worse for myself.

I was given hardly any food or water and was interrogated ceaselessly. Why had I killed Szekeres? What was I looking for? Was I a spy? Was he a spy?

I stuck to my story that I was writing an article about the 'new' Spain for an English magazine. I also insisted that the British Ambassador and his wife knew me well.

'We don't like *ingleses* in this country,' he said, frustrated at the lack of information I was giving him. 'El Caudillo says the Germans will win this war, and they will.'

One morning the door of my cell opened and Comisario García walked in as usual. I presumed he would subject me to another round of pointless questioning.

'You have a friend who wants to speak to you,' he said with a stupid grin.

I was relieved, believing it was someone from the embassy, but my heart sank when I saw that my visitor was none other than Hans Vogel, wearing an SS captain's uniform. All hope of ever seeing my mother again vanished instantly. I was petrified. The *comisario* clapped me in a pair of handcuffs and left, locking the cell door behind him.

'Where is the money?' Vogel asked without any preamble while he paced the cell impatiently. I was relieved to know they had not found it yet.

'What money?' I asked innocently.

'Don't try to fool me! I don't have patience for games. The money that Laszlo had,' he said savagely.

'I don't know what you are talking about. Laszlo was my friend. We used to go out together and have fun. He was just an eccentric and wealthy artist. What do you want from me? My arrest is illegal. I have done nothing. I don't know anything about any money.'

Ignoring my pleas, he took an electric prod out of his pocket and put it to my face.

'Are you going to tell me, or do you want me to stick this up your arse?'

'I don't know anything,' I insisted. At that, he forced the prod into my mouth and I suddenly felt as if my head was about to explode. I started vomiting and blood spurted from my nose and ears. Now I imagined what caused the constant screaming I heard throughout my confinement. I felt as if I were fainting. He started to unbutton my trousers, but I was too weak and dizzy even to react. What he was about to do was too ghastly for words. I felt I would not survive another electric shock.

My screams must have alerted Comisario García because he burst into the cell.

'What the hell do you think you're doing? You cannot torture our prisoners! You have no jurisdiction here! You are not in Berlin! I warned you!' He shook his head sorrowfully.

The *comisario* was furious and ordered a police officer to drag Captain Vogel out in spite of his protests and threats.

'You're going to regret this! Our countries have a pact! I shall inform the minister! I shall have you fired!' The police officer undid the handcuffs and gave me some water to drink. I felt dreadful.

'When are you going to let me out of here?' I asked the *comisario*.

'You will be leaving tomorrow. Your embassy has just secured your release,' he replied with a stern face.

'Tomorrow morning you will be driven to Gibraltar and put on a boat in a convoy bound for England,' Captain Hillgarth told me with a strained, worried expression on his face. 'You should consider yourself lucky. Tonight you will be the ambassador's guest at the residence but please, for your own good, do not mention to anyone that you are leaving.'

'I must go then and collect my things at the hotel and pack.'

'I'm afraid that will not be possible, Rodney. The Gestapo has already been there and there is nothing left except for these two paintings.' He pointed at the two oils I had bought from Pelayo Herentals.

'So they haven't found the money yet?'

'Yes, they have.'

'Oh my God! That is terrible! Poor Laszlo! He paid with his life, trying to prevent the money from falling into German hands, and all for nothing. Hans Thomsen and Captain Vogel are responsible for his murder.'

'There is nothing we can do about that, at least for the moment. The money has not fallen into German hands, but into Franco's. What was left of it. Franco just got lucky.'

'So there'll be no coup against him, then?'

'Exactly. He has already moved against all the royalist generals and has had them purged. Sainz Rodriguez, whom Don Juan had chosen as prime minister of his resistance government, has been ordered into exile to Fuerteventura. Eugenio Vegas has also been ordered out of the country and has joined the prince in Lausanne. I am afraid to say that, quite unintentionally we have damaged any chances that the prince had of regaining the throne. From what we know of Franco and his wife, they despise him now, and they are people who never forget.'

'Alan...'

'Yes, Rodney.'

'I need to ask you a big favour. Promise me that you will protect Felisin. I know this is something that I should not be asking. However, I have to. Can you get her out of the country, please? Send her to England. If necessary I will marry her.'

'That is out of the question. And would she want to leave?' Alan asked gravely. 'You love her, don't you? What you are asking is most honourable but I cannot let you marry a prostitute. The ambassador will never allow it. It is impossible. I am sorry.'

'I don't know, but I would feel terrible if something happened to her. Please promise...' I pleaded.

'What you are asking is extremely difficult but I promise I will look into it and do what I can to protect her.'

11. GOING HOME

I left Madrid without having the chance to say goodbye to any of my friends, not even Felisin, whose love I longed for. I promised myself that if Alan could not manage to get her to England I would return after the war to look for her and give her the life she so much deserved.

The trip to Gibraltar was uneventful, but the one to England was a terrifying ordeal as the food convoy was bombed several times by German Stukas.

As planned, I arrived in London and went straight to Fort Monckton, where I received intense training for over four months before joining 'the firm', as it was called. I found the training tough, as I was not too good with discipline and order, although I worked hard at it. We were woken at dawn and were kept very busy until we collapsed into bed at about eight in the evening.

I had not been able to save any money from my stay in Madrid and was virtually broke. Nobody had any news of my mother who was officially still at the displaced persons' camp in Foix. I longed to see her.

August 1942 saw the start of what was to be known as the Battle of Stalingrad. This fierce battle took a devastating death toll in both the Red Army and the Nazis, and by the end of January the Russians had defeated the hitherto invincible Germans.

After my intense training I returned to London in October, but was quite unprepared for the devastation I found there. The city had suffered greatly during the Blitz; nothing had been spared, not even Buckingham Palace or the Houses of Parliament. Thousands of Londoners lost their lives, and many more were now homeless. Everything was rationed, except for fish, but at least there was enough food to go around for everybody. Yet in spite of the shortages and suffering there was a sense of purpose and resistance against the common enemy that seemed difficult to erase.

Of course, extreme situations create seedy characters and a new breed of men appeared in those difficult days. Known as the spivs, they controlled the black market and as a result became quite prosperous and went to many of London's nightspots to show off their new acquired wealth. They were flamboyant characters, most of them young men discharged from the front on medical grounds.

My work in London was similar to what I had done in Madrid. Our government had interned Sir Oswald Mosley, his wife Diana and other fascist sympathisers. Mosley had many followers, as he preached a unique form of fascism. Its main policies rested on the concept of a united British Empire, which appealed to those older members of society who had served that empire. Mosley was a brilliant politician who had always advocated peace and negotiations with Hitler as a way of solving the problems affecting Europe since the Treaty of Versailles at the end of the First World War. He had followers within the British establishment, who provided funds in secret, and my job was to find out who those people were. By now, I was extremely well suited for the job.

I took a small apartment in South Kensington and started going out and enjoying London's social life.

News from Spain was quite encouraging. In September, Franco finally declared the neutrality of Spain. Operation Torch was launched in November with the American and British governments having assured Franco that Spain's sovereignty would be respected. The disembarking in North Africa was successful and there was hope the tide would change in our favour.

One evening, as I was having a drink at the bar of the Renaissance Club, I noticed a very attractive woman sitting by herself. I, of course, was not in uniform, which was rare for a young man in those days. I approached her and looked straight into her eyes.

'My name is Rodney Mundy. And yours?'

'Phryne Alabaster,' she replied with a laugh, and offered to buy me a drink, which I found rather odd but attributed to her just reaffirming her independence.

That night we had dinner together. We talked, danced and clicked immediately as it happened we even had a friend in common, Rafael Valls. I told her about my adventures since escaping from Foix, but omitted any references to MI6. One could never be too careful.

It was love at first sight. We enjoyed each other's company immensely and often went down at weekends to the Old Bell at Hurley, where Raf Valls and his girlfriend, Joanna Kinlock-Jones, often joined us. I knew that Raf was with MI6 and he obviously knew that I was, too, but in all our years of friendship we never once discussed it. Joanna was soon to leave Raf and become romantically involved with her boss. She was personal assistant to 'M', who was also my boss, and who would be immortalised in the James Bond books and films.

In London we went regularly to the Milroy, which was frequented by Bing Crosby and Frank Sinatra when they were in town. Though we still lived in separate apartments, I felt my relationship with Phryne was healthy, calm, and steady, and so did she.

My cover was that I was working at the Ministry of Aircraft Production and with the job came the privilege of a car—something very rare in those days.

To my surprise, M asked me one day to bring Phryne along to meet him. At the time, she was working at the Yugoslavian Embassy. We met at the Savoy for tea. M was in his mid-fifties, a tall, attractive man with keen eyes and a face like a hawk. To my utter astonishment, he told Phryne all about my work and then said he was certain she could be trusted and could be very helpful to me. He told her never to acknowledge him in public, which of course she never did.

In those days, I had many reports to write and usually prepared them very late at night, thereby indulging in the pleasure of getting up at noon. I went to many cocktail parties and dinners where I mingled with all sorts of people. As in Madrid, I quickly became very popular in the London party scene. I had just turned twenty and was now adept at flirting and charming people into talking. I could be a communist, a fascist or gay if the situation demanded it. I had become a master of disguise and deception, and I enjoyed myself immensely. However, I gathered so much valuable information that my reports were becoming longer and longer, with the result that I was sleeping less and less.

The news from Cairo was upsetting. The embassy and the military headquarters were forced to burn all their papers when an attack by Rommel had seemed inevitable—thus that the 1st of July was known as Ash Wednesday, because the air was thick with smoke and ashes when our forces prepared to evacuate the city. The shopkeepers and hoteliers had been seen preparing red, white and black streamers and bunting. The pictures of Churchill disappeared, while those of Rommel and their Mohammed Haider popped up everywhere. Mobs took to the streets, chanting 'Rommel! Rommel! Rommel!' I felt sorry for the Jewish population in Cairo and Alexandria left stranded there by the British to face their fate. I also wondered what fate awaited Irene and Helen, who had done so much for us. All of this disgusted me, as they had all been loyal allies. Fortunately for the Egyptians and for the free world, Rommel never made it into Cairo. Had the Germans entered, King Farouk, who was only twenty-two, would undoubtedly have been deposed and the pro-Nazi Prince Abbas Halim placed on the throne.

On 26 July 1943, Italy was overjoyed with the news that their king had finally dismissed the Duce and ordered his arrest. This was very good news for the Allies, as it meant that Italy would most probably seek immediate peace, but it was too late for poor Victor Emmanuel to save his crown.

Around this time, Phryne and I invited Fred Kempler for a drink. He was now working for General de Gaulle's Free French Government based in London and I had not seen him since Madrid. We went to a well-known club off Park Lane that was ran by an extremely funny black man who, showing a mass of gold teeth, laughed in six languages while he spent the night playing darts as he drank and laughed. Another evening we went to the Vanity Fair Club in Mayfair, as Phryne was a member. It was the most exclusive club in the city. I met Prince Philip there and told him that our fathers had been very close friends.

Nightclubbing was an important part of my job because after a few drinks I always managed to elicit some important information. We went regularly to the Milroy, the Four Hundred, and the Sweevy, which was at the Berkeley Hotel. This club was a rather dangerous place and it was finally closed down as it was considered a security risk.

I finally moved into Phryne's mews flat where we were very happy despite my heavy workload. I was thrilled when, just before the Christmas holidays, I received the best present I could have wished for. Finally, my mother, Uncle Jack and Princess Jane were going to be released from a camp in Albi where they had spent the past two years. A few days later, I received my mother's first letter in almost three years. It was a very emotional moment. She asked me to rent a furnished flat for the three of them, as they would be arriving in London soon. I found one not far from Sloane Avenue.

The day of their arrival finally came and Phryne and I went to Victoria Station to pick them up. We embraced for a long time. Mother looked wonderful, bubbling over with conversation. Her overwhelming personality had obviously been what had kept their spirits up during all these trying years. Uncle Jack looked even more like Maurice Chevalier than before while Princess Jane looked beautiful with her perfectly set blonde hair and her lively blue eyes. I realised how much I had missed her husky, blasé English voice. I was overjoyed at being reunited with my family.

We all wanted to know everything that had happened since we had last seen each other, so we spent all night celebrating our reunion and recounting our trials and tribulations. I told them my story since my escape from Foix, and mother seemed very impressed with my adventures.

'You're a man now, Rodney,' she said proudly, as she drank to my health.

Over the next few months, I was extremely busy, as a lot was happening on the front. Phryne and I met Lillian Craig at the cinema where she worked and immediately became good friends. She was a petite woman with great charm and personality, who later we later introduced to Prince Bertil of Sweden. Theirs was to be one of those love stories that made headlines. It was only many years later, when the Prince's nephew, King Charles Gustav, married and had children that they were finally allowed to marry. As Princess Lillian of Sweden she has gained the love and respect of the Swedes.

I had, however, little time to spend with Phryne or my mother, but I was lucky they were very understanding and supportive. On 6 June 1944, British and Allied forces landed on the coast of Normandy in an unprecedented offensive against the Germans and their allies. On 20 July, Hitler survived an assassination attempt, led by a group of German conservatives who wanted to overthrow the Nazi regime. Things were happening at such speed that we all felt victory was not far off.

Late that summer, the British and American forces with the aid of Free French troops finally liberated Paris. How I would have loved to have been in my adored Paris and joined the French in their celebrations!

Time flew and soon it was Christmas. The Germans were desperately trying to stop the Allied advance and the Battle of the Bulge was their last major attempt to do so. After that, victory would be just a matter of a few months.

M was always full of surprises. He would summon me through coded messages to meet him in the oddest places, the zoo being one of his favourites. So one cold December morning in 1944, I found myself feeding the monkeys with him while he explained my next mission.

'Rodney, I need to talk to you about looted art.'

'I know nothing about it.'

'We've been aware of the scale of looting that has gone on since the very beginning of the war, and last year the War Office set up a specialist department which is responsible to the director of civil affairs. We have created an Archaeological Advisor's Branch with orders to draw up an inventory of all national art treasures and Jewish private collections in German-occupied countries. A formidable task, I might add,'

'And how can I be of any use?' I asked.

'Does Klaus von Jellenbach ring a bell?'

'I met him some years back.'

'That is precisely why you are the man for this job. This charming character has amassed a very important art collection that he has looted from the Jews. As you probably know, and if you do not you can read this file, numerous art works have been looted from France, Belgium and the Netherlands. Before the war Hitler dreamt of installing the best art collection in the world in a museum in his hometown, and Jellenbach and Goering have been working hard on this project, using every conceivable method to acquire the works of their choice.'

I listened with interest.

'What sort of paintings does that monster like?' I asked out of curiosity.

'Old masters! We know he loathes late-nineteenth-century and twentieth-century French paintings. He considers Impressionism degenerate, and consequently he has forbidden importing such paintings into Germany. IN spite of this, we know the Germans have looted many paintings from this period and then used them as payment for other works of art more to their taste.'

I had not been aware of any of this.

'Until quite recently the baron has been Goering's art advisor, a position he has used to acquire, behind his back, a vast private collection for himself, mainly from Poland, Hungary and Czechoslovakia. The Reichsmarschall also has a large number of agents in the occupied territories who keep him supplied with information about Jewish art collections. As the second most influential man in the Third Reich, he has used his position of power to his own advantage breaking, whenever it suited him, most German laws, those of the neutral countries, and those of Germany's allies. He is a cruel bully who has no qualm about using the Gestapo for his own benefit.'

'Does Hitler know about this?'

'Probably not. Goering keeps him happy by giving him some of his paintings as presents every now and then.'

'Is Jellenbach with him most of the time?' I asked.

'Well, they do spend a fair amount of time together. He travels with him when Goering is in an acquisitive mood, which, I might add, is most of the time. Jellenbach carries out all the negotiations and makes all the final decisions on acquisitions. Well, that was until recently. Over the past few years he has been very busy satisfying Goering's vast appetite for art, and in the process has kept for him some magnificent pieces that he has not shown his boss.'

'How did he manage that?' I asked, unable to believe what I was being told.

'Most of his collection was obtained before the war even started. In those days Jellenbach had many wealthy Jewish friends in Germany, Poland and Hungary, and knowing what Hitler had in mind, he went to see them one by one and persuaded many of them to hand over to him their unique collections for safekeeping. He can be a very charming man when he wants. After agreeing to do so, the Jews were then taken away by the Gestapo and have all disappeared.'

I remembered then the conversation I had had that first night I went to the Herentals' home in Madrid with dear Laszlo. It all made sense now.

'What do you mean by "until recently"?' I was slightly confused.

'Well, according to our informants, a few weeks ago Göering found out what the baron had been up to, and he was livid. The thought that Jellenbach might have a collection better than his own makes the fat pig sick to the stomach. The baron, probably fearing for his life, has now vanished and so, we imagine, has his collection.'

'Sounds like a jolly nice chap! I never did feel very comfortable in his presence, and he was certainly anything but charming. What sort of agreement did the two of them have?'

'Goering had promised to appoint him director of his collection at Karinhall, and until now he was acting as his buyer while remaining an independent dealer and retaining the right to any work of art that the Reichsmarschall did not wish to acquire. Being under the wing of the second most powerful man in the Third Reich, he has been free to travel and has had access to all the art collections in the occupied territories. He has also had access to as much foreign currency as he has needed.

'The war is in its final stages and it is clear now that we will win. We would like you to find out, and I know it will be complicated, where the baron is and where the paintings are. You should leave for Paris tomorrow?'

'OK, M, I shall.' I was delighted at the prospect of returning to Paris.

'Here,' he said with a straight face, 'have some more peanuts.' And we both laughed.

12. A SHORT VISIT TO PARIS AND THE END OF THE SECOND WORLD WAR

Paris! It felt wonderful to be back! I stayed at the Powers Hotel on Rue François I, my home in the city of lights even in my old age.

The first thing I did was to call Claude at the Tour d'Argent and make an appointment for dinner. I found him in great shape and the Parisians in a festive mood after liberation. Over a glass of champagne, he explained how he had hidden most of his wine behind a brick wall, out of the sight of the heavily German clientele. The city had not suffered too much during the war but, being so proud, most Parisians had had great difficulty in accepting the Germans as their masters.

That evening we went to all the nightclubs and I drank more than I should have, but I was overjoyed at seeing my friends again.

The following morning I went with a slight hangover to the British Embassy, where I was introduced to a group of highly qualified art historians who were also seasoned interrogators and wise to the intricacies of the art market. James Plaut was in charge of the newly set up Art Looting Unit of the office of Strategic Services. Another member, Theodore Rousseau, had worked at the National Gallery, and Laine Faisan was professor of art history at Williams College. Their combined knowledge overwhelmed me.

They explained that they had only just started their investigation but had already ascertained that the former German Ambassador to France, Otto Abetz, had been one of the principal architects of the looting programme and had reserved works by Monet, Degas, Bonnard and Braque to grace his own home and offices. When he had fled Paris, he gave orders to ship these paintings to Germany. The group also had information that Joachim von Ribbentrop, the German Foreign Minister, had hung his Berlin offices with paintings by these same masters looted from Jewish collections in France.

Goering had organised the Einsatzstab Reichsleiter Rosenberg, which he had entrusted to Alfred Rosenberg, the chief party ideologue. From his Paris office Rosenberg was to take charge of the confiscation of Jewish collections, which ended up in Goering's private collection.

I wonder why it is that, throughout human history, people on the winning side, in any conflict, have always considered themselves entitled to any spoils of war. This is obviously a very primitive and basic instinct.

The dedicated members of the Art Looting Unit informed me that von Jellenbach had not been seen in Paris since Rosenberg had taken on the Reichsmarschall's affairs in France. So probably only a fraction of his collection came from looted French art, unless he had acquired some pieces in Germany, but Plaut thought this was highly unlikely.

My investigation would be more complicated than I had foreseen, because central Europe was still occupied. These countries would eventually be 'liberated' by the Russians, who would in turn plunder whatever was left. Thus, I never had the opportunity of travelling to Budapest or Warsaw to continue with my investigation.

It was no secret that many Jews in Germany, Poland and Hungary had owned excellent collections and that Jewish Hungarians were particularly passionate about art. The baron had been to Hungary before the German invasion in March 1944, and it was known that he had been able to convince some of his friends to hand over their collections to him. Baron Ferenc Hatvany, for example, had turned over some of his French Impressionist paintings. An art professor, who saw the entire collection before von Jellenbach arrived on the scene, wrote, 'There were ten Manets, eight Courbets, twenty Corots and six Ingres, in addition to twenty-five portfolios, each with twenty-five French masters.'

I found out much later on that von Jellenbach had at least had the decency to help the baron escape alive. I presumed that he had merely been protecting another aristocrat from certain death, though it was clear that he must have been very satisfied with the paintings he had stolen from him. After the war, Baron Hatvany had placed sixty of his most valuable paintings in a bank vault, under the non-Jewish name of his secretary, in order to keep them safe from the Germans. However, in January and

February 1945 when the Red Army arrived in Budapest, they had opened all the bank vaults and sent the paintings and everything else they had found to Moscow.

Another renowned pre-war collection was that of Simon Stern, whose father had established a large commercial bank at the turn of the century. He not only had a magnificent collection of old masters, which included five El Grecos and three Tintorettos, but also had paintings by Degas, Monet, and Renoir. All Plaut could tell me about this collection was that some of the paintings had been confiscated by the pro-Nazi Hungarian government and were exhibited at the Museum of Fine Arts in Budapest.

What a tragedy for all these magnificent central European countries to be liberated, only to be placed under the Russian boot for decades. I always thought it was most unfair, and I believe Churchill made a terrible mistake not invading Russia after the fall of Germany. Russia was so devastated by the war and her government was so weak that it would have been an easy matter to install a democratic monarchy under the Romanovs that could have saved us all from the Cold War years that were to follow.

I was back in London a couple of days later and decided that I would return to Madrid as soon as the war was over.

Something extraordinary happened just before Christmas when I went on my own for lunch to Bentley's Oyster Bar and there, sitting by himself, was Mr. Scheuel, the disgraced consul. I walked up to his table and smiled. 'Hello, old boy. How are you?' He was rather stunned. Seeing that he did not recognise me, I introduced myself as Meynell Phillips.

'My name is Schubert,' he lied.

'We met at a few receptions in Barcelona,' I said, in order to satisfy his curiosity. 'Do you mind if I join you for lunch?' I asked politely.

We drank some excellent Pouilly and had two-dozen oysters each. By the end of the meal we were the best of friends, and I asked him for his address and phone number, which he was happy to give me. I passed the details on to M and my dear friend Scheuel was never seen again.

I celebrated Christmas and New Year with my family and Phryne. Everybody felt that the Germans would soon be defeated. The January liberation of the Auschwitz concentration camp by the Russians revealed to the world the full extent of Nazi cruelty and the unbelievable horrors they had perpetrated.

Hundreds of thousands of Jews had been used as guinea pigs in the most appalling pseudo-scientific experiments and many more had perished in the gas chambers. In the camp lay piles of dead bodies waiting to be cremated. The survivors were in a pathetic state: walking corpses who had somehow survived the very worst of nightmares. Similar scenes were repeated at the extermination camps of Belsen and Buchenwald.

Phryne and I cried when we first saw those images. How could human beings be so utterly cruel and cause suffering to such a degree? The full details of the Holocaust were gradually revealed to the world as the German troops retreated.

It must have been in early February, around the time of the Yalta Conference, when I had one of my regular meetings with M. He popped by our mews flat for a cup of tea and was in a particularly cheerful mood.

'Rodney, do you know who Simon Stern is?'

'The name rings a bell. Isn't he that Hungarian art collector?'

'Bingo! He was liberated from Auschwitz and will soon be sent to a hospital in London. His health is very poor and the doctors do not know if he will survive. The moment he arrives, I want you to go and visit him and make friends with him. At the moment he is not speaking to anyone, but I am sure you will be able to change that, my dear chap.'

Things were moving fast on the war front. On 25 April, American Forces met the remains of the Nazi Army at Torgau and managed to cut the Third Reich in half. Five days later, Adolf Hitler, one of the most abominable criminals the world has ever seen, committed suicide in his Berlin bunker. By 7 May, the war was over and we rejoiced and partied hard. We cried with joy at the end of so much suffering, heartbreak and pain. It had all been such a nightmare that we could only hope that we had all learnt our lesson and that such a tragedy would never happen again. At a personal level, I was also happy because soon I was going to return to Spain to continue with my investigation.

It was wonderful to be able to tear down the blackout curtains after more than four years. Our eyes had become so accustomed to complete darkness at night that it was almost painful to see so many lights, and we felt quite dazzled. London's streets looked like a fairyland! Restrictions naturally continued for a few more years until we were all back on our feet again. In fact, after the war there was nothing. Everything was rationed and scarce. During the war, the government had made the enormous effort to keep the morale high, but when it was over it seemed they did not care any more. There were coupons for clothes, for petrol, for everything, so the spivs became even more notorious as the black market flourished everywhere. I still clearly remember the line of spivs selling nylon stockings on Oxford Street.

Soon after, I received a call from Sister Mary, who had good news. Simon Stern was finally on the mend and had regained some strength; so the doctors believed that fairly soon the time would be right to make his acquaintance.

I was not surprised to learn from M that many Spaniards, including high-ranking members of the army and Franco's government, had reacted to Hitler's death by going to the German Embassy and signing the condolence book. I felt that Franco's regime would not last long and that the allies would finally restore the monarchy in the figure of Don Juan. Franco had only broken diplomatic relations with the Third Reich on 8 May, in a desperate attempt to save his regime.

'Our sources in Spain,' M told me, 'inform us that the dictator has given orders to conceal Nazi assets there, which have been placed under an embargo. Apparently over ten million dollars have been transferred to private individuals, and Falangist volunteers have helped to destroy compromising documents from the German Embassy and consulates. Over 250 million dollars' worth of German business assets have been transferred to stooges, and hundreds of Germans who were working for Hitler in Spain have stayed on, having been granted Spanish nationality.' I could see that his temperature was rising.

'And now Franco is hailed by the Spanish press for his neutrality during the war! He even has the audacity to state publicly that he never supported the Axis, in an attempt to wash away his Axis stain!'

'But surely we will be able to get rid of him,' I said, sharing M's indignation.

'That will depend on the politicians. If it were up to me, I would have him prosecuted and executed. Just imagine—in order not to be accused of having granted asylum to war criminals, he has given them Spanish nationality. We've complained to the Spanish authorities, but our complaints just fall on deaf ears.'

'It's a scandal! Is there nothing we can do?' I asked.

'I'm afraid not.' After a short pause he continued, 'You should go and see Stern as soon as you can. I will arrange everything. Now then, when do you plan to go to Madrid?' He took a long sip of his tea.

'As soon as I win his confidence.'

I went to the King Edward VII Hospital for Officers, to visit Simon Stern. One of the nursing sisters took me to the ward. I had my first glance of him from behind a screen. He was sleeping, but the expression on his face was that of profound suffering, even as he rested. He looked like a very old man, yet he was only in his late forties. A white blanket covered his frail body. I felt a wave of compassion for him.

I gave the sister my telephone number and soon began my regular visits to the hospital. I spent every afternoon at his bedside. I realised I would have to be extremely patient if I were to succeed in my mission, but luckily I had a comfortable chair in which to sit, and while I waited I dozed intermittently.

'Who are you and what are you doing here?'

The sound of a man's voice drew me back from that pleasant state into which the mind drifts before falling asleep. For over two weeks I had been sitting for hours in a chair beside Simon Stern's bed and had been completely ignored. We had exchanged glances, but neither of us had uttered a word.

Shaking off my drowsiness, I now sat up. 'I am a friend, Mr. Stern.'

'But I don't know you. I've never seen you before,' he said wearily. 'Or have I?'

'The British government has asked me to become your friend in England and to help you recover.'

'What is your name?' he asked, in a heavy Hungarian accent.

'Rodney.'

'Mine is Simon.' I could feel that he wanted to talk, but I was ill prepared for all I was to hear over the next few hours.

'If you are indeed my friend, I need to ask you a great favour.'

'Please do.'

'You see, I was taken to Auschwitz with my wife and my beautiful daughter, Rita. She was the liveliest of little girls. When we got there, we were separated and I have never heard from them again. I cannot bear to think that they are dead. Maybe you can help me find out what happened to them.' He was close to tears and his voice was feeble.

'I will get to work immediately, and I promise you that we will find out where they are. Mr Stern, would you mind telling me about the events that lead up to your confinement in Auschwitz? That will probably help me in my investigation.'

'If we are going to be friends, you should call me Simon.'

'I shall.'

'Very well, then. Make yourself comfortable, because it is a long story.'

I settled into my chair, and within minutes, I was immersed in a terrible story of suffering and loss.

'It all started, or rather ended, depending on how you look at it, with the ill-fated attempt by King Carl to recover his throne from the regent. Unfortunately, the attempt failed and His Majesty had to flee the country, never to return. Admiral Nicholas von Horthy was then free to rule as he pleased, and he soon put Hungary under the influence of the new National Socialist government in Berlin. This was because Hitler had promised to return territory in Romania, Bohemia and Slovakia that had been Hungarian before the First World War. Do you follow me?'

'Yes, of course.' He was eager to tell me everything, which was exactly what I had come for.

'At the end of the nineteenth century my father had established a bank, which soon became one of the leading commercial banks in the country. He believed in the monarchy and supported the Crown financially and, for his services, he was to be given a title. Unfortunately the First World War shattered these plans and my father's dream. The king and Queen Zita were very compassionate people and would have been wonderful rulers had the situation been different.

'My father was also an art lover and had started a collection that, together with the purchases I myself made later, became probably one of the finest in Hungary.'

'What happened to that collection?'

'By the late thirties the government had passed anti-Jewish laws that severely limited our activities. By the early forties, with Hungary now one of the Axis powers, thousands of non-Hungarian Jews were rounded up. Some were exiled and most were murdered. We felt that things would only get worse, and we were not wrong. The time had come to act.

'I resigned as president of the bank and let the other board members, mostly Hungarian aristocrats, assume control, as I knew that had I stayed on the bank would have been taken over.

'My next move was to save my art collection. As I was certain that the pro-Nazi Hungarian government would eventually pay me a visit, I decided to place the most valuable pieces in the safekeeping of a good friend of mine who was German; the rest were kept at home.

'About a year ago some men knocked on the door and proceeded to confiscate most of the paintings in the house. They had them sent to the Museum of Fine Arts in Budapest, where I suppose they still are if the Nazis have not taken them to Berlin.'

'What was the name of your German friend?' I asked. I knew full well the answer.

'Baron Klaus von Jellenbach.'

'How did you arrange this?'

'My wife, Sarah—she is English, you know—and I were trying to think of ways of hiding the best pieces in our collection—five—Grecos, three Tintorettos, some major works by Degas, Monet, and Renoir—when who should suddenly telephone? Klaus. He was a charming man and I knew him quite well socially. He said he was staying at the Gellert Hotel and had urgent business to discuss with me; so I invited him over for tea that same afternoon.

'As soon as he sat down, Klaus told me that he had come all the way to Budapest to warn me about Hitler's plan to invade the country and to advise me to place my most important art pieces in his custody, as he was the only person who could guarantee their safety. He kept insisting that he was taking a great risk in safeguarding my collection but that he was prepared to do so for a friend.

'I really did not have many options. So, two days later, I handed over to him my treasures. He signed a document, which my wife sent to her family in England, so maybe one day...' his voice trailed off.

'He did the same thing with many other of his Jewish friends,' I said.

'By early March,' Stern said, resuming his story, 'German troops had occupied Budapest and we were arrested and taken to Auschwitz.' His kind expression changed to one of terror by the sole mention of the extermination camps. I felt so sorry for him. 'Would you mind handing me another pillow, please?' I helped him sit up in bed, and he began to recount his personal trip to hell.

'Things were going from bad to worse, so I had made plans to leave the country with Sarah and Rita and go to England. Some of my aristocratic friends from the bank were willing to help us, but by then it was too late.

'The night before our planned escape we were woken up with great violence and given five minutes to pack our belongings. I feared the worst, but tried to remain calm for the sake of my family. We were put on a lorry with other Jewish families and taken to a train station outside the city.'

'You must have been terrified,' I said.

'Nobody knew where we were being taken. At the station, we were made to wait for several hours in sub-zero temperatures. Finally, we were crowded into wagons like cattle, fifty people to a wagon, without food or water. The train journey was the beginning of a terrible ordeal, only made worst by the hours of darkness and the bitterly cold early spring nights. I lost count of the number of days that we spent like this. By the time we reached our destination, several people in the wagon were dead. I had to carry Rita, who pleaded weakly for water. My little princess was only four years old!' His voice broke down, and he started to cry. I felt so sorry for him. It was several minutes before he could resume his story. He was a man with a broken heart.

'All the men who were considered physically fit were immediately rounded up, and we later discovered that we had been chosen to work for the Third Reich. The elderly and the weak were taken to a special section of the camp and were never seen again while the women and children were taken to the women's camp. I was heartbroken when my wife and my daughter were dragged, crying, from my side. I have not seen them since then and do not know if they have survived.' He sobbed for a while.

A profound silence took over the room. Simon Stern closed his eyes.

'British Intelligence is now investigating what happened to them. Simon, you have my word that you will be informed as soon as we have something.'

'Please, Rodney!' he pleaded. 'Life in the camp was a nightmare from beginning to end. We were stripped of all our belongings. Can you imagine being deprived of everyone you love and everything you own? Even your name? Well, that is how our life in the camp began.'

'I can't even start to imagine how awful it must have been!' I interrupted.

'No one can. We were branded and given a number, thus, ceasing to have an identity. We were allocated bunks—two men to a narrow, lice-infested bunk, and given instructions. Everything was forbidden. Once a day we were given a bowl of a disgusting soup, but never any water. We were always thirsty. To survive, some of us ate insects, which was considered a crime punishable by death. We were nothing but slaves, working very long hours, seven days a week. Those who could not keep up were taken away and replaced by new arrivals. The cold was unbearable and they often forced us to stand outside, naked, for hours on end.

'Each block had a block clerk. Though prisoners like us, they were German and common criminals and, for some reason that I will never understand, were even crueller than our jailers were. As camp officials, they did not have to work but merely gave orders, and they could be as ruthless as they pleased. They wielded absolute power over the life and death of their fellow prisoners.

'One day, our block clerk handpicked my bunk companion and me, and took us to a large room in the crematorium, where there were huge piles of corpses. Three prisoners were carefully undressing them while a fourth was removing any gold teeth with a pair of pliers and placing them in a tin. I felt sick, having never touched a dead body before, but if you wanted to survive in Auschwitz, you did as told, however awful that might be.

'For days we worked stripping bodies, before dragging them into the ovens to be cremated. Finally, two of the prisoners could not take it any longer and refused to continue. They got down on their knees and pleaded, but the block clerk beat them savagely with his truncheon, screaming, "You God damned lazy bastards! I'll show you what happens to scum like you!" But they refused to move. I will never forget that scene until the end of my days.'

I could see how hard it was for Simon to speak about what he had witnessed. He was trembling.

'The two men knelt motionless, still sobbing. The guards then pulled them roughly to their feet, swung open the oven doors and pushed them inside. We were ordered to continue filling the oven with corpses, and then the clerk switched the oven on. The screams of the two men, as they burnt alive will haunt me forever. You have no idea.'

After a short pause, Stern went on. 'At one point they decided that there were too many prisoners so the new arrivals were forced to undress before being taken straight to the gas chambers. The SS officers had discovered it was easier than stripping the corpses afterwards. Next, they decided that it was simpler to send prisoners directly to the ovens, without gassing them first. The screams, the moans, the desperate banging on the oven doors were heartbreaking and terrifying. I felt overwhelming horror. Were there no limits to their cruelty?

'However, this was not the only way in which they got rid of new arrivals. When groups of less than 200 prisoners arrived they forced them to undress, and then shot them in the back of the head in front of the others. Considering other things that I witnessed, this was a far less painful way to go.'

'You should write a book,' I suggested, 'and tell the world in your own words what some human beings are capable of doing to others. The world must know and hopefully something so utterly horrendous will never happen again.'

'Maybe I shall, one day. Because of starvation my health has seriously suffered, and in the camp I became thinner and thinner. Then, I had a stroke of luck. Even in the most awful situations, one's luck can change for the better.

'The *Kapo* asked around for someone who was good at accounts. The selected few were given a test and finally I was chosen for the job. Working in the camp offices meant less strenuous work and slightly better food.

'Nevertheless, shortly after starting my job in the office, I became very ill with a serious stomach infection and they took me to Ka-Be, the camp clinic. I was probably sent there because the *Kapo* found my accounting skills very useful. Otherwise, they would have shot me on the spot, as there was no place for weakness or failure in that hell. We were turned into non-men, who marched and laboured in silence. They emptied us even of the capacity to feel or to suffer.

'Every now and then they gave us delousing orders, which were a cruel joke. For example, they expected us to show the SS officers a shirt that was free of lice or risk death. However, as our bunks, shirts, and bodies were infested with the creatures, it was virtually impossible to be lice-free, and many prisoners ended up being shot.

'By late spring, Hungarian had become the second language in the camp after Yiddish, as the Nazis were sending all the Hungarian Jews there. By August, after less than five months, I, and those who had arrived at the same time were considered "the old ones". The thought of the impending winter made us all shudder. We knew what winter meant. A large percentage of the prisoners would not survive the extreme cold.

'The camp was seriously overcrowded, and in order to return to more manageable numbers, hundreds of inmates were sent to the gas chambers. The crematorium chimney never stopped smoking. When they finally released me from the clinic, another inmate had my accounting job in the office, so I had to return to the impossibly hard manual labour.

'Christmas came and went. The New Year bought rumours that the Russian troops were advancing fast and that the Germans would soon be abandoning the camp. They eventually did and I was confused as to what to do. Most of the healthy prisoners, about 20,000 in total, vanished during the evacuation march, but I was too weak. So I decided to take advantage of the chaos and hide in the clinic.

'We did not know what would happen to us because some SS officers had remained behind. That night, Russian bombs hit the camp. With the buildings on fire, the remaining prisoners ran outside into the freezing night. Most of us had barely any clothes, and some had no shoes, and deep snow lay on the ground.

'The Germans had vanished. No one appeared for eight days and we were free to roam around and search for food and wood to burn. I felt very ill, not knowing that I was suffering from typhoid fever.

'Some days later, armed SS officers suddenly reappeared in the abandoned camp and promptly shot all those who had moved into what had previously been their dining room. Many men were dying of dysentery and the camp was littered with frozen corpses. Finally, the Russians arrived, and we were taken to a provisional hospital that had been hastily erected outside the camp. I was one of the lucky ones, as most of the inmates perished.'

Simon Stern fell silent, exhausted at having had to relive such suffering.

'I only saw him once… but I shall never forget that face,' he said suddenly, lost in thought.

'Whose face?' I asked.

'The camp commandant! He was responsible for all those deaths and his face was the picture of pure evil.'

After a dramatic pause, he continued. 'Rodney. Please find my wife and daughter! Please!' He leaned forward in the bed and held out his hand. I clasped it in mine for a few minutes while tears coursed freely down his cheeks.

'You have my word, Simon.'

'How could anybody give the orders for such a diabolical plan?' he asked, not expecting a reply.

13. THE NIGHTMARE WAS OVER

Phryne and I got our visas for France and Spain. We packed our Speed 6 Bentley and drove straight to Paris, where we stayed for a couple of nights. We then headed for Switzerland to change our money as we doubled it by changing into Swiss francs and then returning to France and changing the Swiss francs back into French ones.

As we drove south, I felt how wonderful it was to be back in France with the woman I loved and to whom I then felt so close. We enjoyed every moment of our trip, stopping for a refreshing *pastis* in the beautiful old village of Cagne, perched up in the mountains between Nice and Cannes. It was June '46 and we were taking our first holiday after the end of the nightmare.

On our arrival in Cannes we saw that some buildings had been destroyed, but this was nothing compared to London. Everybody still remembered me, and welcomed us with great affection. My good friend Freddy McEvoy had come back, and we frequently sailed on his superb Black Swan with Porfirio Rubirosa and his famous wife Danielle Darrieux. It was such a pleasure to see him again. We had so much to catch up with.

For some incomprehensible reason, mother had sold our house, so we stayed at the Martinez Hotel while we looked for a house to rent. We found Villa Paul on Avenue Benefiat, high up in the town, behind the Martinez. It had five double rooms and three bathrooms, plus an enormous living room, a dining room and, of course, servants' quarters. There was a lovely garden with a swimming pool, and the house came complete with an Italian cook, a butler and a gardener.

I needed to spend some time with Phryne away from M and London and to free myself from the war's shadow, which was suddenly unbearable. I guess I wanted to go back to July 1937 and recover that part of myself that died in the war.

I decided that we would use Villa Paul as our home and that I would only return to London when necessary. Spain was close enough and I planned to go there at the beginning of September. In the meantime, I was determined to lead a carefree life and enjoy it to the fullest; after all, you could never know whether death would call at your door.

Most evenings we had drinks on board Stewart Granger and Michael Wilding's boat. I remember meeting Vivien Leigh and Elizabeth Taylor, both in their late teens. Vivien was a vivacious young woman and Liz had a remarkable sense of humour. Her violet eyes were mesmerising. We all got on splendidly well and they came to lunch and dine at Villa Paul on several occasions.

Raf Valls and Diana, his new girlfriend, came to stay with us. We often took them to Eden Rock, a luxury club perched on the hillside near Cap d'Antibes and the in place to go. Aristotle Onassis, the Greek tycoon, could be seen there almost every day, and fantastic yachts, two- and three-masted schooners, and even large steam yachts, were often anchored nearby, next to the odd seaplane.

To see the sun again and the bright blue skies was very energising. The emerald and sapphire colour of the sea reflected on the rocks, and the umbrella pines buzzed with chattering tree frogs. Life was simply wonderful again.

When we were not sailing we used to go to Tahiti Beach, just past St Tropez. The three kilometres of sandy beach were almost deserted and the few people there were in the nude, scattered about in small groups with large spaces in between. We went with friends to enjoy delicious picnics, chilled wine, and refreshing dips in the ocean, while the gendarmes, sitting on the sand dunes behind the beach, watched us through their binoculars. Occasionally they would swoop down and ask us to cover ourselves up, but they enjoyed watching all the pretty girls, and thus they did not sound very convincing. The whole thing was rather civilised.

We laughed all summer every time Diana and Phryne recounted an incident when, walking along the beach, both looking stunning in nothing but G-strings, Diana had asked a naked young man who walked past them for the time. Upon thanking him for the information, the man replied, 'the pleasure is mine, madam. I'm so pleased to meet you.' She laughed as she looked at his private parts, and said, 'I can see you are!'

The summer was coming to an end when my mother, Uncle Jack and Princess Jane suddenly announced their imminent arrival and asked us to postpone our trip to Madrid and spend a couple of nights with them at the Palace Hotel in Monte Carlo. An old friend introduced my mother to Barbara Hutton, who was lavishly entertaining a group of about twenty friends. She was wearing a stunning emerald necklace that I immediately recognised as the one I had sold for Princess Niloufer Mourad at Van Cleef's. What an amazing twist of fate!

The train journey to Madrid was a nightmare. Not only was it hot as hell but also the wagon was packed, and we had to stand for fourteen hours. At one point, a priest gave Phryne his case for her to sit on for a while.

We arrived in Madrid filthy and exhausted, and went straight to the Palace Hotel, where they received us warmly. Although they knew me well, for the sake of appearances we had to take two separate rooms, as in ultra-conservative Spain, it was unlawful for unmarried couples to share a bedroom.

I had come to Madrid on a mission, that of discovering the whereabouts of Klaus von Jellenbach and the art collection he had looted.

Once Spain's neutrality had been guaranteed, Captain Hillgarth had been sent to command naval intelligence in Eastern Europe, where he worked with top-level interceptors. When the war ended, he left the navy and moved to Tangiers to publish an English language newspaper with his friend, Ian Fleming, who later was famous for his James Bond novels. In fact, through him, M became a fiction character.

Samuel Hoare returned to England soon after I had left Madrid, and the king knighted him and he became Viscount Templewood. Thus, when I paid a courtesy visit to the embassy, I found I only knew a few of the secretaries.

On our first night in Madrid, I called Pepe Ruiz-Gimenez, who invited us to dine at Jockey, one of the best restaurants in town. We gossiped about the Spanish friends we had in common and he told me how the Count of Herentals, devastated by the Nazis' defeat, had followed Hitler's example and committed suicide. I was flabbergasted, and next morning I called the count's sons, Pelayo and Gonzaga, who were eager to meet us for lunch.

The brothers immediately fell for Phryne and talked to her about all sorts of things in their perfect English. They both looked well, if more mature, and were in a very talkative mood, even shy Pelayo.

After ordering some drinks and our food, I asked them how their family were.

'Mother is now a merry widow because father shot himself last year. He just couldn't cope with an Allied victory!'

'I know. Pepe told me. I'm terribly sorry,' I said, feeling something for their loss.

'Actually, we're much better off without him. He made our lives a misery. Now Gonzaga is the new count, and I am free to paint and study at the *Academia de Bellas Artes.*'

'So it was you who painted those two lovely oil paintings that Rodney bought from Spain? They are hanging in our living room in London,' Phryne exclaimed admiringly.

Pelayo grinned with pleasure at the compliment. And Gonzaga raised his glass in a toast, 'To friendship!'

'Gonzaga, now that the war is over, what do you know about your father's dealings with the Germans?'

'Father admired the Third Reich and what the Führer wanted to achieve. Even Franco did,' he added as a matter of justification. 'This is why he offered his services to the German Embassy.

'And what exactly did he do for them?'

'He organised parties in their honour and passed them information about his pro-ally friends. He helped them in whatever capacity he could, as he was devoted to their cause. For example, when Göering wanted to sell about sixty paintings to the Prado Museum, my father arranged a secret meeting between two of his friends, José Uyarte, Director of the Museum, and a friend of Dad's called Klaus von Jellenbach.'

It was a sheer stroke of naked luck. I was right on track.

'And did the deal go through?' I asked.

'No. In spite of my father's assurances as to the legitimacy of ownership, Uyarte was not convinced and refused to continue with the negotiations.'

'I met the baron the very first time I went to your house. Whatever happened to him?'

'Oh, he came back to Madrid just before the end of the war. He managed to bring with him a large number of crates containing his entire collection, which we kept in our cellar until he disappeared.'

'What do you mean?'

'I heard my father tell mother that the baron had fallen from grace and could not return to Germany. His life was in danger if he did so. He stayed with us for several months, and it was my father who asked Franco to grant him a Spanish passport, which he did.'

'Why would Franco do something like that when by that time he must have known that we would win the war?'

'Well, I heard he received a magnificent painting as a gift.'

'How did the baron disappear? It must have been difficult without the Gestapo's aid?'

'Don't forget that by then he was Spanish and very wealthy. We think he simply left for South America as soon as the war was over, taking advantage of his Spanish nationality. Father was furious at his leaving without even bothering to say goodbye or thank him for his hospitality. He left like a thief, taking everything with him when father and mother were in the countryside. He bribed his way out of the country.'

Phryne and Pelayo were silent, listening with interest to our conversation.

'Do you know if he changed his name?'

'Yes, of course he did. He changed his name to Claudio Jiménez de Bach. Our father made us call him 'Uncle Claudio'.'

My plan was to stay in Madrid for a couple of weeks before flying back to London, and I intended, in those two weeks, to make Phryne love Spain as much as I did.

I took her to visit the Monasterio de El Escorial and the Roman Aqueduct in Segovia. I also took her to her first bullfight, at which the hitherto novillero, Luis Miguel Dominguín, took his *alternativa* at the hands of Aruza and became a matador[1]. He and I were to become friends, and I was later to meet him on many occasions in London in the company of Ava Gardner.

To my relief Phryne was really enjoying Spain and its people. She loved

---

[1] Novice bullfighter

her stay at the Ruiz-Gimenez country estate, outside Madrid, where we went boar hunting. Pepe was a charming man and an excellent host.

As soon as I had an opportunity, I called Felisin. I had never mentioned her to Phryne, and I was not about to do so at this stage. I had asked the Herentals brothers but they did not seem to know. I could not get through to her, so while Phryne went shopping I walked form the Palace Hotel to her apartment nearby. The doorman recognised me immediately, as I had been generous with my tips in the past.

'Señor Mundy. It has been a long time. Where have you been?'

'In London, Antonio. How is Señora Felisin?'

'Oh, Señor Mundy. You did not hear about the tragedy?'

My heart skipped a beat.

'What tragedy?'

Antonio passed his arm around my back and whispered, 'Señora Felisin was murdered about two years ago. She was shot in the back of the head.'

I was speechless and felt utterly devastated. My tears began to flow as I remembered all the good times we had spent together. I recalled her sweet laughter and sense of humour. She was such an extraordinary woman, beautiful and full of the finest human values, and I had failed her.

After a few minutes, Antonio brought me a glass of water and patted me on the back. 'I know how fond of you she was,' he said.

'Was anybody prosecuted?' I asked.

'No, Señor Mundy. The investigation was closed after a few days.'

I knew it must have been Vogel. If only she had listened to me, she would be alive now, but the temptation of 100,000 wretched pesetas had been too great. I spent the next few hours walking in the Retiro Park, alone with my thoughts, reflecting on what my life had been until then. I realised that I had really loved her and I cried in silence again at the loss. I was so angry with myself, at Alan, for failing to protect her as he had promised. It was a pain that would never leave me.

14. A MARRIED MAN

It was already October and we were back in London. Phryne had not felt too well during our stay in Madrid, so as soon as we got back to London I took her to the doctor who told us she was pregnant with a dead baby. This was devastating for her, especially as I was not sympathetic enough, for I had never really thought of becoming a father, and I felt overwhelmed by the whole situation. I guess, at the time, those shoes were too big for me to wear.

My mother, Uncle Jack, and Princess Jane had returned to London in time for my birthday on the 27th. It only took her a few days to sell our magnificent estate in Farnham and buy a beautiful large house in London, at 76 Cadogan Place on Lord Cadogan's estate. She moved in with all our furniture from both Farnham and the South of France.

M was delighted with my information on the whereabouts of Klaus von Jellenbach, now going by the name of Claudio Jiménez de Bach. He believed that eventually our secret services would track him down wherever he was in South America.

The Nuremberg hearings had been going on since November 1945 but, unfortunately, many important Nazi figures were being tried 'in absentia' as they had mostly disappeared to South America where the local dictators received them with open arms. Those brought to trial had been chosen largely to ensure representation of all major administrative groupings of the Reich. However, the lawyers, the press and the public came to focus mainly on the human dimension of Nuremberg, considering it a trial of humiliated Nazi bosses and a record of their victims' sufferings.

I went to see Simon Stern who, though still in hospital, was to be soon discharged as he had made a remarkable recovery. I regaled him with stories about the South of France and for the first time since his death I spoke to someone about my father.

'Do you know, Simon, I have just remembered sitting by the fireplace when I was home on holiday, and my father telling me fascinating stories about when he was young. He had been a very close friend of Prince Andrew of Greece[1]. They had both been wild in their early manhood and had spent a lot of time together in Paris, mostly broke. Known as the *Papillon Gris* because of their grey hair at such an early age, they had modelled for a well-known artist in order to make ends meet. The result was a famous bronze statue of two polo riders!'

'Your father comes alive every time you think of him, as do my adored wife and my little Rita,' Simon said sadly.

I really liked him. He had a good sense of humour in spite of his underlying sadness, and he, like my father, was a true gentleman. I yearned to give him news about his family. He had such a generous spirit that he never again mentioned them, but his silence was more eloquent than words. Then one day, just before Christmas and to my relief, I was finally able to give some news, albeit bittersweet.

M called me to tell me Rita was alive and living in an orphanage outside Budapest. She was to be flown to England. As her mother had been British, the girl, now nearly seven, was a British subject. God alone knew what ordeals she had endured. She had survived the camp due to a stroke of luck; the childless wife of a German captain had found her adorable and had arranged for her 'adoption'. Fortunately for Rita, her devoted new parents had abandoned her when they hurriedly vacated the camp. Her mother, sadly, had ended her days in the gas chamber.

Upon his release from hospital, Simon Stern rented a room in the home of a Polish refugee couple now living in London. Tadeusz and Malgorzata Zawidski had a small boarding house at 86 Onslow Gardens. I was to become very close to them; they were the loveliest of people.

The Zawidskis had been members of the Polish underground of whom over 200,000 had died in their desperate fight against the Germans and, unknown to them at the time, also against their allies, the Russians. They had managed to reach safety by walking through the city sewers, full of human waste that sometimes reached up to their necks. They had walked

---

[1] Prince Andrew was the father of HRH The Duke of Edinburgh, husband to Queen Elizabeth II

for over a day and, like many of their companions, they had lost their sight for several days due to the fumes given off by the sewage.

I visited Simon at their flat, which was beautifully decorated for Christmas. The moment I walked in Tadeusz offered me a glass of Polish vodka while Mrs Zawidski went to tell Simon Stern he had a visitor.

No words were necessary between us. As he entered the living room and saw my smile, he asked in disbelief, 'Have they found her?'

'Yes, Simon. She will be in London for Christmas.'

'What about my wife?'

'I'm afraid we have no information about her. We have to assume she has perished.'

I believed the time had come to leave MI6. I had concluded my mission and was planning to marry Phryne. I felt I wanted to start my own business and make real money, so I went to see M at his office and handed in my resignation.

'Once you are MI6, you will always be MI6,' he said, making it sound like a courteous expression of formality, as if we belonged to a prestigious fraternity. At the time, I could not grasp the full meaning of his words.

Our wedding was set for 28 April, my mother's birthday. It was a very quiet affair at the Kensington Register Office, and it was only then that I discovered Phryne was four years older than I was. We had a family lunch at the superb Belfrey Club and in the evening we threw a large party for about forty-five friends, including M, at Raf and Diana's flat.

Having no job, I soon ran out of money, so we went to live with my mother at Cadogan Place while we planned a tourism venture in Santa Margherita in Italy.

It soon became clear that the United States did not intend to permit the spread of communism, once more, throughout Spain. President Truman had concluded that, in spite of Franco's continuous human rights abuses, he was a lesser evil as he was, at least, ferociously anti-communist. One of the paradoxes of history is that Stalin's policies were to keep the Spanish dictator in power until he died of old age in 1975. Within a few months, Spain tried unsuccessfully to be part of the reconstruction project known as the Marshall Plan though in the end as a ploy against communism and to the relief of General Franco the regime was allowed to survive. I really felt sorry for the Spanish democrats and for Don Juan, whose chances of recovering the throne were now shattered, probably for ever.

In 1947 Phryne moved to Italy to get everything organised, and I followed in late July. Things began going well for us until the British Government suddenly passed a law that cut the travel allowance right down to £25 per head, which was virtually nothing. Nobody could go abroad on such a pittance so our new business venture was sacrificed at infancy.

Without a business, we were soon broke, and I had to leave Phryne at the hotel and go to Milan in order to get some money to pay our hotel's bill, as it was promptly closing for the winter.

With some money still left in our pockets, Phryne and I left for Cervinia, a mountain resort on the Italian side of the Matterhorn. I enjoyed skiing and teaching Phryne how to do so immensely. By the end of our Alpine holiday, we were again practically penniless, so in order to pay for two first-class tickets on the Orient Express to Paris, Phryne sold her gold watch and some ruby earrings. One precarious and exciting adventure was over, but another was just about to start.

To celebrate my twenty-fifth birthday, I took Phryne to the Scala in Milan to hear Di Stefano make his debut in Massenet's *Manon*. It was a memorable evening. My mother inculcated me with the love of opera from a very tender age and I spent many evenings with my father sitting by her piano while she played and sang her favourite arias.

Our first-class couchette on board the Orient Express adjoined that of Jacques Fath, the well-known gay couturier from Paris, who spent the whole night trying to seduce the guard on the Wagon Lits. It was very entertaining listening to their conversation while we dined, and I feel sure he succeeded in the end. As we could not afford to go to the restaurant car we had bought a bottle of Chianti, a loaf of bread, some salami, and a dozen oysters plus a lemon to eat in our compartment. It was a perfect arrangement, as far as we were concerned, for it provided a romantic night with jolting love sessions on board a train quite unlike any other in the world.

We arrived in Paris in November with exactly 50 lire and 2,000 francs and went straight to the Powers Hotel where we were welcomed with open arms. We took a beautiful light and airy room in the attic with a slanting roof, chintz curtains and a large bathroom. Whenever we ran out of money, which was very often, we would order a bottle of champagne to see if our luck changed. We would drink it in our room laughing and chatting over our latest adventure.

However, our luck was not quick to change and, at one point, we were stuck in the charming hotel for over three weeks. I loved France and was determined not to return to England. I was not missing my work at MI6, and in spite of our precarious financial situation, we were having a great time enjoying every moment.

Finally, my lucky break came when one day, of all people, I ran into dear Fred Kempler. It was wonderful to see him again. He was now living in Paris and made a living by wheeling and dealing. He immediately lent me some money and we ventured into the cloth business together.

In France things like material, except goods destined for export, were still rationed. So at least on paper I became an English agent. Fred would buy the cloth for manufacture and then he would export it to England through me. However, what actually happened was that Fred bought the material very cheaply and then promptly flogged it by the baleful on the black market for a small fortune. The material never saw a manufacturer and never ever left France, while Fred and I split the profits of our highly lucrative business. I knew he was doing on the side all sorts of dodgy deals, but preferred not to know too much about them.

After a month in the cloth business, Phryne and I moved into a divine little house with a garage and a garden at 10 Rue Donne, very near the Bois de Boulogne. Beautifully decorated, it even had three Renoirs on the walls. We rented the house for an entire year, as the owners had gone to the United States to sell a theatre curtain painted by Picasso, which they had managed to smuggle out with them!

Business was booming and we gave many parties. Edith Piaf and Yves Montand were regulars. She was an amazingly scruffy little person, always dressed in black, but what a lovely voice and personality she had!

One day Fred came roaring into the house, saying that the authorities had caught a partner of his in some other business for some tax fiddle. He suggested that I return to England for a while until things cooled down, in case they came asking awkward questions. Thinking this a sensible idea, I returned to England, leaving Phryne with quite a bit of money and a garage full of material. Fortunately, nothing happened.

After I had been in London for only a few days, Phryne phoned me, sounding desperate. The French government had suddenly called in all 5,000 Franc notes. I rang Fred and arranged for him to go to the house and collect all the notes in that denomination. I sympathised with Phryne. She had a hard job ahead of her as the bank notes were hidden away between the pages of over 100 books on the bookshelves in the drawing room and bedroom.

I was very relieved when the next day Fred told me that he had successfully changed the money through a South American Embassy. I guess Porfirio Rubirosa helped him.

Time flew and soon an entire year had passed since we moved into 10 Rue Donne. We were now moving out. Phryne was pregnant and we decided to spend the summer at Villa Paul, but at the end of September we returned to England, as I wanted the baby to be born there. I reasoned that if the baby was a son and born in France, he would be due for military service.

My son was born on my birthday, which was the very best gift I could have wished for. I named him Simon after Simon Stern. However, Phryne suffered from post-natal depression, which made living together rather a strain.

By February, I needed a holiday and was ready to go skiing, so I persuaded Phryne to leave Simon with her sister, and off we went to Alp d'Huez, about fifty kilometres from Grenoble.

Within a year I was flat broke again. My mother and Uncle Jack had been living well beyond their means for some time, so she decided to sell her lovely house and we all moved into a flat in Sloane Square. Most of the furniture had to be sold as there was very little room, but this did not include the Blüthner piano, and we still enjoyed many a musical evening.

My relationship with Phryne was becoming rather tense. What made matters worse was that we could not take any holidays because we had no money. To escape from the very unpleasant situation at home, I began playing golf at the weekends. My mother, as usual, gave me enough money to make ends meet until she decided to return to the South of France.

By now, I was in £600 of debt and there seemed no alternative but to get myself a proper job, especially as I now had family responsibilities, so I entered the motorcar business. My friend Ian Metcalfe and I became sole distributors in the United Kingdom for the Borgward, a German car.

Things soon changed for the better. I paid off my debts and we were able to live quite well despite many things such as material, clothes, and petrol still being rationed. Life with Phryne improved considerably and in the summer of 1951 we returned to the South of France for a long family holiday, this time in St Maxime, in the Villa Le Mas de Saccade, right up in the hills.

We sailed on a daily basis on the Black Swan, until one day Fred announced that he would be sailing back to Australia with his beautiful and wealthy girlfriend. He went down to Marseille and, having difficulties finding personnel for such a long trip, he got himself a rather dubious crew. He then filled the vessel with all the jewellery and furniture he possibly could, and set a date for their departure. When the day came it was very stormy, and he was advised to delay the trip a few days, but being a seasoned sailor, he insisted in leaving.

We were shocked to read in the newspapers the following day that the Black Swan had sunk and Fred and Marianne had drowned. How could that have happened when both of them were excellent swimmers and, strangely enough, all the crew had managed to swim ashore? The police, once they found their bodies tied to the mast, finally concluded the crew had murdered them, but it was too late, as by then they had disappeared taking all the jewellery with them. It was a tragic ending for a wonderful friend.

After the summer, I had an argument with Phryne because we had not been making love regularly. She blamed it on the fact that she was now a mother, but insisted that she still loved me. As proof of her love, she gave me the green light to see other women, with the sole condition that I did not fall in love.

We used to go to many parties at Raf and Diana's. One evening, Ava Gardner and Luis Miguel Dominguín were there, as well as the Spanish Ambassador. Ava walked straight up to the ambassador, kissed him on the lips and then sat on his lap! That night I was introduced to a beautiful young Spanish student who was staying at Raf and Diana's. She was called Pepita and was stunning, with a vivacious personality. She reminded me of Liz Taylor, as they had exactly the same eyes. Pepita was a friend of Jorge Juan, a young Spanish lawyer who was doing his articles in international law at Raf's office, and the two of them soon joined Phryne and me regularly for cocktails and picnics.

A few weeks later Raf asked us if Pepita could stay with us as a paying guest, to which we naturally agreed. However, after a few weeks I had to accept the inevitable: Pepita and I had fallen madly in love with each other. Pepita left the house but we were unable to stop the fire once it had been ignited, no matter how hard she tried.

One night, after spending a blissful evening at Pepita's new apartment, I drove round the corner only to see Phryne standing there. I drove a short way past, then pulled up and waited for her to come alongside. Opening the door, I told her to get in.

'I want to walk home. Don't you remember we have a son?' she said on the verge of tears.

Back home, we had a terrible scene. In her rage, Phryne threatened to shoot Pepita, but soon she calmed down and we agreed to continue living together for at least another year, for Simon's sake. I tried everything to get Pepita out of my system but failed miserably. She was the woman I loved.

In 1952, as a result of our policy in Egypt, King Farouk, (who in his frustration of being practically powerless had become a debauched monarch only interested in heavy eating and sex), was deposed by the army. I felt really saddened by the news. He had been a good king in many ways. He had been very active in inter-Arab politics, had increased the Arab orientation of Egypt, developed the League of Arab states, which had their headquarters in Cairo, and had taken a keen interest in the aspirations of the Palestinian people. Egypt had developed economically during his reign and he had founded many institutes of higher learning. It was a great shame.

It was soon May 1952. I sent Phryne and Simon to St Maxime to stay with my mother and Uncle Jack, and joined them a few weeks later in a last attempt to salvage my marriage. We spent most of the days with Gregory Peck, who had rented the villa next to ours. By then I really could not face being alone with Phryne, and always tried to surround myself with friends.

A few months after this holiday we got divorced. Our break-up was very difficult for her, but we have managed to stay friends all through the years. Soon afterwards, she moved to the Costa Brava and ended up having an affair with Jorge Juan, Pepita's friend. She has lived there ever since.

Pepita took a room at the Zawidskis' boarding house and we saw each other every day. By then Simon Stern had left the country. The Zawidskis were very fond of her and we used to sit with them over a glass of their excellent Polish vodka and listen to what they had to say about Poland's past and present hardships. They were very embittered about Churchill having sold Poland's freedom to Stalin. Their country had fought the German war machine for sixty-three days with no outside help until the resistance was crushed and Warsaw completely destroyed as a lesson to the rest of Europe. We felt extremely sorry for them because they had both suffered enormously, and their deep-set nostalgia for their country would never leave them.

Pepita and I were very much in love, but she always felt guilty and blamed herself for the break-up of my marriage to Phryne. She came from a conservative Catholic family and was very religious in her own way. I was glad that she got on well with my mother and Uncle Jack, as that made things easier for everybody.

I finally proposed to her and she accepted. However, there were quite a few problems to solve before we could get married. I belonged to the Church of England, and the Catholic Church was against marriages between different faiths. To make matters worse, I was divorced, which was equally unacceptable. As far as Pepita's family was concerned, I was quite unsuitable as a husband for all the above reasons and because I had a son.

After much consultation, a lawyer specialising in Vatican Law gave us the good news: as far as the Catholic Church was concerned, I had never been married to Phryne at all, because she had been a divorcee at the time. Therefore, the Church considered her still married to her previous husband; in the Church's eyes, our marriage had never existed. This was an amazing way of erasing ten years of our lives, but it suited us just fine.

In the summer of 1954, I invited Pepita's mother and her sister to the South of France to spend a few weeks with us in the delightful atmosphere of the Mediterranean. Everything went very smoothly as our respective mothers sat down to arrange the details of our wedding, which was to be celebrated in the Church of Nuestra Señora de Begoña in Bilbao in the spring. I was very excited.

The wedding was an incredibly lavish affair with over 500 guests. As I stood waiting for over half an hour at the altar of the Basilica, which Pepita's mother had decorated with hundreds of white flowers, I felt rather uneasy. Had Pepita changed her mind?

Luckily, she had not. She arrived at the church holding Uncle Jack's arm and looking ravishing in her stunning mauve long-tailed wedding dress. The

Duke of Primo de Rivera, Spanish Ambassador to Britain, Ian Metcalfe, and José Luis de Arrese, Pepita's uncle, all signed as witnesses, together with other friends.

That night after the banquet, we drove to San Sebastian where we stayed at the Hotel de Londres and then travelled through France.

Back in London, we stayed for a few weeks at the Zawidskis', who by now had become very close friends. Every Christmas we went to see them with our children. We all enjoyed listening to their old Polish tales.

As the motorcar business was thriving, we decided to buy a beautiful house in Putney, 9 Westleigh Avenue, which was to be our home until we left England. Pepita hired Spanish staff, and we entertained constantly.

My son Carlos was born in May 1956. Pepita went to Bilbao to give birth in order to be close to her mother. I had not been too keen on the idea, myself, but she was a stubborn woman and insisted on giving birth to all four of our children in her hometown.

I received a heavy blow just before my second son was born. My mother died from a stroke while taking a nap. I would miss her very much, as she had been such an important person in my life. Not only had she been an excellent mother, but also one of my closest friends.

For the next few years, I led a life of domestic bliss, until one day the harmony was shattered and the past returned to haunt me.

15. THE SIXTIES

Life in London in the Swinging Sixties was great fun. If the sixties were a social revolution, London was the centre. Yuri Gagarin's becoming the first man in space in 1961 had led to a new way of thinking. People somehow felt they were no longer limited exclusively to this planet, and this idea of greater space and freedom reflected in everything else.

We entered the decade in black and white and we came out in colour. Mary Quant had invented the mini skirt, and the Beatles and the Rolling Stones had taken the music world by storm. The British Establishment was reeling with shock, having been quite unprepared for such a radical change, a change that was visible everywhere. Everything was now geared to the taste of the younger generation.

With the Bay of Pigs incident, the world had been poised on the brink of a major conflict, and President Kennedy's assassination a year later in 1963 came as a dreadful shock.

I feared MI6 would come knocking on my door, but luckily they failed to materialise and allowed me to continue living my life in peace. I heard through Raf Valls that M had finally retired, as by then my contact with the firm was non-existent.

I was enjoying life in the company of my beautiful wife and children. Simon was attending King's College in Canterbury and I saw him on occasional weekends and on holidays.

Time flew, and in 1965 Winston Churchill, the greatest political leader of the twentieth century, died. The entire nation went into mourning. I admired him enormously, considering him a keystone to the Allied victory in the war. But I am sure history will also judge him for his mistakes, especially that of handing half of Europe over to Stalin.

Back in 1947 Simon Wiesenthal, a Jewish Holocaust survivor, and thirty others had formed the Jewish Historical Documentation Centre, based in the town of Linz in Austria. The centre's aim was to compile evidence in the hope of bringing Nazi war criminals to trial.

M had passed Klaus von Jellenbach's file on to the centre years ago and for a while I waited for his detention, but by now I thought the case had been forgotten. Although the original office had closed in 1959, Wiesenthal had carried on with his investigative work and had opened the Jewish Documentation Centre in Vienna, concentrating his efforts exclusively on hunting down Nazi war criminals. His painstaking efforts and investigations were soon to prove very fruitful.

Not only was Wiesenthal responsible for the capture of Adolf Eichmann, the man who had supervised the implementation of the Final Solution and who had been living happily in Buenos Aires as Ricardo Klement, but in October 1966 he had nine SS officers arrested and tried in Stuttgart for their part in the extermination of Jews in Lvov. A year later, after three years' patient undercover work in Brazil, Wiesenthal had Franz Stangl arrested and sentenced to life imprisonment. Stangl had been the commandant of Treblinka and Sobibor concentration camps.

After Stangl's arrest, the international press ran articles about him and the luxury in which he had been living. In one of the photographs taken in his home, I recognised a painting that had been part of Simon Stern's collection and was included in the list of works he had given the baron for safekeeping. My heart beat fast at the discovery. I contacted the Jewish Documentation Centre in Vienna and gave them the information that was to lead to the baron's arrest.

Fleeing from Spain as Claudio Jiménez de Bach, the baron had settled in Asunción, Paraguay, where many high-ranking Nazis joined him, seeking the protection of President Stroessner, who had turned his country into a home for ageing Nazis. The baron soon became a Paraguayan citizen and changed his name once again, as the name given him by Franco made him very easy to trace. He also underwent plastic surgery to erase any features that might remind anyone of Klaus von Jellenbach.

As Gerardo Echevarría, he lived in style in Asunción and was a prominent member of Paraguayan society. He had become a patron of the arts. His donation of some of the minor works in his collection to the city's art museum had won him the favour of the dictator and to add lustre to his altruism he sponsored young Paraguayan artists.

It was thanks to Stangl's testimony that the Jewish Documentation Centre was able to trace the baron, but bringing him to trial in Israel was not so easy. The Paraguayan authorities, as was to be expected, refused either to arrest him or grant his extradition. To them, officially, Gerardo Echevarría had been born in Asunción and could not possibly be a war criminal. However irrefutable the proof presented by Israel, it was all to no avail.

The Israeli Government finally lost its patience and decided to act. Israeli agents promptly abducted the baron on his return from spending a weekend with his wife and son at his country estate in the north. It was there that he kept his magnificent art collection for the enjoyment of his family and closest friends.

I knew the capture of Klaus von Jellenbach would land me once again with MI6, although I hoped they had forgotten me. A few days later, however, someone from the firm came to see me at my office. His name was Miles.

'Mr Mundy, the Israeli Government has requested that you go to Jerusalem to attend Mr von Jellenbach's trial once a date is set. And as you are a former member of this organisation, we also request that, when the time comes, you attend the trial.'

'But these events took place over twenty years ago!' I protested. 'I only met Jellenbach a few times and I don't even recognise him now in the photographs.'

'You were involved in the investigation that took place at the time and you became a good friend of Simon Stern, so I think you owe it to him, at least. Your testimony will certainly help to get that bastard convicted!' Miles added, forcefully.

'All right then. I'll do it,' I conceded. 'Tell me, whatever happened to Stern?'

'He finally moved to Costa Rica with his daughter. He died a few years ago. The suffering he endured in those camps must have finally taken its toll.'

'What will happen to the baron's art collection?' I asked.

'Stroessner is so indignant at what has happened that he refuses to admit that his buddy was a former Nazi. The official position is that the collection belongs to Paraguay. We will do everything legally possible to have the paintings returned to the families of their former owners, although it is going to be difficult and costly.'

'Very well, then. I shall have to speak to my wife, of course, who will no doubt be none too happy that I have never mentioned any of this to her.'

'Rodney, one more thing... We would like you to go and live in Spain. Franco cannot live for ever and we need you there.'

I could not believe it! I was back in MI6 again!

To my surprise, Pepita was most understanding. She loathed the Nazis with a passion, influenced no doubt by the Zawidskis' horrific stories about what went on in Poland. I, myself, believe that sometimes one must let go of hate in order for the wounds to heal, but, of course, every human being is a world unto himself.

Pepita decided she would accompany me to Jerusalem whenever the trial would take place; moreover, she was willing to go and live in Madrid and be closer to her family.

We stored our furniture in a warehouse, put Westleigh Avenue up for sale, and made our arrangements to travel back to Spain, to Playa de Berria, not far away from Santander, where every summer we spent the holidays with Pepita's mother and her sister's family.

When the summer was over, we settled into our new home at Calle Cinca 16, in the residential district of El Viso. Pepita had chosen a nice big house with garden so that our children would not feel too unsettled by the move. Madrid had changed enormously since my last visit and a new air of freedom could be sensed everywhere. Franco was getting old, and in time, there would be a change of regime. As soon as I arrived, I called Joaquín and Pepe who were now prominent members of society. They loved Pepita.

As a cover, MI6 had arranged for me to work for a company called Hierros y Aceros Europeos, which was a subsidiary of Harlow & Jones. Our job was to advise the Spanish steelworks on the purchase of scrap metal from the US, the UK and other European countries, chiefly Belgium and the Netherlands. Initially I knew absolutely nothing about scrap metal nor did I have the slightest interest, but I soon learnt to enjoy it and eventually became very good at it. To cap it all, I got a generous salary and I had a charming assistant, Count Peter Potocki, whose family had given Poland several kings and who was now living in exile in Madrid.

My work for MI6 was once again to infiltrate Spanish society and find out who would support the restoration of the monarchy, because a lot of support would be necessary if the institution was to survive, and it was feared the extremists would react against it. Neither Santiago Carrillo's outlawed Communist Party nor the Socialists wanted a monarchy, and they both mocked the future King from their headquarters in exile. They referred to him as Juan Carlos 'the brief'! On the other hand, Franco's acolytes were not very keen on the idea of the monarchy either, although they said nothing in public. MI6 had briefed me that they feared that when Franco died there was a real danger of another civil war breaking out.

Pepita was a great asset in my work because after only a month in Madrid she started giving her extravagant and amusing dinner parties, which became the talk of the town, and which our *madrileño* friends found very entertaining.

I was in contact with Miles through my office and I told him everything I learnt, which, in truth, was not very much, because nobody wanted to discuss the future. After so many years of Franco, during which a reasonable level of prosperity had been achieved, people were apprehensive of any change, and they all agreed that the king's task would be anything but easy.

No date had yet been set for the trial in Jerusalem, so at Easter we decided to rent a house in a sleepy fishing village on the Costa del Sol, called Torremolinos. We took the children and their Spanish governess, Beatriz, with us. Pepita and I were planning to go afterwards to Seville for the April Feria, having been invited by Pablo Atienza; she took most of her very valuable jewellery with her.

One afternoon we drove with the children and the governess to the nearby village of Marbella to visit some friends. On our return, we found that the house had been broken into. The place had been ransacked and, naturally, Pepita's jewellery was missing. She was very upset by the loss, as many of the pieces had been gifts from her mother; others were Mundy heirlooms and the rest were expensive gifts from a devoted husband.

The police concluded that the thieves were just common criminals who had had a stroke of luck, but I knew better. From the way in which they had searched the apartment, I knew the burglars had to be former Nazis. I said nothing about my fears to my wife but, instead, contacted Miles, who told me that the date for the trial had been set for October of the following year. Now I understood.

In the spring of 1968 France was in turmoil. The students had taken to the streets of Paris en masse and were bringing about a veritable revolution.

Naturally, the Spanish press censored all news from Paris, while giving ample coverage to the communist regime's brutal repression of the pro-democracy movement in Prague.

Spanish summers were three months long, so we prepared to shut up the house in Cinca for the holidays. It was a lot of hard work; all the furniture and paintings had to be covered with sheets to protect them from dust, and the smaller objects wrapped in newspaper, but under Pepita's guidance, the servants managed to get everything done.

As every summer, we went to Santander, driving up in two cars.

In mid-August, feeling like a change of scenery, Pepita and I accepted an invitation to spend a few days in La Manga del Mar Menor in Murcia. We took Carlos with us and drove down, stopping in Madrid for an overnight stay in Cinca. Madrid was unbearable hot, and the house felt ghostly. We enjoyed our week in La Manga, which had only recently begun to be developed. Our host, who would eventually marry Pepita's niece, took good care of us.

For our return journey, we planned the same route, once again with a stopover in Madrid. However, the minute we arrived at Cinca, I knew there was something terribly wrong. The front door had been forced open, but my worst fears were nothing compared to nightmarish sight we found inside. Whoever had broken in had turned the house upside down with premeditated violence; they had slashed all the valuable paintings, destroyed and thrown about many of the children's toys. The mess left behind was unbelievable. Pepita broke down in tears. We called the police and booked into a hotel.

The police thought it most likely that a group of Gypsies had broken in and stayed for a few days, as there were signs that led them to believe they had cooked themselves meals and slept in the house. As one would have thought in a burglary many priceless objects, including the rest of Pepita's jewellery, were missing but what was not in character was the evident hate factor. Why had they destroyed the paintings rather than steal them? Littered around the house were packets that looked like gifts, but when the police opened them they turned out to be full of human excrement. I realised that whoever these people were, they were delivering a message on behalf of others who passionately hated me and wished to intimidate me. Once again I kept my thoughts to myself, as Pepita was worried enough as it was.

We decided for safety's sake to move to a rented, huge, flat on Raimundo

Fernández Villaverde 61, and had the rest of our furniture sent out from London. It was already late September, and shortly we would have to fly to Jerusalem for the trial.

It was then that I started receiving hate mail and threatening phone calls at the office and I became seriously worried. I naturally had to speak to Pepita, who pleaded with me to forget the whole affair and not go to Israel. I was obliged to explain that I was active with MI6 again, at which she became extremely upset and seriously concerned about the children's safety.

'You had no right to hide that from me. We are a team,' she said. 'These Nazis won't stop at anything to achieve their goals. And their goal is that you stay here.'

'I know that, my love, but I have to go.'

'Fine! In that case, you can go alone. I do not want to have anything to do with it. I shall take the children to Bilbao, to my mother's, until it is all over. I hope you never live to regret this decision.' She stormed out, slamming the door behind her. It was our first major row since our marriage.

In a few days hence, I would be on my way to Jerusalem. In the meantime, the British Embassy provided some guards to protect my family.

The day before my departure I invited Pepita to lunch at Horcher. She was barely speaking to me, but I needed her blessing before I left, as I knew that my stay in Jerusalem would not be easy. She accepted and we walked into Horcher at exactly two-thirty.

We sat at an excellent table and the maitre placed a cushion under Pepita's feet. I ordered a bottle of vintage Krug and we drank a toast.

We were chatting away happily, when I noticed an elderly man sitting by himself. He was fairly close to us. The face was very familiar and after observing him, I realised that he was Vogel. He was probably following me, and I was certain he was responsible for everything that had happened to us. Instinctively, I got up and walked over to his table. Though he of course knew very well who I was, he pretended otherwise, feigning surprised.

'Hello Hans. It's been a long time.' He was an excellent actor and continued to act as if he did not know me.

'Tell whoever is in charge to get off my back,' I said firmly, but in a whisper. 'If you hurt my family I'll destroy you.'

He started rambling in French, 'But, monsieur, you are crazy, I am a

French tourist, my name is not Hans and I have never met you. My name is Pierre Dupont. You must be mistaken.'

Vogel started calling the *maître* and complained about my harassment in fluent French and without a trace of his former heavy German accent. I turned and, without another word, walked back to my table. The sight of him had greatly disturbed me. I remembered poor Laszlo, and how he had been murdered.

'What was all that about?' asked my wife. I recounted the whole story. 'I told you before, Rodney, these people are really dangerous and will stop at nothing to save the baron. What do you intend to do? You cannot possibly go to Israel. You have to think of your family.'

'My love, I have to do my duty. I shall inform my boss in London, and the Simon Wiesenthal Centre.'

'What about your duty to your family?' Tears rolled down her beautiful cheeks. I could not bear witnessing her pain. However, I had no choice.

16. THE BARON'S TRIAL

Pepita had taken a night train to Bilbao with the children and Bea as planned. She had made me promise that I would be back for my birthday, although I was not at all certain that the trial would be over by then.

The flight to Lod airport was uneventful. The Israeli Government had bought me a first class ticket on El Al, the national carrier, and on arrival the British Consul and several members of the Mossad collected me.

The weather was delightful. It was sunny and warm, as only Mediterranean capitals can be in autumn. We drove to Jerusalem, the city of peace, and they took me straight to the King David Hotel, where a comfortable suite was waiting for me. I called Pepita, who had arrived safely in Bilbao. I felt a faint sensation of uneasiness and promised myself that this would be the last mission of this type. My work in Madrid was not dangerous, so in future I would just stick to that.

Isaac, a member of the Mossad, had been assigned to me during my stay, and when I had unpacked, he escorted me to the Consulate, where members of the Israeli secret service would brief me on the details of the trial.

The residence of the British Consul was situated in one of the best areas of the city. As we drove there, I marvelled at Jerusalem, a city that was 3,000 years old and sacred to the world's three most widespread religions. I hoped I would have time to do some sightseeing during my stay.

Talbot Mundy, the great author, who as a sign of friendship to my parents had taken our family name as his *nom de plume*, wrote in the twenties that Jerusalem was ludicrous, uproarious, dignified, pious, sinful, naively confidential, secretive, altruistic and realistic. A city proud of its name and its unique history and I could not agree with him more.

The gates of the residence opened as the car approached. After we passed security, I was escorted to the consul's study. He rose from his chair as we entered, looking distinctly worried.

'Welcome to Jerusalem, Mr Mundy,' he said somewhat gravely, and I realised all was not well.

'Please call me Rodney.'

Isaac and two other members of the Israeli Secret Service sat down and the consul introduced me to the ambassador.

'Rodney, I am afraid I have news from Spain that you are not going to like.'

My heart sank and my distress was clearly visible to everybody in the room.

'Your family is fine,' he quickly reassured me. 'However, your ex-wife has contacted the embassy in Madrid to inform them that Simon was threatened by a middle-aged German man.'

'What did he want? Is my son all right? I was beyond myself with worry. How could I have put duty before my family?

The ambassador rose from his chair and approached me. 'Whoever it was, wants you to return to Spain and not to testify.'

'I can't go ahead with this,' I said as I was overcome by a feeling of gloom.

'You have a duty to perform, Rodney. You must stay. Both your family in Bilbao and your ex-wife and elder son now have extra protection and they are fine. They will be safe!' He said trying to be as reassuring as possible.

'That's not much of a relief! I would never be able to forgive myself if anything happened to them.'

'The man told your son that he was an old friend of yours. Do you have a clue as to who he could be?' the Consul asked.

'Yes. He is probably Vogel. He was a member of the Gestapo: a cold-blooded, ruthless murderer. How is it possible that these Nazis move around with such impunity? It's been over twenty years since the Reich collapsed!' I cried out in exasperation.

'Though very discrete, the Nazis are still very active. We know they have a clandestine organisation that operates worldwide, but it is so impenetrable that we have been unable to infiltrate it. We do not even know where it is based. Former members of the Gestapo, the SS, and Nazi sympathisers belong to it. They have vast amounts of money, which they managed to get out of Germany mainly through Spain, and they use it to help those in need to protect their identities and they finance neo-Nazi groups. Their main goal, of course, is to establish the Fourth Reich. So you see, Rodney, the Nazis are still a formidable enemy, which is why you must stay for the trial.'

'Why are they so concerned about the baron? After all, he is a disgraced Nazi.'

'Well, after the fall of the Reich he used his money and influences to regain the organisation's respect.'

'Ambassador, Captain Vogel murdered two good friends of mine. I would like us to do whatever it takes to have him arrested and prosecuted for his crimes.'

'I will speak to the Israel Government and to our Secret Services and hopefully we will find him.'

'I saw him in a Madrid restaurant only two days ago. He is pretending to be French, and if he was with my son yesterday he is probably still in Barcelona.'

The trial was set to begin on the morning of 17 July. Jerusalem was abuzz with expectation and very strict security measures were in place everywhere. Hundreds of journalists from all over the world had come to cover what had been dubbed 'The Trial of the Decade'. To add to the excitement, it was going to be televised, as the Israeli Prime Minister, Levi Eshkol, wanted to ensure that the world did not forget the atrocities committed by the Nazis.

This would be the second Nazi trial to be televised, the first having been that of Adolf Eichmann. There were similarities between the two cases, in that both men had been kidnapped, rather than being arrested, in South America, and both had been brought to trial by a Jewish court in Israel. The difference was in the scale of their crimes. Eichmann had been responsible for the deaths of millions of Jews and had been the mastermind behind the Final Solution, whereas the baron had arranged for the disposal of some of his wealthy Jewish friends out of pure greed.

I walked into the courtroom and sat at the designated place. I looked around to see if I knew anybody. Over in a corner I spotted a very attractive blonde woman in her thirties, accompanied by a boy of about twelve, who looked the perfect Aryan. He looked very much like the baron when I had first met him in the south of France. It had to be his son and it only confirmed that this man, about to be tried for crimes against the

Jewish people, was none other than Klaus von Jellenbach, whatever the Paraguayan government said.

The accused entered the courtroom and took his place inside a glass booth to protect him. I had to admit that he had changed beyond recognition, his piercing blue eyes being the only vestige of his former self.

The chief judge entered the courtroom, and the proceedings began. He read out the accusations and asked the accused if he declared himself guilty or innocent.

He stood up defiantly and said, 'You have made a mistake! I am not the man you say I am! My name is Gerardo Echevarría and I am a citizen of Paraguay.'

His German defence lawyer, who had defended many former Nazis, asked to speak to the judge. After a few minutes, the judge spoke again.

'As the identity of the accused is in doubt and the representatives of the Government of Paraguay insist that the accused is in fact Mr Gerardo Echevarría, the court will subject him to some tests in order to establish his identity and will study the documents submitted by the Paraguayan authorities. The trial is thereby adjourned for five days while the experts reach a conclusion.'

I was rather put out by this decision, as a delay meant that I would probably be unable to keep my promise to my wife, but Isaac reassured me, saying it would only take a few days for the baron's identity to be proved beyond doubt.

'Although he has allegedly had much plastic surgery performed on his face, in addition to dental work, we are submitting photographs of the baron as a young man and pictures of him today, to an eminent German forensic expert who has developed the PIK ear identification. The baron can't have changed his ears!' he said, with a touch of humour.

'What other tests will they do?'

'He has no fingerprints, so they will do graph logical tests too. We are not worried, as we know who he is and we will prove it beyond a doubt. If it shows positive, the PIK test is irrefutable.'

I spent the next few days sightseeing with Isaac, eating kosher food, and enjoying one of the most fascinating cities in the world. The dinner with the consul was very pleasant. Every day I spoke to Pepita, who was fine, and I heard through the embassy that Phryne and Simon were also well. I had given him instructions not to return to university until after the trial.

Five days later, we were back in the courtroom. The silence was absolute. The judge entered, at last, with a broad smile on his face.

'The identity of the accused has been established beyond doubt.' He paused for greater dramatic effect, and I could see he was quite a character. Handsome and in his early fifties, he had a boyish look that was enhanced by his straight blond hair, but I felt certain that behind his amiable and mild-mannered expression lay an acute mind.

'In view of the fact that there are no fingerprints or dental records, we have had to hire the services of Dr Moritz Furtmayr, who has developed the PIK test, which compares the anatomical points of the ear. For a person's identity to be confirmed, a minimum of twelve points must be identical. The professor has compared photographs of the right ear of the young baron with photographs of the right ear of Gerardo Echevarría, and he has found fifteen identical anatomical points. Therefore, the trial will now proceed.'

There was uproar of approval in the courtroom. Only Mrs. Echevarría and her son looked miserable. In fact, she was devastated. After all, she had not known to whom she had been married all these years, I felt sorry for her as she too had been deceived.

'Do you have anything to add?' the judge asked the accused. The baron remained silent.

The prosecution called on several witnesses who recounted everything they knew about the baron's activities, and whose testimonies the defence lawyer weakly refuted. Many of them were descendants of the baron's victims and, deprived of their inheritance, lived in semi poverty while trying unsuccessfully to obtain compensation from the German Republic. The outcome of this trial could change their lives, as it would enable them to recover eventually some of their works of art.

Then Gonzaga Pérez de Sanchís was called to the witness stand. To my surprise, it was Gonzaga Herentals, but addressed by his family name. I had not seen him in years, as both brothers had left Madrid and gone to live in New York. He looked well and was still very handsome. I hoped I would have the chance to talk to him, but the witnesses were kept rather isolated and we could not mingle with one another.

Gonzaga told the court about his father's relationship with the baron, and how he had secured a Spanish passport for him just before the end of the war. He recounted everything he knew, including detailed information on the crates of paintings that had been kept at the Herentals palace.

The trial was adjourned until the following day. Things seemed to be going smoothly, and the defence lawyer's attempts to discredit the witnesses presented by the prosecution were all proving unsuccessful.

The next morning I was called to the stand. I confirmed Gonzaga's testimony and recounted how I had first met von Jellenbach and became aware of his activities. I also told the court what Simon Stern had told me about the baron's acquiring part of his collection, which of course was now in Paraguay, an indisputable proof of his guilt. There was no doubt to anyone present that the accused was guilty, and it looked as if the trial would be a brief one.

On the third day, after listening to over fifty witnesses, the judge asked the accused to make a deposition. The baron stood up in his glass booth and in a dignified manner proceeded to defend himself. After a sip of water, he cleared his throat.

'My detention is illegal. It was an act of terrorism. I am the victim of an error of judgement. The Mossad have kidnapped me and brought me here against my will, which makes this trial illegal. My lawyer has already explained to the court how President Stroessner's Government has filed a lawsuit against the Israeli Government. I trust the judges will consider these facts.

'In my defence, I can only say that I never persecuted Jews with avidity and passion. In fact, I never persecuted Jews at all. I, myself, had many Jewish friends, whose names have been mentioned in this trial. I tried to save them through my close relationship with Reichsmarschall Goering who, like me, was a lover of art. My intentions were honourable. I tried to protect my friends by warning them about what was going to happen and by protecting their collections.'

A roar of disapproval greeted his words. He paused and took another sip of water. I could see that he was only too aware of the importance of what he was saying. He knew his life depended on it.

'In those days I was art advisor to the Reichsmarschall and I merely obeyed orders. We all did. If I am guilty of anything, it is only of obeying orders.'

The speech was rather similar to the one Eichmann had made at his own trial a few years earlier, were he had been found guilty of crimes against humanity and had been hanged.

'When I discovered what was happening, I was horrified by the extent of the killing of Jews. I did not hear about the Final Solution until just before the end of the war, and I was so disgusted that I left the Third Reich and moved to South America. It would be a grave error if the court were to believe that I had anything to do with those fanatics. I assure you that during my days of service to the Third Reich I never had the power or responsibility to have anyone killed. I have always lived my life according to ethical principles.'

A laugh was heard somewhere in the courtroom.

Though the baron was giving an excellent performance and he sounded quite convincing, I, of course, knew better.

'I have a son whom I love and a wonderful wife whom I cherish. I am a respected member of society in Paraguay, a patron of the arts. I am no danger to anybody. I beg this court to consider this. If I am declared innocent, I shall ask the Government of Paraguay to permit the export of those paintings that were given to me by my friends for safekeeping.'

An irritated elderly man cried out, 'It's a bit late for that!'

The judge demanded silence in the court and then addressed the accused.

'Baron Klaus von Jellenbach, have you finished?'

'Yes.'

'Very well then, the court is adjourned until tomorrow at ten, when the verdict will be given and sentence passed.'

The next day the courtroom was buzzing with excitement. Although it was clear that the baron had not murdered anybody himself, there was overwhelming evidence of his involvement in the disappearance of some of the most prominent Jewish art collectors in Europe. I very much doubted that the sentence would be a mild one.

We all, including the accused, rose to our feet as the three judges entered the room, with the verdict inside an envelope. The excitement was palpable.

The chief judge ceremoniously opened the envelope and, with even greater solemnity than on previous days, proceeded to read the verdict.

'When deciding upon the appropriate sentence for the accused, this court has been more than aware of the great burden of responsibility laid upon it. In view of the fact that the accused has enjoyed over twenty years impunity under a false identity, the court has decided to give him the maximum sentence permitted by the laws of the State of Israel.

'In its judgement, the court has detailed the crimes in which the accused took part. Although it is a fact that he is not directly responsible for the murder of the Jewish art collectors whom he insists on calling his friends, the accused has been found guilty of stealing their collections before they were sent to extermination camps. As the court is well aware, most of these Jews did not survive their ordeal.

When considering the sentence to be passed, this court has also, and perhaps most importantly, taken into account the injuries inflicted on the victims of these crimes as individuals, and the immeasurable anguish which they and their families have endured and still suffer to this very day.

Whether the accused was following orders or whether he acted out of irrepressible greed is largely immaterial. The fact is he acquired one of the best art collections in the world by illegal means. If, as he claims, he did so out of altruism, he should have returned all the paintings after the war. Had that been the case, this court might conceivably have treated him with greater leniency.

'Therefore, after due consideration of the testimonies presented, this court hereby sentences Baron Klaus von Jellenbach to life imprisonment for crimes against the Jewish people, and for the theft of art collections owned by Jews. He has also been found guilty of membership of an organisation that is hostile to Jews and to the State of Israel.

'This is the court's verdict and sentence. Baron von Jellenbach is entitled to appeal, and has ten working days in which to do so. I declare this trial closed.'

The crowd burst into applause. Only his deceived wife was sobbing. She was well aware that she had suddenly become a social pariah. Her son sat there expressionless.

The judges left the courtroom and everybody started talking at once. I was relieved that everything had gone so fast, as it meant that I would be flying back to Madrid the next day, in time to celebrate my birthday with my family. It was all over, at last.

17. AN IRREPARABLE LOSS

My return to Madrid was uneventful. Pepita and the children arrived from the North so that they were home for my arrival. She had arranged a surprise party as only she knew how to do, and to all our friends were invited to celebrate my forty-sixth birthday.

Less than a fortnight later, I was having breakfast when the maid brought me the morning paper, the ABC. On the cover was a photograph of Baron Klaus von Jellenbach. The article said that, after losing his appeal against the sentence, the baron had been found dead in a pool of blood in his cell. He had apparently cut his own throat with a Boy Scout knife that his son had somehow managed to give him before returning to Asunción.

'What a finale!' I thought. I felt sorry for the baroness or Mrs Echevarría. Until her husband's abduction, she had not been aware of his identity or his activities.

The next few months went by very quickly. I had to travel extensively for the company and every now and then, I would send a report to Miles.

However, in early June I once again started receiving threatening letters and phone calls, so I immediately notified London. The long arm of the hostile organisation that I had heard about in Jerusalem seemed to be quite active. In the letters, I was insulted and called a murderer, while the voices on the phone kept repeating that I should always look behind me. It made me so uneasy that I again requested protection for my family and for Simon, who was now studying in Germany.

Pepita was beside herself with worry and told me she could no longer live like this. Neither could I, so I promised her that by the end of the year I would definitely quit my espionage activities.

We decided to spend our summer holidays in the North as usual, but starting in late May, so we set about closing the house. I decided that if for any reason I had to return to the office during the summer, I would stay at a hotel.

The summer was glorious and the weather excellent, which was not too common in the north of Spain, where rain and cool temperatures are the norm. We fell into a delightful routine of swimming, fishing, going for long walks, playing golf and dining in excellent rural restaurants. My sons, Carlos and Ivan, were sent to Broadlands in Hampshire to improve both their English and their riding, and would be back by mid-August. The girls remained with us, enjoying the company of their cousins, aunt, and grandmother.

That summer we watched the amazing feat of men walking on the moon, and no one can deny that the sixties were exceptionally historic years for humankind.

In early September, Pepita and I were ready to return to Madrid to reopen the flat. We took two cars. For the children's sake we always drove separately as a precaution against both of us being involved in an accident. We did not take Carlos with us, despite his insistence, and he was very upset when we drove off without him.

In those days the roads in Spain were decidedly second-rate, so we stopped for the night in Burgos. The Hostal Landa had a charming atmosphere and offered excellent food, and that night Pepita and I made love with a passion that surprised us both.

We spent two days in Madrid, busily preparing the house for the family's arrival, before driving north again, via Burgos. That night at the Hostal we had a major fight, the second in our entire marriage. Pepita blamed me for all the stress she was under, due to my activities with MI6, and threatened to leave me if I did not stop the minute we returned to Madrid. I tried to calm her down but was not too successful. In the end, she fell asleep in my arms. I felt terrible at being the cause of all her worry and anguish.

The following morning we awoke to appalling weather and heavy rain. 'Drive carefully,' I said, as I kissed her tenderly on the lips. 'I love you.'

The weather was foul all day, with pouring rain and strong winds, and it took me five hours to reach the North. The children were happy to see me, and I to see them.

'Daddy! Daddy! Did you bring me a present?' asked my lovely little girls, as their grandmother looked on, smiling indulgently.

'Has Pepita arrived?' I asked.

'No, not yet,' my mother-in-law replied.

'Well, she should be here very soon, as we left at the same time. She's probably taking extra care because of the rain,' I said.

An hour passed with no sign of Pepita, then another and another. By then we were seriously worried, and I called the Civil Guard to find out if any accidents had been reported. They promised to call back as soon as they knew.

Shortly afterwards, the phone rang. 'Señor, I'm afraid a car with the description you gave me has gone off a cliff in the mountain pass of Los Tornos. Your wife has been taken in an ambulance to Bilbao.'

'How is she?'

'I am sorry to tell you that she is in a critical condition.'

'Pepita! Pepita! No! Please hang on!' I muttered to myself. From the tears running down my cheeks, my mother-in-law and Carmen knew that something was terribly wrong. We hugged and cried until I managed to regain my composure. I called Dr. José Mari Herrasti, who had been Pepita's gynaecologist and was a close friend of the family, and asked him to go to the hospital.

I did not want to tell the children anything until we knew more about the situation, so we left them with a neighbour, their cousins and of course the faithful Bea.

Before leaving for Bilbao, I went to say goodbye to them.

'What's happened?' Carlos asked. He was already thirteen and very intuitive.

'Everything is fine. Your mother has had an accident, but she will soon be OK. Don't worry. Now, make sure you take good care of your brother and sisters. OK?'

'OK, Papa.' I knew he did not believe me because he started to cry. He was heartbroken.

My sister-in-law drove her mother and me to Bilbao. It was only a distance of sixty-eight kilometres but it took us nearly two hours because of the rain and the bad state of the roads. Dr. Herrasti was waiting for us at the hospital with a gloomy expression on his face.

'I'm afraid it doesn't look good at all,' he told us, 'Pepita is in a coma, in intensive care. There is only about a ten per cent chance that she will survive.'

My mother-in-law, usually a paradigm of strength, half fainted.

'The best thing is for you to go home and fetch the children. And pray.'

'May I see her?' I asked.

'I wouldn't recommend it. Please trust me.'

As the situation began to sink in, I started asking myself many questions. Why had she taken that particular mountain pass, which was dangerous even in the best of weather? Did the threatening letters and phone calls have anything to do with the accident? I called London from my mother-in-law's flat and informed my superiors.

'She has been murdered, Miles. I just know it. It's the dark hand of Nazism.'

'Rodney, don't jump to conclusions like that. We will send a team of experts to work with the Spanish police and the Civil Guard and I will get a report to you as soon as we know anything.'

'But, Miles, those letters and the phone calls… They are making me pay for Jellenbach's death. Fuck, Miles, it is your responsibility. This was not supposed to happen. You gave me guarantees!'

'Calm down Rodney. Let us just wait for the results of the investigation before you jump to any conclusion. Just remain calm and we will contact you soon.'

I was broken inside and felt an uncontrollable rage inside me. I promised that if they were behind this, I would seek them out and destroy them even if it was the last thing I did in my life

I took refuge in my work for the company, and visited the steel works, spending very little time at home. The children were in Bilbao, but I hardly saw them. I just could not face them. I ate in restaurants and tried to hide my pain. However, when I came home late at night my mother-in-law berated me, saying that my behaviour was disgraceful and that my children needed their father. I knew she was right but my distress was so great that I did not know how to cope with it. The idea of losing Pepita was driving me crazy.

A week after the accident, and without her ever regaining consciousness, Pepita's heart failed her. We were all devastated. My world crumbled under me. I felt as if my life had no meaning any more. Only the thought of my young children kept me focused.

My beloved wife was buried in her mother's family vault. A few days later, a requiem Mass was held at the Basilica de Nuestra Señora de Begoña where we had been married. Hundreds of our friends attended. I went through the motions like a zombie, only managing to cope with the ordeal thanks to the tranquillisers given me by Dr. Herrasti.

Miles was there and I remember him telling me that all the evidence pointed towards an accident. His experts said that the car had not been tampered with, and the Civil Guard and police agreed. Pepita had simply taken the wrong road and, due to poor visibility, fog and rain, had gone off a cliff. The report was final and the findings somehow made me feel less miserable.

As soon as all the funeral ceremonies were over, I returned to Madrid with the children. It was already late September and, for the sake of my family, life had to go on.

After the conclusions of the investigation, I was ill-prepared for the letter that Rafael, the porter, handed me on our arrival in Madrid. Written in capitals, the letter said: 'We *told you so…*'

I was so confused I did not know what to believe any more. I called Miles. I was very, very angry and frightened.

'Don't let this bother you. All they are doing is playing mind games. They know you are very vulnerable, and these notes are simply to undermine you. They want you to break down,' he said, trying to reassure me.

'But after all these years, how can they still be active?'

'Rodney, you know as well as I do that one of the Nazis' specialities used to be psychological torture. They just want to drive you insane. So please try to stay calm. Be reasonable. There is no doubt whatsoever that your wife's death was a most unfortunate and terrible accident.'

'That's an easy thing to say from London!'

I was now beginning to become furious and I felt very lost. The formula to personal disaster Why hadn't I killed those bastards when I'd had the chance? Vogel, Gisela… every one of them! However, Miles was right. They were just trying to make me lose it and I was not going to let them. I had to be strong and keep my bearings.

Returning to the flat with Pepita gone was not easy. I had four young children to take care of and had no idea how I was going to manage. I took Carlos under my wing, for he was terribly distressed by his mother's death; he was depressed, and for some reason blamed himself.

Nevertheless, time cures all, and after a few months, although I missed Pepita dreadfully, I was back leading my usual life. I had loads of work in the office and I travelled a great deal, having taken an extended leave from MI6.

My in-laws came to visit the children on several occasions. I could feel a certain tension in our relationship, which I could not understand, as I had always enjoyed their company and felt genuine affection for them.

They began to put pressure on me to send the children to live with them in Bilbao, but I refused. I had already lost my wife and was not prepared to lose my sons and daughters as well. However, eventually, as a compromise, I agreed to send my two daughters to spend a year with them and see how it went. I would always regret that decision, not because they were not good to the girls but because I later realised that a father must be with his children, especially at that age.

I bought a 1,000-square-metre flat on Calle Rafael Calvo 7, to be our new home, and moved my office there, too. It was a lovely apartment with a huge terrace, and I felt we could be happy there.

Simon had now finished his studies and I asked him to come and work for me in Madrid. The boys were very excited at the idea of their elder brother whom they hardly knew coming to live with us. They all got along splendidly from the start, and he was a great support to them and still is.

The governess had taken over the household and now managed everything and I really did not know what I would have done without her.

18. STARTING AGAIN

I am a man who needs a woman by his side in life, and I started dating a delightful widow, but she had four children of her own and the relationship failed to take off. However, soon another woman entered my life. Pepita and I had often played golf and dined with her among other friends. We both shared a love for golf, the opera and travel, and I found her very attractive.

My sons got on quite well with her from the beginning, but for some reason the girls did not warm up to her; so it came as something of a respite for me when my daughters finally went to live in Bilbao, whereupon I fired Beatriz, who promptly joined them.

I travelled to Bilbao every week on business, so I saw my daughters regularly, but I could feel I was gradually losing their love. They were too small to understand my situation, and unfortunately, I was too selfish to understand theirs.

At the beginning of 1972 I asked her to marry me. I did not dare tell my daughters other than through a letter to their aunt, in which I informed her of my marriage and asked her to pass the news to the girls in the most delicate of manners.

My new wife had not siblings nor had she had any children in her previous marriage. Living in a big household with teenagers became too much of a strain for her so we built a house in the country, twenty-five kilometres outside the city, and went to live there, leaving my three sons in the flat, with a cook and a butler. They were free to do as they pleased and I gave them plenty of money, which in hindsight was a big mistake.

By now I felt half-Spanish and really loved my adopted country so, as Franco's health was deteriorating rapidly, I resumed my work for MI6.

The Generalissimo had become a pathetic and fragile old man who clung to power despite the changing world around him. This fragility was an ideal breeding ground for all sorts of intrigues, such as the arranged match in

March 1971 between his granddaughter Carmen and Alfonso de Borbón Dampierre, the eldest grandson of King Alfonso XIII. Despite Alfonso's having no rights to the Spanish throne, the wedding was organised with all the pomp and ceremony of a royal one and opened a completely new world of worrisome possibilities.

To me it seemed improbable that Franco would renege on his designation of Prince Juan Carlos, son of Don Juan, as his successor. However, through some friends of mine within the regime, I found out that Franco's inner circle, comprising his wife, Doña Carmen, his son-in-law, the Marquis of Villaverde, together with the most extremist of the falangistas, were putting great pressure on the ailing dictator to designate Alfonso de Borbón as his successor. What better way to continue the regime than placing on the throne the grandchildren of both Franco and the late King? London was very worried, fearing that if this were to happen it might lead to a revolution shortly after Franco's death or worse, another civil war.

In spite of very tight censorship, things in Spain were changing rapidly. This was partly due to the tourist boom, as in summer Spaniards mingled with the increasing number of foreigners who came to the coasts. The Spanish people were waiting patiently and in silence for the freedom and democracy they so desired, while the most important of the banned political parties—the Socialists and Communists—were likewise biding their time before reappearing on the scene and fighting for their goals.

Prince Juan Carlos had very little support within the regime but if he ever became king, he would inherit absolute power, enabling him to go in whatever direction he wished if he managed to stay in power long enough to do so.

The royalists, the monarchy's natural supporters, were divided among themselves. The traditionalists would not accept Prince Juan Carlos as king unless Don Juan abdicated, while others, whom I called the practical, wanted the restoration of the monarchy at all costs, even if this meant sacrificing Don Juan. The only thing they had in common was their loathing of the Don Alfonso option.

In the summer of 1973, Franco named a prime minister for the first time, Admiral Carrero Blanco whom ETA, the terrorist group, assassinated three months later. At least that was the official version then. I had my doubts, as the murder of Carrero was incredibly well planned. I doubted that ETA had the means to carry out such an attack on the regime.

Considering that Carrero Blanco, with the Army behind him, would have blocked any democratisation of the regime under the young King, it is obvious that he was an obstacle for democracy. I asked Miles in several occasions if he really knew who was behind the assassination and he always shrugged his shoulders and smiled. I believed then and still do that it was a CIA operation, probably with some help from us.

Influenced by his inner circle of family members, Franco then chose Carlos Arias Navarro as the new prime minister. This was a blow for the monarchists, as it was common knowledge that the hardliner Arias was utterly opposed to the idea of the restoration. The prince now found himself in a difficult situation. Franco was very ill, old, had little will of his own, and his family were not prepared to lose their privileges, everyone having ambitions of their own. Alfonso de Borbón, however, instead of remaining loyal to his family and the institution, went along with them and with the hostile prime minister.

By the summer of 1974, Franco was so ill that he named Prince Juan Carlos as acting head of state. In the inner circles of Madrid, we knew that his wife and son-in-law were furious at this decision. Their weight was felt when, only five weeks later, Franco decided he was well enough to resume his responsibilities as head of state. Everyone knew better and the situation became very tense, with rumours and jokes abounding.

I believed that the prince stood a very good chance of remaining king if he democratised the regime shortly after the dictator's death. Although I had only met him once, at a golf tournament, I had chatted to him for some time during the game and he had left me with a very favourable impression of his capabilities.

On the 20 November 1975 the dictator died. Parliament proclaimed Juan Carlos as King of Spain. His father, Don Juan, remained silent in Portugal, waiting to see how events turned out. If this attempt at restoring the monarchy failed, as he was the legitimate king, the throne could eventually be restored on him.

After a year of brilliant political decisions in the midst of great tension the young king legalised all political parties and announced that democratic elections would be held in June 1977. By doing this, the monarchy was bringing democracy to Spain in a move that would guarantee its survival.

After seeing his lifelong dream realised, and democracy finally established in Spain, Don Juan, who was primarily a great patriot, abdicated in favour of his son, thereby granting him dynastic legitimacy. It was an act of great love and personal sacrifice, and it touched and moved me profoundly. He was a truly extraordinary man. A man who had lived most of his life in exile, despised and insulted by the regime, and who had always put his life at the service of Spain before any other consideration. With this simple but emotional ceremony he had passed on the flame to his beloved son.

I had played golf with him a few times and I admired him greatly for his values and his patriotism. He was also a very charming man with an extremely good sense of humour, a true gentleman, as had been his father, King Alfonso XIII, my father's friend.

A week later, having accomplished my mission, I finally and definitely handed in my resignation.

The following year I had the great honour of being received by His Majesty in the Zarzuela Palace accompanied by my son Carlos. I was very proud.

Marbella, Summer 1980

By 1954, the year the Marbella Club opened, two men with an eye for business had bought up most of the property and orange groves between the charming sleepy fishing village of Marbella and the Guadalmina River.

One of them was Prince Alfonso von Hohenlohe, whose father, Prince Max, had tried so eagerly to persuade the British Embassy to sign a peace treaty with Germany during the war. The family discovered Marbella soon after the war, immediately saw its potential and bought a large amount of land. Prince Alfonso's idea was to build a haven by the sea for all his rich and famous friends, which is precisely what the Marbella Club would become.

The other astute businessman was Norberto Goizueta, who bought all the land between the village of San Pedro de Alcántara and Guadalmina, where he developed the Guadalmina Golf and Hotel and sold plots of land to all his wealthy conservative Spanish friends. In fact, we ourselves have a lovely flat there, overlooking the sea, where we spend three months every summer.

1970 saw the construction of Puerto Banús, a splendid leisure port against a stunning backdrop, the mountain of La Concha. The port would soon attract some of the largest yachts in the world.

It was during the seventies and eighties that Marbella enjoyed its heyday. During those fun years, some extraordinary characters appeared on the scene and dominated the nightlife. Pepe Moreno's discotheque catered mainly for the Guadalmina crowd, while Menchu Escobar established her equally famous Menchu's Bar in Puerto Banús. I had met her years before in London, when she had struck me as a beautiful redhead with a very outgoing personality. My wife and I used to go to her bar nearly every evening, as the mixture of people from Guadalmina and the Marbella Club made it very entertaining. Everybody went there, and it was a matter of great importance where Menchu sat you.

One evening in the summer of 1980 I went to Menchu's Bar by myself. Even though the place was packed, Menchu gave me our usual table on the terrace. A few minutes later, she returned, accompanied by an extravagantly dressed woman in an enormous straw hat that completely hid her face.

'Let me introduce you to my dear friend from Paris, Mimi St Claire.' The faceless lady extended her hand for me to kiss. 'Are you alone tonight?' Menchu asked. 'If you are, I'd like to ask you to invite Mimi to your table.'

'Yes, I am. Please, Mimi, take a seat,' I said, moving a chair back.

'Champagne is on the house!' said Menchu, pleased with herself.

After Menchu left, the mysterious Mimi made herself comfortable and proceeded to take off her hat. She had not yet said a word when I saw her face and immediately recognised her. She had quite a few wrinkles, though not as many as I would have expected for a women in her seventies, but those unforgettable sensual green eyes and red hair were still there.

'Gisela!' I cried, quite startled.

'Monsieur!' she paused for suspense. 'You are mistaken. My name is Mimi,' she said in exquisite French with no trace of a German accent.

Surprised, I said, 'Cut the crap, Gisela, and let's try to have a drink in a civilised manner. It's been a long time.'

A pretty waitress uncorked the champagne and filled our glasses. I knew the waitress well, as her father, Brian Walmsley, was a good friend. Her name was Tessa, and I introduced her to Mimi. She now runs a fashionable restaurant in Madrid called La Parra in Calle Montesquinza.

'Her father was MI6,' I said after Tessa left.

'And so were you,' she added softly and then sighed.

'So you knew!'

'We knew everything, my dear. As I suppose you did, too. Anyway, in those days you either fought or spied, so it was rather obvious. It was all a big game.'

'A terrible game! So many lives were lost. Over fifty million people! I've often wondered how you could all work for such a monster as Hitler.'

'We elected Hitler to power because his promises of a greater Germany were very appealing to most of us. We longed for the greatness of the Kaiser and it seemed that this was what the Nazis were offering. I am going to be quite honest with you. We knew that the Jews were being taken to work camps, but we never knew what they were doing to them until much later on in the war. When I found out, I was appalled. I had quite a few Jewish friends in Berlin before the war, but not a single one survived.'

'But you worked for them.'

'Don't be mistaken. I worked for Germany in the same way that you worked for Britain.'

'Yes, but I worked for freedom, while you worked for a despicable and murderous state.'

'Things are not always what they seem. I'm going to tell you a secret that I haven't told anyone. Two of my closest friends were Count Klaus von Stauffenberg and Erwin Rommel.'

'The first name rings a bell, and naturally one cannot help feeling a certain admiration for Rommel. He was a formidable enemy,' I said, fascinated by the turn the conversation was taking.

'The count was the mastermind behind the plot to kill Hitler and Erwin was seriously implicated. Klaus placed a briefcase with a bomb in it at a staff meeting. But it all went wrong. Hitler survived and poor Klaus was promptly executed the next day. He is really a very tragic hero.'

'I know that but I was not aware of Rommel's involvement, not only was he never implicated in the plot, but he received a hero's funeral with full military honours, if my memory does not deceive me,' I said.

'They forced him to commit suicide at the hospital in Ulm. Hitler knew that he was too popular to degrade his memory. Did you know, Rodney, that poor Erwin was about the only German commander not to be involved in any war crimes? He was a real gentleman.' Her tone of voice was one of certain nostalgia and had a tone of sadness.

'We did hear in those days that during the North African Campaign he often cut the water rations of his troops so that the prisoners of war could survive. He must have been quite a man. You should consider yourself lucky to have known him. Were you involved in the plot?'

'Yes. I was one of the few who were not caught. By then, we were all so disgusted by Hitler and what he was doing to our country.'

'I have to say I'm impressed. I thought you were nothing but a cold-blooded bitch. How did you manage to leave the service?'

'I stayed on until after the war, but gave them hardly any information or, at most, misleading tips. I had to pretend I still worked for them because my life was at stake. After the war I managed to get to France, where a friend turned me into Mimi. My involvement in the plot to assassinate Hitler saved me from prosecution and landed me with a French passport.' She fell silent, lost in thought.

'Gisela, I have hated you for many years. I was in Laszlo's apartment when you murdered him.'

'I had nothing to do with his death. Yes, I was there when it happened. 'But I must tell you that it was Vogel and one of his men who pushed poor Laszlo off the balcony. I was very fond of him in fact,' she said, sighing.

'In that case, how come your diamond brooch was under a chair?

'When poor Laszlo realised he was going to be thrown to his death, he struggled and held on to anything within reach, and that's when my brooch must have fallen off.' Gisela was trembling as the memories of that incident flooded back, so I took her hand. 'You see,' she went on after the briefest of pauses, 'Laszlo and I had been lovers. If it could buy information, sex was just part of my job.'

'And part of mine, too.'

We both suddenly laughed and it helped ease the pain of our memories of a time long gone.

'I'll return your brooch to you.'

'No, keep it as a souvenir. I never want to see it again.'

'But you can always sell the diamonds,' I insisted.

'Rodney, Mimi St Claire is a very wealthy woman.'

'I've always enjoyed having rich friends.' I winked at her and she winked back.

'I have longed for you for many years,' she said, turning flirtatious as she raised her glass of champagne and we drank a toast to us both.

'You have always been on my mind, Rodney. Sex with you is something a woman does not easily forget.' She placed her hand on my knee and moved it upwards, and although it made me feel rather uncomfortable, I did not stop her. 'Had our circumstances been different, I would have made you my lover and you would have learnt some very exciting techniques!'

We both laughed again at the idea.

'I have to admit that the sex we had was probably the best ever, but it all happened long ago. By the way, whatever happened to Francisco de Beaumont?'

'Do you remember the night in the houseboat?' she asked, surprised.

'I have never forgotten. What did they put in the champagne?'

'A very strong narcotic. It was all Francisco's idea, but sex was not part of the plan. It all just got out of hand. We were supposed to knock you out and try to find out what you were really up to. I think we all got a bit carried away by the sensual atmosphere.'

'I think Francisco nearly lost the plot. You know, he more or less kidnapped me and tried to make me his sex slave!'

'Don't be absurd, Rodney. He saved your life. He was besotted by you! He would never have allowed any harm to come your way. The Nazis wanted you dead.'

'So they knew?'

'Of course we knew. First in Madrid, then in Cairo, and so well connected... what else could you have been, darling?'

'Where is Francisco now?' I asked with curiosity.

'He returned to Germany at the end of the forties. The pearl trade had suffered and his mother was not well. I have seen him on and off throughout the years. Ever so charming, he always spoke of you as his long-lost love. You know, he never married. He died in his sleep just a couple of years ago.'

'I'm sorry for him. I really found him charming and entertaining. He was extremely refined but, unfortunately, he was not my type!' We both laughed.

'I know that, Rodney!'

'And the American spy, Paul Roberts?'

Gisela took a sip of her champagne. She now seemed to be enjoying remembering those long-forgotten days.

'He was not American. He was one of us, in fact, born in Berlin. He was taken in the same day they arrested Naima and handed over to the Americans. He was rather harmless, the poor fellow.'

'Not so harmless! He nearly killed me!'

'He was sentenced to death.' Gisela sighed.

We both took a sip of our champagne and then Gisela returned to her favourite topic.

'Well, maybe you and I could make love once again for old time's sake,' she suggested seductively. 'I am staying at the Marbella Club.'

'I think not, my dear. It would not be wise. I'm a married man now, and they say in England that it's not a good idea to heat up a cold soup!'

'Too bad,' she said smiling. 'At least I can still fantasise with the memories.'

'You are quite naughty for a lady your age,' I said jokingly.

'I'd never have imagined that a gentleman like you would say something so rude!' She pretended to blush. 'We girls have our needs, my dear, just like you boys do, I suppose.' We refilled our glasses and giggled.

The bar was full of celebrities, like Gunther Sachs and his wife, and Princess Soraya, the former Empress of Persia, but that night it seemed to both of us that we were the only people there.

'You must have been very pleased to have Jellenbach prosecuted,' she went on.

'Well, it was a job well done and a stroke of naked luck,' I said.

'He was an immoral crook, alas, with good manners. He gave me the creeps. I never liked him and I was delighted when I heard the news. He was responsible for the deaths of a few of my Jewish friends. You see, my father was also a collector and they all knew each other.'

'You should have been an actress! You really misled me. I thought he was a friend of yours.'

'That was part of the job... misleading the enemy. I was highly skilled at it in those days.'

'I have to confess, Gisela, that during that trial I felt sorry for his wife, who had no idea who her husband really was. Poor woman! By the way, whatever happened to Vogel? I saw him once in a restaurant in Madrid before the trial and I am certain he was harassing me at the time.'

'You, and a few others!'

'What do you mean? '

'Hansi was a real monster. He was a sadist who loved his work. I have not heard from him in years. He escaped prosecution. The top exiled Nazis would not admit him into Odessa. He apparently became so obsessed with the survival of the Reich that he founded a small organisation with a few other hardliners. This I know because he tried to recruit me. They acted in very bizarre ways and were a bunch of crazy and dangerous fools.'

'But Laszlo told me that you two had been lovers.'

'Poor Laszlo. How he loved to gossip! We were only lovers for a few days until I discovered what a cruel monster he was.'

'He should be history by now,' I said. Then, realising it was close to eleven and that I had to hurry home, I added, 'It's been a pleasure spending the evening with you, Mimi. I would love to see you in Paris, and would introduce you to my wife if we were to meet again.'

'What a lovely idea,' she said, passing me her card, 'but you had better make it soon, as, after all, I am not that young any more.'

19. GHOSTS FROM THE PAST

It was early October 1980. I was soon to turn fifty-eight and I felt wonderful. My wife was planning a birthday dinner party at our home in the country, at which all my children would be present, and I was very much looking forward to the occasion.

A few weeks earlier, however, as I arrived one morning at the office, I noticed a very strange-looking old man swaggering about. He was wearing an old-fashioned trench coat that reached down to his ankles and a hat that dated back to the forties. He was standing on the corner, reading a newspaper and trying to look inconspicuous. I presumed that he was just a beggar and never gave him a second thought.

That is, until I saw him again as I was leaving Balmoral, my favourite bar, on Calle Hermosilla. He looked quite harmless and I wondered if it was just a coincidence. I chose to think it was, and I pushed him from my mind, once again.

Nevertheless, the following morning he was standing across the street from my home, and it was then that I decided to call a friend of mine in the police.

Inspector Vega asked me to go and see him in his office at the *Dirección General de Seguridad*. He was a charming young man who had the bad habit of chain-smoking. I had been a heavy smoker myself until I turned forty, and other people smoking now bothered me, so I opened fire at once.

'I shall assign someone to protect you while we try to find out who this person is,' he said reassuringly. 'I'm sure there's nothing to worry about.'

'I hope so too, Vega. Many thanks.'

However, just as he had appeared, the mysterious man disappeared, and I did not see him again; so, after only a couple of days, my bodyguard was withdrawn.

The evening before my birthday, my youngest daughter came over for a drink. I always enjoy her company as she is in a permanent good mood and full of life. There is never a dull moment when she is around.

'Papa, there's a very odd-looking old man in the street. Is he your new beggar?' she asked jokingly. I looked out of the window and there he was again, in the same old coat and hat, only this time his hair was white and he wore a ridiculous fake moustache.

'Yes, he does look odd,' I agreed, drawing the curtains closed.

I went into my bedroom and called Inspector Vega.

'He's back,' I said.

'Who's back?'

'The stalker.'

'OK, Señor Mundy, I shall get you another officer. Just don't worry.'

I walked my young daughter to her car, but by then the old man had disappeared.

The next day I dropped by the office for a couple of hours before taking my wife out to lunch. I was aware of the presence of the plainclothes police officer, whom Vega had assigned to protect me, but once again the stalker was nowhere to be seen. It looked as if he had disappeared again.

After lunch, we went out to our country house to prepare for the evening's celebrations. At about half-past eight the children arrived and we drank to my health with champagne. We hardly managed to spend much time together and it was a wonderful feeling to have all of my sons and daughters with me. However, about an hour later, just as we were sitting down to dinner, the doorbell rang, which was rather strange, as we were not expecting anyone. The maid went to open the door and returned a few minutes later.

'Señor, there is a gentleman who says he must speak to you immediately.'

'What is his name?'

'I don't know, Señor. I shall go and ask him.'

She returned a few moments later.

'It is Adolf Dumas, Señor. I think he is a bit strange.'

I got up from the table to find out who he was. I was stunned to see him standing in my doorway.

'Who the hell are you?' I demanded, 'Why have you been following me?' I had no idea who he could be. His face was not at all familiar. Maria was right; he did seem unbalanced.

He started rambling on in German and I realised he was saying something about Klaus von Jellenbach.

'I think you had better leave,' I said, very annoyed.

The old man had his hands in his coat pockets. He looked like a caricature out of an American detective film, and had it not been for the circumstances, I probably would have laughed

'Don't worry, I shall leave very soon,' he now said in surprisingly perfect English.

Without a warning, he pulled a pistol out of his pocket and pointed it straight at me.

'Happy birthday, Herr Mundy.'

I reacted in a flash and pushed him to one side. The gun went off, the noise alerting my whole family who immediately rushed into the hall. My assailant had fallen to the ground and my eldest son, who was an expert at martial arts, leapt on him and held him pinned to the floor. He had not much difficulty as the man was well passed his prime. I immediately called Vega and asked for instructions, as I had given my bodyguard the evening off.

'Lock him up in a bathroom. We'll be there as soon as possible.' With the help of my sons I locked him into the small guest bathroom. It was rather difficult as, though he was frail, he behaved like a wild animal. His strength was outrageous for a man of his age.

'I think we had better sit down for dinner until the police arrive,' I said, as we trooped back into the dining room in a state of utter shock. Obviously, the children and my wife wanted to discuss the incident and bombarded me with questions, which I avoided answering. We just left it as the act of a lunatic but I knew better. I would certainly never forget this birthday, for I had been reborn.

No noise came out of the bathroom.

I had just managed to blow out my candles when Inspector Vega arrived with two other police officers.

'Where is he?' he asked.

I escorted him to the bathroom and gave him the key. The man was lying on the floor. Vega knelt down and examined him.

'I'm afraid he is dead. What did you do to him?'

'What do you mean, do to him?' He tried to kill me! We did not use any violence against him.'

Vega called an ambulance and before midnight, they took the body away to the morgue for an autopsy.

'I shall let you know who he was as soon as we find out. Meanwhile, happy birthday, Señor Mundy.'

On 30 October, Inspector Vega called me and asked me to go to the police headquarters. I took a taxi and was soon sitting in his smoke-filled office.

'What did you find out?' I asked impatiently.

'Your friend was not called Adolf Dumas, although he did have a false French passport with that name. His fingerprints had been erased and the only clue we have as to who he might have been is this old photograph we found in his wallet.'

'May I see it?'

The inspector handed me the picture. It was an old black-and-white photograph of a young man in a SS uniform.

'Oh my god!' I exclaimed.

'What is it?' asked the Inspector, lighting yet another cigarette.

'This man is Hans Vogel. He was an important member of the Gestapo in Spain during the war.' I told him part of the story. 'How did he die?'

I waited impatiently as Vega stubbed his half-smoked cigarette out in an already overflowing ashtray. The stench of cheap black tobacco was nauseating.

'Cyanide poisoning.'

'They all carried cyanide pills after the war. Death was considered preferable to arrest. What would I tell my family?'

Vega sensing my worries, said, 'Do not worry, Señor Mundy. The official story will be that Dumas was deranged. No connection to you whatsoever. Trust me. It has all been taken care of.'

'Thank you, my friend.' I was relieved.

20. CARLOS AND I

Carlos had listened to my story without a single interruption. When I finished he remained speechless, his features soft and handsome in the flickering candlelight. What a Christmas gift I had given him!

'So what do you think of my life?' I asked at last, not knowing how he would react.

'Why didn't you ever tell us? I can't believe you didn't share this with us.'

'Well, some things are best left unsaid. It was a way of protecting you all but, under the present circumstances, I felt I had to.'

'What present circumstances?'

'Carlos, I think that Martin Jiménez could be a Nazi. I never forget a face and I know I have seen him before. I don't know, maybe I'm just getting old.'

'Oh come on, Papa. I am sure it is not that. It could just be a coincidence. Two people could be similar and remind us of others. It happens all the time. It all happened so long ago.'

'Carlos, don't ask me why, but I have the gut feeling that he means trouble. Look at all the strange things that have been happening, and let's not forget the shaman's warnings!'

'You heard Mauricio, the Indians are quite superstitious. Come on, Dad, don't worry! The guy gives me the creeps but he can't be a Nazi. He is too young.' Carlos tried to calm my fears. 'It looks as if we're in for quite an adventure. You should write a book about your life. It would make a great story. It's just amazing! Promise me that you will one day.'

'I'll think about it, but I won't promise anything. I'm just too upset right now to be able to think about anything except getting out of here.'

It was past midnight and time to go; all the other guests had already gone. Miss Edith came out to wish us goodnight, giving us both a large kiss on either cheek, and we set off in the direction of our hotel along a dark path beside the beach. The small beach bars were having their own Christmas parties, and the voice of Bob Marley blasted out from some rather second-rate amplifiers.

I do not know if I was being paranoid but I had the feeling that someone was following us. I had always possessed a sixth sense, that of 'feeling', and although I did actually not hear or see anything, I could feel someone was following us on our track. I told Carlos, and we decided to stop off in a bar called El Ancla. Ethiopian flags and large posters of Emperor Haile Selassie hung everywhere.

I ordered two beers from a spaced-out *mestizo*[1] and went to the gents, which turned out to be a shack in an open field. While I planned my next move, I somehow felt exhilarated, feeling young again.

Following my familiar old instincts, I circled the building and placed myself behind our pursuer, who I could see hiding behind a palm tree and taking a good look at the table where my son sat. I edged forward like a sleuth to get a better look. He was quite tall, maybe six foot, and he held a machete in his right hand.

Suddenly, I leapt forward and fell on him with all my strength. At sixty-nine, I was still fit, agile and fairly strong. We fell to the ground and I managed to pin his head down. However, he spun around with amazing ferocity and I felt his fist crash into my jaw. As I fell backwards, I could taste the salty flavour of my own blood. I saw him pick up the machete, but, just as he raised an arm to strike, a large man stopped him from behind.

'Are you crazy, man? This gentleman is a friend of Miss Edith's.'

By now we were surrounded by the people from the bar, including Carlos, who helped me to my feet. Taking advantage of the confusion, my assailant took off with his machete.

'We know who he is. He works for Señor Jiménez, the owner of a lodge. He was probably just after your money. There is quite a big drug problem here,' said the big guy who had just saved my life.

'You don't need to cut someone's throat to get their money. Who are you, anyway? I owe you my life.'

[1] Person of mixed blood

'I am Miss Edith's son. She asked me to keep an eye on you. I am glad I did. You see, Mama sees things before they happen.'

'Maybe it would be a good idea to call the police,' I said without thinking.

'We'd better not, Papa. Don't forget the call and why we're here!' Carlos said with great logic.

'Maybe we should all have a drink,' I said, trying to sound cheerful.

We all returned to the bar, where I put some ice on my painful jaw and invited everyone to a beer.

The next morning at dawn we drove back to San José. On the way we stopped at a phone both in a small village, and Carlos called our friends in San José. I thought our well-connected friends would know something about the identity of our protector, but I was wrong. Our story shocked them, and said they would make some calls and try to investigate.

Back in San José, we checked again into the Gran Hotel. There was a message from our friends saying that they would be picking us up for Christmas lunch at 1.30 p.m. We had a very pleasant meal at their beautiful home, answering all of their questions, but we were left without a clue as to who our guardian angel was.

Carlos decided to spend the rest of the afternoon with our hosts and I ordered a taxi to return to the hotel and take a nap. I felt I needed a little rest and some time on my own. I was tired from the sleepless nights, and I planned to start packing, as the next day we had to catch a midday flight to Kingston. I had just started snoozing off when I received a phone call.

'Señor Mundy, I have a message for you,' said the receptionist in the sweetest and softest of voices. 'Señora Blasco will be waiting for you outside the hotel in fifteen minutes. She will be driving a red Range Rover. She insisted that you accompany her. It seems to be very important.'

I was not sure if I was up for more mysteries; but I got up, dressed, and prepared to meet my blind date. The red vehicle was waiting outside, with a fragile, dark-haired woman in her fifties behind the steering wheel. She was elegantly dressed and wore a string of excellent pearls around a long, lovely neck. She had an aquiline nose and deep-set black eyes, her skin was translucent and she looked anything but hostile. I got in and, without a word, she started the engine and we drove off.

'I must apologise for arranging a meeting in such an unorthodox fashion. My name is Rita Stern. I am the daughter of Simon Stern, who you met after the war.'

'I can't believe it!' I cried. 'I last saw you as a little girl in London with your father.'

'I am sure you have many questions to ask me, and I shall be happy to answer them.' Taking my hand affectionately, she smiled. 'My father always cherished your memory and was very grateful for what you did for our family.'

'I know he passed away.'

'Yes, in 1961. His health never fully recovered after Auschwitz.'

'I am really sorry to hear that. Your father was a very good man, and I became close to him. But what brought you here?'

'My father had a sister living in San José, and as we had so little money and nothing to keep us in England, we emigrated. We needed a fresh start and this is a wonderful country.'

'I agree. The people are so friendly, with a couple of exceptions.'

I waited for her reaction, but she said nothing.

'Why don't we have a drink at the terrace bar in the hotel?' I suggested.

'I'd love to.' She turned the car around and we drove back to the hotel. As the Avenida Central was closed to traffic because of some processions that were to take place shortly, we took side streets. When we arrived, Rita gave the car keys to the porter.

The terrace bar was in front of the Teatro Nacional. In a small flea market in the square, ticos and Indians sold their merchandise while a group of musicians played local tunes. It was cool and very pleasant. We ordered some fresh papaya juice and I settled comfortably into my chair, waiting for Rita to speak.

'And what bought you to Costa Rica, Rodney, if may I ask?'

'I am on holiday with my son. But how did you find me?'

'Let me explain. I have a son called Rodney. He is now twenty,' she said at last.

'And I have one called Simon.'

She smiled at me candidly. 'My husband is a high-ranking official in the police force. As your name has been mentioned so many times at home, a couple of days ago he told me there was going to be a drug raid and that a foreigner with the same name as yours was somehow involved. Was it possible? Was it you? For all I heard my father say about you, I could not believe that you could possible be involved in drugs or any unlawful activities. I pleaded with my husband to find out if the man who reunited me with my father was the same man, and if he was, to help you. I was so insistent that he investigated. Your embassy here confirmed you were above any suspicion and convinced my husband that you were up to no wrongdoing. He concluded it was a set-up; so he took immediate action and had one of his men call your son and save you from a very unpleasant situation.'

'But why weren't we told what was happening? It would have saved us a lot of anxiety.'

'Well. I understand, but that was not possible because it would have ruined the investigation that is now being carried on.'

'I am so thankful, anyway. I can't even imagine the nightmare it would have been'

'It is us who can't thank you enough. You made it possible for my father to find me, and not only that but I also became a very wealthy woman after I recovered his art collection.'

'Rita, but who tried to get us framed?

'My husband is investigating that. When your room was raided this morning, they found fifty kilograms of marihuana which, somehow, someone placed there, and that is big crime here.'

'Do you know Martin Jiménez?'

'Yes, he is married to an acquaintance and is the owner of the Toucan Lodge. Do you think he is involved?'

'Well, I'm not sure but it did all happen at his place.'

'Why would he harm you? You don't know him, do you?

'No, I don't, but his face is disturbingly familiar, and since we arrived at the lodge strange things started to happen.'

'What things, Rodney?'

I told Rita about the snake, which now I suspected was an attempt on Carlos's life, and the attack in Cahuita by someone who worked for Martin Jiménez. Rita was horrified.

'I think you better tell my husband. This might help him in the investigation. I'll call him right now.' Rita got up and went to make the call.

When she returned a few minutes later she said, 'He will meet us in a couple of hours at home. He took Rodney to his parent's home.'

'Great. I will feel better to get this off my chest. So tell me, what do you know about him?'

'Not much. He spends most of the time on the coast and seldom is in San José. I don't think he and his wife are very close.'

'Do they have any children?' I asked.

'No. He is quite a loner. I would say an odd type. Always keeps to himself. Apparently, both his parents committed suicide when he was only a child. He has a reason for being so different, I suppose.'

'But is he Costa Rican?' I enquired.

'No, I think he is originally from Paraguay. We don't really know much about him… it is his wife who has the money, though.'

The mention of Paraguay hit the nail. 'Could it be? The pieces in the puzzle seemed to fit, 'but why did their names not match?

'Are you all right, Rodney?'

'Yes, sorry. I am just very confused. Rita, why didn't you go to the trial?'

'What trial? My question took her by surprise.

'Klaus von Jellenbach's!'

'Oh God! I should have gone, but I was only a child when all those terrible events took place, and I could not face reliving all the pain.' She paused and shuddered ever so slightly. 'So Rodney, are you still in the Secret Service?'

'Oh no my dear, I now work for my son Carlos as the financial director of his model agency. It's a wonderful job for an old man as I get to go to all the model contests. It's fun and it keeps me young.'

'I'm sure it does. Dad told me you had quite a reputation with the ladies!'

'When I was younger I did.' I was glad that Rita had given me the opportunity to change the subject of the conversation. I really preferred to speak to her husband.

'You still look like you can break a few hearts,' she replied jokingly.

'Now my hobby is antiques. I adore going antique hunting in England.'

The conversation was very friendly and we both felt a sort of empathy. After all, we had known each other for many years.

'I love antiques too. Let us go to my shop now, and then we can go home to see Antonio, and you can meet Rodney, my son. The shop is closed today so we can have it for ourselves. It is just near the house.'

'That sounds like a wonderful idea.'

We drove off to an area with lovely houses, not too far from the centre of town, or that is what it seemed to me as we chit-chatted all the way until we stopped in front of a lovely modern antique shop. Rita parked the car.

'We live in the house next door,' she said as she got out, and she pointed to a magnificent wooden mansion, which had been designed by one of the most prominent young Costa Rican architects.

'Charming neighbourhood,' I said.

Rita unlocked the door of the shop and we passed through a stunning courtyard filled with flowers and she invited me to come in, locking the door from the inside after her.

She put on the lights and I followed to the back of the store where she displayed what she said was part of her private collection. The quality of her pottery collection amazed me.

'I really can't have it all on display at home,' she said, trying to justify her treasure trove. 'And of course, most of these pieces I will one day donate to Costa Rica, which always made my father and I so welcome.'

'I'm very impressed. Where have you found such exquisite pieces?'

'Dad persuaded me to start collecting. You know it was his passion. My first piece was a gift from him and then I bought at auctions, private sales, and in my travels around the world. You know... by the way, I have a present for you. It was one of Dad's favourite pieces. Here, come, follow me.'

We went to the far end of the room, and in a prominent place was one of the most beautiful pieces I had ever seen. The pale green and blue tones had an incredible intensity.

'Here it is. Do you like it?'

Rita was pointing to a beautiful eleventh-century Korean Celadon vase, which was worth a small fortune.

'I can't accept such a treasure, my dear. But I'm touched and grateful for the gesture.'

'It would have made Daddy immensely happy. It is yours. I insist.'

I kissed her on the forehead. Her gesture really moved me.

'It's settled then! Look at the designs—the chrysanthemums symbolise health and well-being; the lotus, the sun and the mercy of the Buddha; the butterfly, happiness and harmony, and—'

'The phoenix symbolises good omens!' I interrupted her, and we both laughed.

'You know your pottery, Rodney! I can say that. I will get it shipped to Spain. Do you have a business card?'

'I'm afraid I don't.'

'I'll go to get mine and bring you a piece of paper and a pen.'

Rita went to the front of the store while I admired the wonderful present I had just received.

As she was handing me the piece of paper, the silence was broken by the sound of a doorbell.

'It must be Antonio. He is early, though! I'll be right back.'

Rita left and went to meet her husband.

I heard a scream and the sound of an object crashing and breaking into thousand pieces. Rita entered the room in a state of shock followed by a man whom I instantly recognised. It was Martin Jiménez, out of his mind. He carried a gun.

Shouting, he ordered Rita to fetch a chair where, at point blank, I was forced to sit. Pointing his weapon at her, she made her tie my hands behind the back of the chair and my ankles to its legs.

'Sit down beside your friend, bitch!' He was in a state of rage. Rita did as told and she sat on the floor.

'Please, Martin, put the gun down. I am sure we can talk this over. What is bothering you?'

'Close your fucking mouth!'

We were in real danger. The thought of Vogel on my birthday came to my mind, and I gestured to Rita to say no more.

'I never thought I would live to see this day. You killed my father and mother.'

'What are you talking about?' I finally said. 'I don't even know you.' Regretfully, by now, I knew very well who he was.

'Yes you do, you son of a bitch. Does Klaus von Jellenbach ring a bell? I will never forget your smile of satisfaction when my father was condemned.'

Rita looked at me in disbelief.

'But you were only a child!' I exclaimed.

'You shattered our lives. My mother could not cope with the shame you brought on us, and she shot herself, you bastard. And now you are both going to pay for what you did to my family.'

'Martin. Be sensible. You have done nothing yet and I am sure Rita's husband will help you get out of this. Rita is not responsible for anything. Be sensible, please. You have a wife and a life. Try to make the best out of it. There is still time.' I tried to reason with him.

'Yes, Martin. Rodney is right. I will speak to Antonio. Just let us go and we will forget this.' Rita tried to reassure him but to no avail. He despised us profoundly. His wounds were beyond healing.

'It's too late for that. Since that day in Israel I have prayed every day to see you suffer the shame and the pain that we have suffered. As that won't be possible, I will have at least the satisfaction to avenge the death of both my parents. You deserve to die for what you have done to us!' He raised his gun and pointed it towards me. His hand was shaking.

'Please, Martin, please!' Rita pleaded.

Martin, full of rage turned towards Rita and punched her with force on her face. The suddenness of his reaction took her off guard and she fell backward. She moaned as she sat up. A trickle of blood came out of her nose.

'I told you to close your fucking mouth.'

Martin stepped back and, once again, pointed the gun towards me. He was beyond reason. I could see that he was about to pull the trigger. I heard Rita scream. 'No!'

My time had come. During my long life, for some reason or another, I had been on the verge of death on several occasions but my destiny was to stay alive. I had lived on the edge, and now I was certain that I could not be so lucky once more. However, for some reason that only God knows, Martin missed. I felt the bullet passing dangerously close to my head. It hit a shelf full of lovely glass pieces by Lalique that was behind me. They came crushing down, clanging as they hit the floor.

Martin was astounded by the fact that he had missed, and he was about to pull the trigger again when Rita sprang from the floor and hit him in the stomach with her head. He fell backwards and a shot went off and hit the ceiling, bringing a chandelier down that missed me by inches.

Rita was now on top of him. She was a frail, delicate woman over a stocky strong deranged man, struggling to take the gun from him. I was most uncertain of the outcome of such an uneven fight, but I could not do much to help, tied up as I was. Then, she miraculously managed to pick up a small Tibetan bronze horse that was on the floor by her side, and with a force uncommon for a woman, she hit Martin on the head. He lay on the floor, motionless.

'Oh my God, Rodney. I think I've killed him!'

'Rita, please untie me.' Without taking an eye off the inert body, she untied me. I got up and checked Martin. He was breathing and his pulse was normal.

'Don't worry. He should be all right. I think you had better call an ambulance, the police and Antonio. I will make sure he cannot move. Here, take the gun.'

Rita and I waited, lost in our thoughts. I wondered why life kept giving me more opportunities. I had been so close to death so many times.

The paramedics took Martin to hospital, and we both told the police inspector what had just happened when Señor Blasco, Rita's husband, and a handsome young man, Rita's son, Rodney, arrived. We all embraced each other.

'So we finally meet. Merry Christmas Rodney!' Antonio said. 'Let's go home next door and have a drink. It seems that we have something to celebrate and lots to talk about.'

'Indeed we do,' I said as I followed them out of the shop.

EPILOGUE

Madrid, 2 January 2000

I had now lived long enough to be nearly part of two centuries. There was so much fuss about the millennium celebrations that my wife and I decided not to travel anywhere and spend the time at home. Carlos was in India with the Maharajah of Jaipur, and the rest of the children, now all grown up, were scattered around the world in some exotic place or other with their families. Such is life.

Those few quiet days gave me time to reflect on what my life had been and what my wishes were for the future.

I am now seventy-eight years old and have a splendid relationship with all my sons and daughters. Through the very special bond between us, I have finally learnt to express my emotions. If there is one thing in my life that I regret, it is not having yet met my granddaughter Carla, whose mother was a lovely Ecuadorian girl. I still hope to meet her before I die.

I have four other grandchildren. They are all wonderful children and I am a proud grandfather.

I am still happily married and enjoying my old age. I like meeting my children's friends, as I really enjoy the company of younger people. They are so refreshing and always have something to teach you.

I continue to enjoy life, though I feel there is too much competitiveness in the world today and that individuals are lost in the clamour.

Martin von Jellenbach or Martin Jiménez or Echevarría was charged with attempted murder and sentenced to a psychiatric hospital where, shortly after, he followed in his parents' footsteps and hanged himself. It was a tragic ending to a very tragic family story.

I never called Gisela when I went to Paris. I assume she must be dead by now or close to 100, but one never knows, she was a tough one; so she may still be alive. Whatever the case, I hope she finally found the peace of mind she was yearning for.

For so many years, I had been consumed with hatred for her and Vogel. However, later on in life, I learnt from the teachings of the Dalai Lama that my son, Carlos explained to me, that hate and revenge are negative emotions. In the end, we always get what we deserve anyway.

My life has taught me that it is a fool's game to mock the enemy.

I would not like to finish these memories of my life without reflecting on what happened in Spain on 23 February 1981. I was no longer involved in the Secret Service. I followed in disbelief how some disaffected members of the Civil Guard took over the *Congreso**. The plotters made the coup in the name of the king, but I knew from the start that was not possible. What I did not understand was how the CIA and MI6 had not prevented the coup in the first place. I had no doubt in my mind that they had to be aware of the machinations of the Army.

Those were very tense days as during the previous twelve months; ETA (the Basque terrorist group) had murdered over 100 innocent people, many of them members of the army and the security forces. I, like most people in the social and business circles, was aware that the army was fed up with these indiscriminate killings. It was rumoured that certain military circles, close to the old regime, believed that the only solution to solve the ETA problem was the military one, and they thought that the democratic institutions were ill equipped to cope with this state of affairs.

Finally, after a few hours of uncertainty at one in the morning, the young King addressed the nation on television in what would be his most important speech ever.

With this act, the monarch saved the infant Spanish democracy. I felt proud of His Majesty! I am sure Spain will always be grateful to the Crown. Without any doubt, the positive effect of that disgraceful episode was that from 24 February 1981, never again would democracy and the monarchy be questioned.

I have had my own share of suffering, but then, who has not? If I look back on all the good times, I can only feel gratitude for the many gifts life has given me.

Rodney Meynell Mundy died of a brain stroke in his sleep on 18 January 2001. Sadly, life did not grant him his wish of meeting his granddaughter, Carla Mundy Noboa.

* Parliament

www.ingramcontent.com/pod-product-compliance
Lightning Source LLC
Jackson TN
JSHW020019141224
75386JS00025B/602

* 9 7 8 0 8 5 7 2 8 3 8 7 0 *